D0065715

Colored Sugar Water

Also by Venise Berry

All of Me
So Good

Colored Sugar Water

VENISE BERRY

DUTTON

DUTTON
Published by the Penguin Group
Penguin Putnam Inc., 375 Hudson Street, New York, New York 10014, U.S.A.
Penguin Books Ltd, 80 Strand, London WC2R 0RL, England
Penguin Books Australia Ltd, Ringwood, Victoria, Australia
Penguin Books Canada Ltd, 10 Alcorn Avenue, Toronto, Ontario, Canada M4V 3B2
Penguin Books (N.Z.) Ltd, 182-190 Wairau Road, Auckland 10, New Zealand

Penguin Books Ltd, Registered Offices: Harmondsworth, Middlesex, England

Published by Dutton, a member of Penguin Putnam Inc.

First Printing, January, 2002
1   3   5   7   9   10   8   6   4   2

REGISTERED TRADEMARK—MARCA REGISTRADA

LIBRARY OF CONGRESS CATALOGING-IN-PUBLICATION DATA:

Berry, Venise T.
Colored sugar water / Venise Berry.
p.   cm.
ISBN 0-525-94471-0 (acid-free paper)
1. African American women—Fiction. 2. Hotlines (Counseling)—Fiction. 3. Houston (Tex.)—
Fiction. 4. Single women—Fiction. 5. Psychics—Fiction. I. Title.
PS3552.E7496 C35 2002
813'.54—dc21   2001037088

Printed in the United States of America
Set in Simoncini Garamond
Designed by Leonard Telesca

PUBLISHER'S NOTE
This is a work of fiction. Names, characters, places, and incidents either are the products of the
author's imagination or are used fictiously, and any resemblance to actual persons, living or dead,
business establishments, events, or locales is entirely coincidental.

This book is printed on acid-free paper. ∞

Acknowledgments

This story is a tribute to my Lord and Savior Jesus Christ and Toni, my guardian angel.

I want to thank many people for continued love and inspiration:

My family who nurture and empower me: Averi, Jean, Virgil, Steve, and many others in Des Moines, Kansas City, Tulsa, San Diego, and Detroit.

My good friends for their spiritual and technical assistance: Denise, Stephana, Vanessa, ayo, Katrina, Tyna, Pam, Sandi, William, Don, Reverend Dial, Michael, and many others.

Important people in the industry who have guided my success: my agent, Denise Stinson; my editor, Laurie Chittenden; and my publicists, Vanesse Lloyd-Sgambati and Erin Sinesky.

The book clubs, bookstores (especially black booksellers), librarians, sororities (especially Delta Sigma Theta Sorority, Inc.), and my faithful readers and enthusiastic fans.

Colored Sugar Water

What is a man profited,
if he shall gain the whole world
and lose his own soul?

—Luke 9:25

1

*

Suddenly Lucy was running. Her heart smashed against her chest hard and fast. Her feet hit the cement pavement one after the other with arduous thuds. Just like before, she wasn't sure how much time had passed, she didn't know where she was running to, she didn't even know who or what she was running from.

Looking off to each side, Lucy tried to recognize something in the muted images around her; something that might shelter or protect her. She struggled, turning back and forth, but found nothing familiar in the blurred faces and the surrounding darkness.

For a moment a black German shepherd broke its stride and trotted along next to her. He threw his nose into the air as if he were trying to tell her something, but Lucy didn't understand. She turned away to focus on the road, but her eyes were drawn back to the dog. This time there was a second head protruding from the neck of the animal. It was exactly the same as the first head except for the deep, black, empty sockets where eyes should have been.

Lucy screamed and ran even faster. But what was she running

from? Even though she could hear no ominous footsteps or heavy breathing, something was definitely there—something terrifying. She steadied her nerves. On the count of three she would glance around quickly to look. One, two, three—but she didn't turn, she couldn't. Instead she whipped left and jetted down a dark alley, then on through an empty street. She ran, watching the fading darkness, which was eventually overcome by light. She ran, praying for help, anybody's help. She ran until she finally woke up.

Lucy leaped out of bed, trying to remember more details this time. Maybe if she knew where she was or when it was happening she could figure out what the dream was about. She struggled to recall something, anything other than the monstrous fear that moved from her toes up into her knees, past her stomach and heart and finally to the center of her brain.

She opened the book of ten thousand dreams on her nightstand and found the section on running. She read the same passage every time she had this dream. "If you are running away from danger you will soon incur a major loss." There was a spark of memory; the dog, the two-headed dog was something new. In the section of the book on dogs she read that multiple heads suggested spreading something too thin. It warned that success comes only with a concentration of energy. Then she looked up *eyes* and learned that the loss of an eye meant trouble or a threat on the way.

Lucy put the book down and went into the bathroom. She thought more about the dream as she brushed her teeth and washed her face. What could she be so afraid of? She shuffled toward the kitchen, but took a moment in the hallway to inhale the sweetness of this week's flower. White carnations stood erect in the glass vase that had held red roses last week and would maybe hold lilies of the valley next week. After landing her first job out of college, Lucy spontaneously stopped by a florist shop and bought herself a huge bouquet of mixed flowers in celebration. It became a weekly ritual when she discovered how the flowers elevated her moods. This week's white carnations enhanced her spiritual strength and devotion. Next week's lilies of the valley would bring happiness and good luck.

In her small kitchen, Lucy pulled a pitcher of iced tea from the refrigerator and filled a glass half full. She tore open one pink and one blue package of artificial sweetener, dumping them into the liquid. A handful of ice and mountain spring water filled the rest of the glass. After taking a moment to watch the concoction swirl with each turn of the straw, she finally enjoyed a sweet, calming sip.

"Colored sugar water" was what Lucy's grandmother, Madea, called the bland-looking iced tea that Lucy drank every morning. Lucy didn't know exactly why she started drinking her tea like that, but now it was the only way. She truly loved the syrupy taste and cool texture. It was a morning addiction just like her boyfriend, Spencer's, cup of strong black coffee or her best friend, Adel's, can of Diet Pepsi. Although Lucy had yet to realize it, in many ways that glass of colored sugar water also reflected what her life had become; bland and routine, yet sweet and satiating.

Lucy covered her nose as she sneezed. "God bless me, God bless me, God bless me," she chanted three times to save her soul and counteract the bad luck a sneeze could bring. She was about to head for the shower when she noticed that she had knocked over the salt shaker with her elbow.

"Oh no," she moaned while picking up a pinch of salt from the table and throwing it across her left shoulder into the eyes of the Devil. The rest of the salt was brushed into her left hand, taken to the front door of her condo, and sprinkled right outside as a deterrence against any other evil that might be lurking around.

Lucy checked the clock and confirmed what she already knew; the dream had made her late for work again. She hurried into the bathroom, pulled off the oversized T-shirt, leaned into the tub, and turned the right knob clockwise. As she quickly stepped under the icy water that flowed from the massaging showerhead, Lucy's body shivered and jerked, then eventually relaxed and enjoyed the extreme sensation.

Cold water showers were normal for Lucy. Sometimes only cold water flowed through the pipes in the Louisiana home where she was raised. However, it was not until she came to Texas and read somewhere that the cold water helped to close her pores and better protected her skin from extreme heat that she started to appreciate the experience.

The phone rang. Lucy stood still for a moment and listened as each ring blended with the sound of the pulsating water. She decided it would be too much trouble to get out and answer it, so instead she closed her eyes and focused on the force of the water.

It might have been Adel. She was waiting to hear from her about a sleepover they had planned for the weekend. Since Adel married for the second time, they hadn't been able to get together as often as they wanted to. Lucy was worried. She was afraid that this marriage would be a disaster just like the first.

Adel's first husband called himself Lane, an abbreviation for his nickname, The Fast Lane. He was a burnt-out musician looking for someone to take care of him. Adel's Florence Nightingale mentality made her the perfect sucker. It was two years and fifty thousand dollars later before she finally figured it out. She swore her second husband was different, but Lucy wasn't so sure.

The way Lucy saw it, Adel's main problem was that she didn't have a strong sense of self-esteem. It was as if Adel were trying to find her self-worth in a man, which was totally unnecessary since she could more than take care of herself. As the vice president of human resources at American Oil, Adel was on the fast track to a CEO position. She pulled in a six-figure salary with fantasy bonuses of twenty thousand plus, depending on the company's yearly profits.

The call was probably from Spencer. He called every morning

around the same time with the same greeting, "Good morning, love." In the beginning of their relationship it was an endearing action and Lucy couldn't get enough. His consistency and simplicity was exactly what she thought she needed, what she thought she wanted. But now it felt like they were drowning in still water. Lucy was bored after only a couple of years with the man, so how in the world could they consider spending the rest of their lives together?

Still feeling the brisk tingle of her recently dried body, Lucy sat in front of the lighted oak vanity and brushed her short, brown twists into place. Despite the fact that she could see herself moving, it didn't feel like her life was going anywhere. Growing up in Pointe Coupee Parish, Louisiana, had been both a blessing and a curse, because she understood so much more about life's possibilities.

Raised by her grandmother, Madea Mayeaux, a well-known healer in New Roads, Lucy was used to people knocking on the door anytime asking for help. Theirs was a house where strange things like evil eye, superstition, and ghosts were revered. She grew up experiencing the power of magic every day. Wanting to get away from all that, Lucy moved to Houston to attend college, chose to stay after graduation, found a great job, and tried to redirect her life into a more normal pattern.

She met Spencer when she ordered a Big Mac at his McDonald's franchise. She immediately adored his stable and simplistic soul. He always ordered the same dish at whatever restaurant they went to. He could always be found at home after work, sitting up under his television watching some sporting event or messing around in his yard redistributing mulch, planting flowers, mowing the grass, or weeding his garden. He was satisfied making love in the bedroom and usually missionary style. His stability had brought a necessary peace into her life.

Spencer had asked Lucy to marry him twice since Adel's New

Year's Eve party. She didn't say no, but she didn't say yes, either. When she thought about it, she knew her major problem was fear, the fear of change. Permanently hooking up would mean major changes for both of them and Lucy just wasn't ready. Spencer swore nothing would change, but she knew better.

Lucy knew all about change and she didn't like it. Her future had changed dramatically in that one moment when her parents' car was totaled by a tailgating semi outside of St. Louis. At seven years old, her whole life changed when she was moved to a place where plantations were restored for tourists to take a peep into that popular historical event called slavery.

After some consideration, Lucy selected a beige A-line linen skirt and a matching embroidered top to wear. She wiggled into the outfit, slipped on her beige sandals, then headed for the front door. When she stopped to pose in the full-length mirror for a final check, she had to grin, because she looked good. That outfit on her curvy, five-foot-eight, 150-pound body said, "Lucinda Marie Merriweather was all that!"

2

At three minutes past ten o'clock Lucy left her condo in River Oaks and drove toward the downtown fitness center where her office was located. It was eighty-eight degrees already in the August heat and she could feel the sweat that had begun to seep through her thin top. The temperature would reach an expected high of ninety-nine degrees by late afternoon, causing everything in the city from people to trees to pray for a decent breeze.

The Looking Good Fitness Center rented two floors at the bottom of a twelve-story office complex. They were a full-service health spa offering weight rooms, personal trainers, exercise and yoga classes, saunas, whirlpools, and a lap-size swimming pool. Lucy parked her pearl BMW in the space with her name on it behind the smoked-glass building.

As the regional manager of this successful chain of fitness centers, looking good was not only a major part of Lucy's attitude, but also her job. After graduating from college with a degree in business, she eagerly took her first job in sales at the Houston location. Ten years later she was named regional manager of the five

Texas centers: Dallas, Fort Worth, and Austin each had one center and there were two in the Houston area.

Lucy rushed into her office and answered the phone just as it
rang for the third time. Adel said hello on the other end.

"Hey, Adel, what's jiggling?" Lucy asked in between short
breaths, flopping down on her padded armchair designed to correct poor posture.

"What's up with you, old lady? You're breathing awfully hard.
You didn't take your vitamins this morning?" Adel teased.

"Instead of worrying about me, you need to get that limp dick
husband of yours to take some Viagra," Lucy shot back and
laughed. She waited for the comeback she knew would follow.

"Ohhhhh," Adel groaned. "You didn't have to go there, my
sister. It was only once last month. I see I can't tell you nothing."

"Once, twice, three times a loser," Lucy sang.

Adel snorted. "I can't believe you've got the nerve to clown me
this morning about my man! When's the last time you got old
Spencer away from the television set? At least Thad ain't never
told me in the middle of lovemaking to move my head to the left
so he can see the game."

They both burst into uncontrolled laughter. Lucy and Adel
could always laugh easily together. They had been best friends for
almost twenty years. As freshmen they met as roommates at Texas
Southern University. In four years together, the girls discovered so
many similarities that it felt as if they were related. Both were the
only children blessed from their parents' mergers. They were
about the same age, just six months apart. Adel was a Gemini,
born in May, and Lucy's October birthday made her a Libra. Religion was the only major difference between the two, often illuminating itself like the bright yellow sun.

The girls shared stories about their Indian and African ancestors, often talking until the middle of the night. Adel's neu-
tral, unsettled soul was transplanted to Houston from
Chillicothe, Missouri, where her father was a descendent of

Shawnee Indians who founded the Midwestern town in the late 1700s.

She told Lucy many of her father's ramblings, but the story that stood out in her memory took place in the early 1800s. The local Shawnee tribe feared witchcraft was taking over their village, so they burned more than fifty women to death. Each victim was accused of practicing sorcery and their evil deeds were linked to any death, illness, or confusion that arose in the village. The accusations were often based on peculiar sightings of owls, wild dogs, and other animals from the forest. Despite the consistent denials, each woman was tied to a stake and burned. This story had shaped Adel's noncommittal religious upbringing. Her family was never wedded to the idea of religion, so they didn't attend a specific church. The way she explained it to Lucy was that it wasn't a matter of not believing in God, but more a matter of not knowing what or how to believe.

Lucy, on the other hand, was extreme when it came to her spiritual connections. She was taught to believe unconditionally in God and his almighty power. Through her grandmother's work, religion became a diverse credence and Lucy learned to recognize all of the god-like forces in the universe. Through Yoruba tradition she followed the minigods that existed, like Osun, goddess of the river; Shango, god of war; and Ogun, god of the sky. In the practice of voodoo, Agwe, god of the seas; Bade, god of the wind; the serpent god, Domballah; and Sogbu, the god of lightning, were worshipped and respected.

Lucy knew very little about her Indian ancestors, only that they were from the Coushatta tribe located in Southwestern Louisiana. Her favorite story came from her African descendents who were escaped slaves from Haiti. Madea often told the story about Lucy's third cousin Big Beany, who townsfolk swore died a hoodoo death. Madea talked about Big Beany's sudden illness many times. She swore it came from his mistress. His wife rushed him to a clinic in Baton Rouge to see the white doctor when he first complained of a pain in his stomach, but that doctor sent him home because he couldn't find anything wrong.

When Big Beany died a few days later, Madea lit a white candle dressed with blessing oil to light the way to heaven for his two-timing soul. As the story goes, in front of Madea and his wife, three small frogs popped out of Big Beanie's mouth and the candle flickered brightly, a signal that his soul had been released. When the coroner came, he pronounced Big Beany dead from heart complications, but most folks in the parish knew that Big Beany had died a hoodoo death. Lucy never could convince Adel that the story was true even though she put her right hand on the Bible and swore to God several times.

Lucy sighed. "I know Spencer's got his problems, but Thad is a Milk Dud. He acts like a big selfish baby and you let him get away with it," she insisted, then took a deep cautious breath before she continued. "I'm your best friend and I'm always going to tell you the truth, Adel. If your husband would just stop crying and start trying maybe he could get somewhere."

"Well Thad *is* my husband and I've decided to hang in there with the brother. He has potential and I'm going to be a supportive black woman," Adel retorted.

"You don't have to settle for a piece of man to prove you're a good black woman."

Adel hesitated, choosing her words carefully. "Thad and I have a passion that you don't understand, Lucy," she finally replied. "Spencer is just a convenience for you."

"Excuse me!" Lucy answered in an exaggerated manner. "You and Thad might have passion, but Spencer and I have stability. Which one do you think will last longer?"

"You know, that halo that you're always flaunting only has to slip a little bit to turn into a noose," Adel huffed.

Lucy inhaled deeply. "I worry about you, Adel."

Adel exhaled deeply. "You don't have to worry, I'm okay."

"Are we still on for tonight?" Lucy asked, attempting to change the subject.

Adel responded to someone in her office before she answered. "I'll call them back in a minute. Okay. Yeah, Lucy, tonight at seven: dinner, a movie, and a good old-fashioned sleepover."

"I can't wait, girl. I need some time away from Spencer. I'm convinced that he loves his mama, fried chicken, ESPN, and me in that order," Lucy whined.

"You need to quit," Adel said with a chuckle. "Spencer is a great guy and if you don't open your eyes and stop being so selfish you're gonna lose him. Maybe I should take him, so I can finally have a man you approve of."

Lucy grinned. This was familiar banter between the two. "I don't know if Spencer and I are going to make it or not, but if you think you're bad enough to take him, go for what you know, my sister," she teased.

"You know better than to challenge me. You need to be glad I got a husband or your ass would be crying the lost-my-man blues."

Lucy flipped through her Rolodex and scoffed. "I appreciate your high moral and ethical standards and that's why I allow you to hang with me," she said.

Adel moaned. "Get real. You know it's the other way around. You're the one hanging with *me,*" she replied. "Anyway, I've got to go. See you tonight."

Lucy sucked her teeth and clicked over to line two. She dialed and waited, but as usual Spencer didn't answer. She sighed. He was probably out working at the front counter. What was the point of owning a Micky Dee's if he was going to act like one of the employees? She didn't know why she couldn't make Spencer understand that. The machine beeped, waiting for her message.

Lucy pulled up her sexiest voice. "Hey, baby," she teased. "I called to tell you how much I hate not seeing you this weekend. Adel and I are hooking up for the sleepover, then I'm going to finish the proposal for the Austin center on Saturday. But Sunday night you need to be ready because my tumbleweed is gonna rest at your oasis in this desert called love. Bye-bye." She knew it was corny, but Spencer was corny. And he liked it.

Most of Lucy's day was spent checking and rechecking numbers on her report for the upcoming board of directors meeting. She was right on target with her quarterly projections for the Houston market. Both centers were grossing more than a hundred-thousand dollars a week. Dallas and Fort Worth hovered around one hundred and fifty thousand, but the Austin market was still stumbling between fifty to sixty thousand.

She had met with the center's manager, Birch Tallan, last month, which did not make him very happy. He spent most of the hour defending his work and insulting her credibility as regional manager. Last week she was forced to send him a probation slip because the figures had continued to drop.

At five o'clock Lucy changed clothes in the locker room to get ready for her daily workout. It started with a ten-minute stretch, then moved into a well-defined routine. She did three sets of twelve repetitions for her arms and legs with the free weights and fifty crunches for her abs. Each movement was slow and smooth to gain maximum benefits. She wrapped up with a twenty-minute swim.

As her well-toned body slid through the cool water, Spencer floated into her thoughts again. She considered him her six-foot, two-hundred-pound Milky Way because the man satisfied her chocolate jones. He adored Lucy and she was crazy about him too, but she couldn't make the commitment he wanted, not now.

3

*

After filling up on fajitas and margaritas, Lucy and Adel sat in Lucy's den watching *Eve's Bayou* for the second time.

"I still can't believe that somebody could have the kind of power Debbie Morgan had," Adel complained.

"That stuff is real, girl," Lucy assured her. "Madea knows all about it."

"If that's the case we need to get the lottery numbers from her so we can win that fourteen million this week." Adel teased.

Lucy stretched out across the beige carpet on the floor. "It don't work like that," she explained. "And you shouldn't joke about shit you don't understand."

As the tape rewound, Adel flipped through the television channels. "That little girl killed her daddy, but it wasn't the voodoo, it was her mouth," she continued.

Lucy looked up at the vaulted ceiling and stared out into the night through the rectangular skylight. "Maybe it was a little bit of both," she replied.

Adel yawned and checked her watch. It was two o'clock in the morning, but the idea was to stay awake until you dropped off to sleep wherever you were. She continued to flick channels until she got to BET, where music videos played incessantly. Adel and Lucy focused on a very sexy black man pumping his pelvis to a reggae beat. They bobbed their heads with the music until a psychic hotline commercial interrupted.

Lucy took an exaggerated breath. "I should call and see if they have a black male psychic," she joked. "Can you imagine a man with that kind of sensitivity? He could rule the world."

"You trippin', girl," Adel replied, extending her arms in a long stretch.

"Think about it. This would be a man who could know your every need and desire before they even emerge. Lord have mercy!"

"That sounds too good," Adel warned.

"Check this out," Lucy said, snatching up the receiver.

Adel shook her head. "Lucy, don't," she cautioned.

Lucy glanced at the television screen, her eyes bright with adventure. She dialed the number carefully. "Hello," she said when the operator answered. "I want to speak to a black male psychic, if you have one, please." She waited, expecting to be told it wasn't possible, but instead the line went quiet and a phone somewhere began ringing.

"Hello, Kuba here. I'm glad you called Sexy Soul Psychics." The husky voice whirled around in Lucy's head for a moment.

"Hey, Kuba," Lucy finally answered in her sexiest voice. She winked at Adel, who immediately hopped up, grabbed the phone in the kitchen, and held her hand over the mouthpiece.

"Hey yourself, what's your name?" Kuba asked, returning the same seductive tone.

Lucy wasn't sure what happened to her plan to use a phony name when she blurted out the real one. "Lucinda," she said, running her index finger over the telephone cord.

"Lucinda," he repeated, almost as a question, but not quite. "And your birthday, Lucinda?"

"October thirteenth."

"Oh, you're looking at a bright future with love in both your fourth and tenth houses," he told her.

Lucy steadied herself. The man's gravel-like tone was awesome. Each word seemed to seep in and out of her pores and she could feel his spirit suddenly surging like a drug through her veins.

"Tell me something I don't know," she teased.

"Romance is the key to that lock on your heart, Lucinda, and unfortunately your current lover doesn't understand that, does he?"

Lucy took a big gulp of her margarita. Kuba had scored a bull's-eye with that one.

"Ask him what he's wearing," Adel whispered loudly.

Lucy frowned on top of her smile. She had forgotten that Adel was even in the room and didn't appreciate her groove being disturbed.

"Tell your friend to ask me herself if she really wants to know," Kuba replied, almost as a test.

"Will you tell me the truth?" Adel asked in what Lucy noticed was a somewhat provocative tone of her own.

"Of course," Kuba answered. "I'm wearing nothing. I've found that I can channel much better without the interference of clothing."

Kuba's silky phrasing pushed intensely against Lucy's thoughts, and the word *nothing* made her dizzy.

"So, tell me more about this channeling in the nude," Lucy requested. "I might want to try it sometime."

Kuba eased out a slow, sensitive laugh. "I bet you'd be real good at it too, Lucinda; you have what old people call a sixth sense."

Lucy envisioned the flex of his large, tender lips as he spoke.

"You think so?" she asked enticingly, with the liquor making her even bolder.

"I know so," he answered, emitting the same sensual intensity.

Fanning herself from the heat that was inching its way across her body, Lucy wondered at that moment if Kuba could spell R-E-L-I-E-F.

"Lucinda, I need your time of birth," Kuba continued.

"Five twenty-five p.m.," she replied without hesitation. She knew because she had recently dug out a copy of her birth certificate to update her passport for the trip to Paris she was planning over the Christmas holiday.

"Hold on just a second," Kuba said, setting the phone down.

Lucy and Adel sat holding their receivers like two kids waiting to see Santa with long Christmas lists in their hands. Lucy strained to hear what was going on in the background, but she could only distinguish the sound of humming. It was not a song, but a chant of some kind.

"Okay, Lucinda, I need you to listen to me seriously," Kuba said in a somewhat forceful tone when he returned.

"What makes you think I haven't been listening seriously?" she asked.

Kuba ignored the question. "You're someone who endures. You've found success in every other part of your life except love. Do you know why?"

Lucy lifted her eyebrows toward Adel, delivering a silent but well-understood message of sarcasm. "First of all, I don't agree with that statement since I have a good man in my life who loves me, but you tell me what you think is going on, Mr. Kuba."

"Yes, I can see that you have a man in your life, but is he the man you need? You are a woman who goes after what she wants and you're not afraid to work hard for it. But when it comes to love you lack that same aggression, Lucinda. You take the easy route and accept what's convenient."

Lucy twisted the ends of her mouth downward. This was the second time today somebody had suggested Spencer was a convenience. It wasn't true. She loved him. She just wasn't ready to commit.

"You're planning a trip out of the country soon," Kuba added, assuredly.

Lucy jumped at the statement. "Yes," she said automatically.

"You will meet the man you've been looking for before you take that trip. He'll be where you least expect to find him."

"And you want me to believe this stuff is for real?" Lucy asked mockingly.

"It's as real as you want it to be," Kuba responded. His voice was cocky and sure as if he knew he had gotten to her.

"Well, you haven't convinced me yet," Lucy lied. "Do you see anything else in my future? Anything more specific?"

"I can see that you are blocking your sixth sense, trying to ignore it." Kuba stopped and allowed a long pause to hang between them. "It's a big mistake, Lucinda. If you pay attention to your sixth sense it can show you things and help you to work out much of your confusion."

"Yeah, sure," Lucy sneered before he could finish. "I've had fortune cookies tell me more than that."

Kuba laughed. It was a strange laugh that shot through Lucy's ear and down into the depth of her soul.

"Revelations are usually reserved for prophets, Lucinda, but you will have a revelation."

"What kind of revelation?"

"I don't know exactly. But I can tell you that the man I see in your future will be the first man to ever understand the true essence of your being."

Lucy took a deep breath. More gibberish. And now that she thought about it they had been on the phone for a long time. Her phone bill was going to be a bitch! She wanted to hang up, but she had to ask one more question.

"Okay, Mr. Kuba, since you know so much, why don't you tell me about the true essence of my being. What is it?"

He was quiet for a moment. Then, as if he could read her mind, Kuba repeated the one word that had been tumbling around inside it. "Fear, Lucinda," he replied. "The fear of letting go."

She sat in silence. How could he know that? It was true. Her whole life was built around fear. She suddenly wanted to hang up. Lucy didn't like the strange chill that ran through her body. "You know what? I gotta go, Kuba. You've done a great job of keeping me on this phone long enough to make yourself some big money, but this is the end of the gravy train. You have a good evening." Lucy lowered her receiver into the cradle as Adel hustled back into the living room.

"Girl, that was deep," Adel said.

"Yeah, real deep," Lucy replied sarcastically. She finished her margarita in one big gulp.

"I've never talked to a psychic before, but I think he was pretty good, don't you?" Adel continued.

Lucy nodded. "You really have to be careful when you're dealing with people like that."

"So what about this new man who's supposed to come into your life?" Adel asked. "You're the one who usually believes this stuff."

Lucy grunted between denials, still trying to get that hypnotic voice out of her head. She kept hearing the sound of her name as it rolled past his prodding tongue. "I'm not looking for anybody new. Spencer may not be the man of my dreams, but he's a good man and I could do worse."

"It's about time you admitted that," Adel said.

Carrying her glass into the kitchen, Lucy set it in the sink before she replied. "Just because I don't say it out loud all the time, doesn't mean I don't know it."

"What about your trip to Paris?" Adel asked, following Lucy into the kitchen. "How would Kuba know about that?"

"He didn't know I was going to Paris. He just said a trip. And most people will probably go on some kind of trip by the end of the year, especially during the holidays."

"He was very good," Adel admitted again. "He almost got me believing that hocus pocus stuff."

Lucy stood and stared in Adel's direction with a furrowed brow. "Adel, the man on the other end of that line is a con artist. Believing him would be like adding M & M's to a tuna salad: a stupid thing to do!"

4

*

Adel sat stiffly behind her large, mahogany desk, then dropped her aching head into cupped hands. It was Monday morning and she wasn't sure what had happened to the weekend. On Friday she and Lucy hung out all night. They'd had a ball as usual: laughing, drinking and playing with a sexy psychic named Kuba from one of those advertisements on television.

Even though she enjoyed Kuba's phone show, she didn't believe it. She believed that life is what you made it. People create their own destinies, not some omnipresent being from above. She offered as proof the state of the world today: futile ignorance, distorted poverty, unnecessary hunger, and unfathomable pain. If there truly was a guiding force, Adel figured, good people wouldn't constantly have to deal with the craziness of this messed-up world.

Adel and Lucy had gotten up late Saturday morning and eaten silver-dollar pancakes with raspberry syrup for breakfast. Then Adel spent Saturday afternoon running errands. She picked up the dry cleaning, did some grocery shopping, and got her Lexus washed. That evening Thad had come home in a surprisingly lov-

ing, playful mood, so they wrestled for a while before the ex-
ploding heat caused a chain reaction that left both of them tired
but blissful in their queen-size bed.

Most of that Sunday was lost in an angry cleaning frenzy.
Thad's car was jacked up in the driveway as usual, so he had borrowed hers early that morning and did not return until very late
that night. Adel started with the dishes. The directions for the
new dishwasher said they didn't need to be rinsed, but she was a
creature of habit, so she stood in front of the sink, rinsing each
dish carefully and sliding it into the open rack.

Thad had purposely posed the question about borrowing her
car when she was half asleep. He knew sleep was her primary passion for living and she would say yes to almost anything just to be
left alone.

"I got some things to do this morning," he'd whispered just
before he snatched the keys from the top of the dresser and
bopped out of the bedroom.

Adel threw the brown-and-black Egyptian-patterned comforter on the floor before she ripped the ivory cotton sheets and
pillowcases from the master bed. Next she made her way to the
guest room and did the same thing, carrying all of the linen to the
laundry room. She shoved the linen inside the washing machine,
dumped in a cup of soap, and started it.

Thad should have returned before she finished, but, of course,
that didn't happen. When she dialed his cell phone number and
got his voice mail her anger grew. She was stuck in the house all
day Sunday and most of the night with nothing to think about except the shallowness of Thad's promises lately.

She vacuumed, dusted, mopped, waxed, washed, wiped, and
straightened and was admiring a spotless stove when Thad's key
eventually clicked in the front lock and the door opened.

Adel didn't have to look at the clock. She could hear Mel
Zimmerman on television with his weekly consumer report, so it
was definitely after ten. There had been no phone call all day

and, apparently, she realized after looking into Thad's face, no remorse.

"Hey, baby," he said, cheerfully following it with a light peck on the cheek.

"Where the hell have you been all day?" Adel spit out before Thad could get the front door closed.

He immediately recognized her mood and dreaded the argument that was coming. "I told you I had to take care of some things today," he responded coolly, then cautiously stepped around Adel's firmly planted body.

"How are you going to take my car and leave me here all day like that, Thad," she screamed at the back of his head. "No phone call, no consideration, no nothing! What is this insensitive bull-shit?"

"I don't know what you're talking about, Del," he replied dismissively. "You told me last night you didn't have anything to do today."

Adel's lips were trembling. Her fingers felt like numb extensions down by her side. This wasn't about having something to do, it was about not being able to do something if she had wanted or needed to. "That's not the point!" she finally screamed.

"And what is the goddamn point?" Thad turned and asked.

"The point is, you need to get rid of that raggedy, piece-of-shit car out there and get something you can drive."

"Del, you know how I feel about my baby. She's a classic and the one woman who truly understands me."

Adel shuddered. "That's so pathetic, Thad! You know, Confucius say: Man who keep classic car should not complain when he has to push that sorry jalopy home."

He shot her a disgusted look. "As soon as I get the new muffler and brake pads on she'll be fine."

"You're always up under that damn car, Thad. You need to go on and buy something that runs."

He shrugged his shoulders, turned, and walked away.

"Answer a question for me?" Adel continued, arm extended, head cocked to the side and finger pointed at the back of his head. "Can you at least tell me why your cell phone was off and you couldn't even call to see if I needed anything today?"

"What am I supposed to do, Del, check in every hour on the hour?" Thad asked in a nasty tone.

"It's not checking in, Thad, it's checking on . . . me!" Adel hissed.

"It don't sound like that to me. I told you when we first started talking this marriage thing that I'm not going to be hog-tied by anybody. I love you, Del, but I'm a free spirit, always have been, and if you try to cage me, I'll fly away and never come back."

Adel stared at him for a moment. "As long as you don't fly away in my car, I'm not sure I would care right now!" She mumbled.

Thad looked at her coldly. "I had a few things to take care of today, no big deal. I don't borrow your car that often and you weren't going anywhere. As a matter of fact, one of the things I did was fill out a credit application to buy me another car."

Adel watched as his soft brown eyes shifted into their battered-black-male mode. His eyebrows were raised just slightly, his eyelids drooping and heavy, and his pupils glassy with emotion. She had fallen for it when they were first dating and even at the beginning of the marriage, but now she knew it was nothing more than a ploy. She had seen Thad use it too many times for too many reasons.

"I'm not trying to cage you, as you put it, but you have to take more responsibility around here. I'm tired of doing everything."

"Fine, baby, you're right." Thad gave in, hoping to find some peace. "I've been letting too many things fall on your back and I'll do better," he said in a voice that was just a little more compassionate. "This has been a bad year for me, but things are going to turn around."

"I hope so, because if all you have to give me is this kind of bullshit, I don't need it," Adel warned.

Thad raised his hands in the air. "I told you I would do better, now can we drop it, please?" he asked.

"One more thing. I'd appreciate it if you would mow the grass tomorrow. Ours is the only house on the block where the yard looks like a jungle."

"Sure, I'll mow the lawn tomorrow, Del," he replied dryly. "Is there anything else you need?"

Adel sighed, suddenly feeling guilty. "I don't want to always be complaining, Thad, but it seems like I have to complain for something to get done around here."

Thad reached out and pulled her to him. "I know, I know, forgive me," he moaned. "I got so excited about these potential investors for my software package, I didn't think to call. I'm sorry you were stuck here all day. It won't happen again."

Adel clenched her teeth. She knew this was the second part of Thad's act and she wasn't ready to forgive him. He was the charming son of a preacher man and she married him because he could make her feel happy for no reason at all. But during their marriage she had learned that Thad was a chameleon, he could be the sweetest, most lovable soul one minute, then turn around and show all his behind the next.

She stood melting under his gentle touch anyway, knowing deep down that nothing was going to change. When he took her into his arms and kissed her softly, she had to admit that there was nobody to blame but herself. The signs were there, smacking her in the face, begging her to pay attention. Thad was two hours late for their first date with no phone call. And when he finally showed up that night flaunting a charcoal gray Armani suit and cherubic smile, he offered a wilted yellow rose and a heartfelt apology that she readily accepted.

Thad continued his peace-making efforts. "If you don't believe anything else about me, baby, believe that I want you to be happy," he whispered, wrapping his arms around her waist.

Adel's voice cracked. "You say all the right things, but when it comes to action nothing happens. I'm tired, Thad. The job, our marriage, nothing seems to make me happy anymore."

Thad held her tighter and chuckled. "Max warned me that you were high maintenance. He even bet that I couldn't hang with you for more than a year. But I won that twenty dollars, Del, and I'm planning to win fifty more on our five-year anniversary."

Adel pulled back and looked deep into his eyes. "Why would Max say some shit like that? Your brother's such an asshole."

"He's actually on your side. It's psychology. In order to get me to do something he wants, he bets that I can't do it, knowing I will do it because I always have to win the bet."

"You're with me because of a bet?"

"I'm with you because I love you, the bet is between me and my brother."

Adel's frown turned to a smirk. "It sounds weird to me, but whatever works," she mumbled. "Sometimes it seems like I'm the only one trying to make things better."

Thad shook his head. "You make things harder, Del, not better. You need to learn to let go. Try to enjoy life more."

Adel rolled her eyes. "If I had some help and support around here, maybe I could enjoy life more."

"I said I'll try to do better. That's all I can tell you," Thad repeated and let her go.

Adel turned and grabbed him around the waist. "Don't tell me, show me, baby," she whispered while nipping at his earlobe.

Thad moved closer, sliding his lips down the side of her neck. "Like this?" he moaned.

Adel closed her eyes. "Just like that."

"Come on," he said, pulling her toward the couch.

Adel smiled, but resisted. "Sex can't solve our problems, Thad. It just postpones them for a while."

"So let's postpone them," he said, grinning and massaging her breasts.

"Maybe later. I need a shower," she replied with a peck on his cheek.

"At least tell me you love me?" he asked before he let her go.

"Of course, I love you," she replied. "Sometimes I wonder why, but I do love you, Thad."

He allowed a victorious smile to spread across his face, then turned and hustled toward the kitchen. "Well the next best thing to sex is food. Did you make anything for dinner? I'm starved."

Adel followed him, laughing at his hungry-little-boy gestures. "You didn't eat while you were out?" she asked.

"I had a quick hot dog this afternoon. You know, this software idea is finally moving forward. I met with a couple of potential investors who might make all our dreams come true," he said with a wink. "I also saw Lincoln again today. He said I could go to work in sales with him until I get my business off the ground."

"Your degree is in computers. I thought you were going to try and find something in that area?" Adel asked.

"I don't have time to look for a real job. I want to focus on the business. As soon as I get my web page set up things should start flowing."

Adel nodded and smiled slightly.

Thad opened the refrigerator and took out three plastic containers. He popped the top on each one, excited to see smothered pork chops, macaroni and cheese, and sweet candied yams.

He grabbed Adel and kissed her mouth greedily. "You cooked all my favorites!"

Adel laughed and playfully pushed him away. "Last night was so good I thought you deserved a special treat today, then you had to mess everything up. If I hadn't cooked that stuff early, you wouldn't be smacking your lips right now."

Thad heaped the food on his plate and fished a knife and fork out of the silverware drawer.

"You are truly the woman of my dreams," he said. "Smart, beautiful, and a great cook, when you want to cook."

"You didn't marry me for my cooking."

Thad lifted one eyebrow. "You got that right," he confirmed, and slid the plate into the microwave.

Adel sat down at the kitchen table. "You said you filled out the papers for a car today. Where?" She asked.

"I stopped in at the Toyota dealer on North Loop, but if my credit don't go through I may need you to co-sign for me."

Adel stopped smiling on the inside even though her mouth was still formed in that shape on the outside. They had had this conversation before and he knew she didn't want to co-sign for a car for anybody.

"What kind of car is it?" she asked.

Thad pulled the plate out of the microwave and plopped down at the table. He shoveled two spoonfuls of hot macaroni and cheese in his mouth before he spoke. "A red Lexus like yours, about two years old. It's in great shape. I know I can't drive around in a hoopty forever, embarrassing my baby."

Thad walked over to the refrigerator to get the orange juice. Before he sat back down he grabbed Adel's hand and squeezed it.

"I've been out there all day hustling for us, girl," he told her.

She hesitated, then spoke. "Thad, we need to talk about this co-signing thing."

He stopped eating long enough to glare at her, then focused on his plate again. "You said I need a car, didn't you?"

Adel thought carefully about how she could say what needed to be said. "The problem is that you don't always think things through," she stammered.

Thad flashed an offended look in her direction and shoveled more food into his mouth. "That's what you're good at, Adel, identifying problems."

"I just can't afford to have my credit messed up like yours, Thad."

He dropped his fork into the plate with a loud bang. "So what do you want me to do, Adel? I will pay for the damn car! You

don't have to worry about your precious credit. That's the difference between me and you. You'll let that white man kick you in
your ass and thank him for the pain!"

In that moment Adel's attitude changed. There it was again:
everything was the white man's fault. She was sick of hearing that
excuse. "Don't nobody kick me in my ass, black or white. So I
don't know what you're talking about, Thad. You need to stop
blaming everybody else for your choices in life."

"That's right, these are my choices and I'm gonna deal with life
the way I want to deal with it." He snorted, then took a big bite
of the candied yams. "Everything doesn't have to be done your
way, Adel!"

"Fine!" Adel shouted and stood up.

Thad didn't look at her as he spoke. "I've put in an application to get a car that runs, I said I'm going to take on more responsibility around here. That's what you want, right?"

"Right," Adel said before dragging herself into the bedroom.
She bypassed the shower and climbed under the clean, cotton
sheets. When she heard the television click on in the living room,
she was grateful that Thad didn't come straight to bed.

5

*

"Hey, can I come in?" Hunter Newton said at the same time that he popped his head into Adel's office and jarred her away from her thoughts.

"Sure, come on in. I'm just daydreaming about a vacation to the Virgin Islands this winter," she offered, lying.

"Sounds good. And what we need to talk about ties directly in to that," he said, shutting her office door. Hunter sat down on the blue leather couch off to Adel's left side. He slid his feet up on her glass coffee table. "I need to ask you to do what you do best, Adel." He hesitated, noticing for the first time that she had cut her hair. It was midlength, barely brushing her shoulders when she moved. He contemplated briefly, then decided he didn't like it as well as the longer hair. It made her look more professional, but less youthful.

"The company's profit figures have been down all year and with this stagnated economy, we will probably need to let three or four people go."

Adel sat up straighter in her chair. This was the part of her job that she hated. Telling people that through no fault of their own, despite acceptable evaluations and consistent productivity they were laid off, fired, canned, cut, pink-slipped, dumped, discharged, dismissed, and basically screwed.

Hunter continued: "I need for you to analyze each department's assets, meet with the managers, and identify four cuts that can be made by the end of the month without hurting productivity."

Adel didn't listen to what he was saying. Instead she was suddenly conflicted by how supportive he had always been of her. As the CEO of American Oil, Hunter had watched Adel when she first started as a management trainee. He admired her quick wit and efficient organizational skills. He helped her move up from account manager to director and then vice president of human resources. He was dedicated to creating a sense of diversity in his company and he believed that she had the stamina to go all the way. Adel was his protégé, his success story, his multicultural trophy.

Many of his colleagues thought he was nuts. They assumed that Hunter and Adel had a thing going on and that's why he thought he could prepare her to break through the glass ceiling. They joked behind his back that he was like a slave master who, after a taste of that good black stuff, had to move his concubine into the big house.

"Can't we wait another month or two and see if things change?" she asked, hoping that her hesitation would cause Hunter to have some compassion.

"If we're going to get our bonuses at the end of the year it has to happen soon, Adel. Remember your trip to the Virgin Islands."

Adel stared blankly at Hunter's bottom lip. What a sad thing to say. How could he sit there and suggest firing someone for her to have a vacation? Four people are supposed to lose their jobs so that the big boys and girl could get their year-end bonuses.

Adel tried to harness the new anger that flared. It sat firmly on top of the old anger left from Thad that had not yet dissipated.

This was not the first time Hunter had made such a request. It was almost as if the company preferred this method of balancing the haves versus the have nots. Instead of making narrow-minded managers work harder to find new financial opportunities, it was easier to fire somebody because *they* didn't have to do it. *Their* jobs weren't on the line and *their* lives weren't being turned upside down.

Two years ago Hunter had asked Adel to fire two people for the same reason. Not so that the company could stay afloat or so that profits would be in the black rather than the red, but so that the president and five greedy vice presidents, including herself, could enjoy the true meaning of Christmas as it had been defined in the new millennium: opulent elitist spending power.

Only the racist attitudes were worse. Whenever Adel complained Lucy would suggest a meeting with the NAACP or one of Texas' black congressmen. But what would she say to them? That Texaco is not the only oil company with major attitude problems when it comes to black folk? They already know that. They already know that the good ones, those managers whose discrimination practices are second nature, are rarely obvious. The skilled racist could use subjectivity to talk to an unwanted applicant so badly, yet professionally, of course, until that potential applicant would storm out of the building without submitting an application at all.

A young black truck driver had once filed an internal complaint with Adel's office saying he was treated worse than a two-bit ghetto gangster at his interview.

"Do you own your rig?" the manager of the trucking fleet had asked.

"Yes, for the last ten years," the unsuspecting young man responded, dropping his application into the well-manicured hands.

Pretending to skim the document, the manager continued. "We'll need to do an inspection of your rig and your driving record to make sure it is up to par."

"Here are the inspection papers on my rig, my driver's license is current, and I have no tickets or warrants," the young man replied.

The manager stuck out his chest and smirked. "Well, we'll need to send somebody to ride around with you, to check your driving out," he responded.

The young man's eyes burned and his shoulders stiffened. "Is this something that is only done with black drivers? Because a friend of mine was recently hired and no one had to ride around with him," he rebutted.

"I make these decisions as I see fit. Do you have a problem with my judgment?" the manager spit back.

The man reached for his application from the top of the desk and ripped it in half. "No problem," he said and left that office, heading straight to Adel's.

She had listened and tried to help him work through his rage. Her major effort was to avoid a lawsuit, because that was her job. But even as Adel sat there and told the man that there was probably no malice in the manager's comment, just a difference of communication styles, she secretly prayed that he would call her a corporate lackey and file a lawsuit.

Adel sat at her large executive desk wanting to scream. Four people were about to lose their livelihood and that made her nauseous. How was the company supposed to function effectively if they kept firing the people who do most of the work? Many employees were already forced to carry their load and half of somebody else's. American Oil would never sufficiently raise its profit margin like this. Why didn't Hunter and his cronies understand that these people, whom they seem to think so little of, are all that's holding them up? They are the ones filling out reports, maintaining the wells, and coordinating output, while the big boys shelter themselves inside insulated golf deals and politically incorrect jokes.

Hunter cleared his throat. "We do have a little time before it has to happen. I hope things turn around before then, but I want a list of potentials ready just in case. Can you handle that?"

Adel shifted in her seat, but she couldn't get her mouth to move. She wanted to yell "Hell no!" But nothing came out. She tried to say: "This is a terrible thing to do, please let's find another way." But silence reigned supreme. She finally just nodded her head in slow motion.

Hunter stood and stared at Adel, knowing this would be a real challenge for her. If she was going to take over his presidency someday she had to be able to handle the tough things. She had to separate her humanity from business. He wasn't really worried, because despite the attack of ethics she had each time he needed her, Adel would ultimately come through for him. He might only have her fire one or two out of the four once she put the list together. The company could probably get by with half the body bags he was asking for, but he wanted to make this one a little more difficult than the last. He needed to see what Adel was made of.

6

✳

Lucy waited in her car at the agreed-upon spot in Hermann Park. It was near the main entrance with a clear view of the bronze statue of General Samuel Houston, the city's namesake, on his trusty horse. It was the spot where she and Spencer first kissed.

She had talked Spencer into trying a new Mexican restaurant in the area, but was afraid he wouldn't find it. One of Spencer's most annoying traits was his lack of patience, especially when he was doing something he didn't want to. Spencer had lived in Houston all of his life and had a hard time dealing with the unyielding growth of the city. Lucy could see him driving around for five minutes at the most, half-ass looking for the place, then heading home to order a pizza delivery from Domino's.

She watched a pair of headlights bounce up and down as Spencer's blue Chevy Blazer pulled too quickly into the drive. He parked, got out of the car, and ambled toward her.

"Hey, sugar," Spencer said, leaning into the driver's window of her car and snatching a quick kiss.

"Is that all I get after three days?" Lucy teased and wiggled her tongue at him.

Spencer pulled his head back. "Mom is with me. She wanted to try this place out, too."

Lucy glanced over and noticed the shadowy image on the passenger side of the truck for the first time. She held her breath. She was not in the mood tonight to deal with his mother. Not that Mrs. Gray wasn't a nice person. She was okay as mothers went. In her mid-fifties, Mrs. Gray was a very pretty woman with short red hair and chestnut-colored eyes. She respected Lucy and at times even seemed to genuinely like her.

Spencer was actually the problem. He literally worshipped his mother. As far as he was concerned the woman was as close to perfection as anyone could get and Lucy hated trying to measure up.

"You missed her family dinner on Saturday, so I couldn't tell her no tonight, could I?" He leaned back into the window and kissed her softly again. "I had a craving for you this weekend," he added.

"I'll satisfy that craving later tonight, but right now let's go satisfy my craving for food," she replied, starting her engine.

They drove down South Main Street, made a left on Greenbriar, and another left on Old Spanish Trail. Lucy signaled that she was turning into the parking lot and Spencer followed. She waited for them to join her at the front door before entering.

The restaurant offered a typical Spanish design, with large sombreros tilted on the heads of wax cowboys riding bucking broncos next to imitation cactuses. The Hispanic hostess showed the threesome to a booth near the plate glass window in front. Lucy sat on one side by herself opposite Spencer and his mother.

"I'm sorry about missing Saturday, Mrs. Gray," Lucy blurted out. She hoped she could eliminate as much as possible of the lecture she knew was coming.

Mrs. Gray smiled delicately, then delivered her carefully prepared comment in response. "Spencer told me you were finishing a proposal and I understand you have work to do, but I don't understand why you couldn't have stopped for dinner, Lucy."

"Once I get on a roll I like to go ahead and finish up," Lucy responded lamely.

"You know Spencer's father used to tell me all the time that he was working and he couldn't get home for dinner. I believed him until the day he died and his mistress showed up at the funeral with Spencer's half-sister."

Lucy's smile froze. "I'm sorry that happened, Mrs. Gray, but my missing dinner on Saturday doesn't mean I'm having an affair."

Mrs. Gray frowned. "That's not what I'm trying to say, sweetheart. What I'm saying is that you and Spencer don't seem to realize that time is passing by and if you're serious about each other you've got to spend time together," she explained. "I lived with a man for thirty years and we never understood that."

Spencer winced, took a deep breath, then jumped in. "Right now we're trying to set our lives up so that we can have some quality time, Mom."

"You two talk like most young people, like I did. I used to think every day was a confirmed blessing. Believe me, it's not."

The waitress brought their drink order and Lucy grabbed that moment to change the subject.

"I love that necklace you have on, Mrs. Gray. Where did you get it?" she asked. Lucy was not really interested in the gold sapphire pendant. It was much too gaudy for her taste, but she knew it would take Mrs. Gray into two of her favorite conversational areas: shopping and self.

"I got this at a little store down on Montrose. You know the artist's district down there. It only cost eighty dollars, which I thought was a steal. I'm so glad you like it," she purred, fingering the chain.

"Mom, I keep telling you to stop reporting what you pay for everything," Spencer complained. "It makes you sound shallow."

"I'm just being honest, Spencer. It was a good deal. That's all I meant," Mrs. Gray protested.

Lucy took several swallows of her iced tea, which was much too strong. She drank a few more swallows, poured some of her water into the glass, stirred, and sipped again. Much better. As she blocked out the discussion on the seat across from her, Lucy imagined herself ten years down the road as Mrs. Spencer Gray. She would be the one next to the man arguing and his mother would be sitting on the opposite side of the table.

She couldn't wait for dinner to be over. Lucy decided that her usual white wine nightcap would be enjoyed at home just to save some time. Since she lived closest to Spencer's mother, they agreed that he would drop his mother off at home and come back to her place.

When Spencer opened the gate and stepped onto Lucy's back patio he heard a soft, sexy voice.

"Hey, loverboy," Lucy called.

Spencer looked around, but didn't see anything in the masked darkness. He pulled his keys out of his pocket.

"Over here," she called again.

This time Spencer's eyes searched the shadows until he found Lucy's scantily clothed body stretched across a chaise longue. "What in the world?" he mumbled.

Lucy motioned to him, but he didn't move. He stood staring at her in disbelief. "Why are you out here dressed like that?" He finally asked.

"I want you to take me right here and right now, baby," Lucy told him, reaching outward.

Spencer said the first thing that came into his head. "Girl, are you going crazy?" he asked.

"Come on, Milky Way. It will be exciting and different."

"We can't make love on the patio, Lucy. What am I going to do with my legs on that little plastic thing?"

"Just try," Lucy begged.

"Lucy, you know I'm an old-fashioned kind of guy when it comes to food, sex, and family."

"But I need something different tonight," Lucy groaned, sliding her thighs open.

Spencer felt his manhood waking up, so he quickly slipped his key in the lock, shoved the back door open, and headed in Lucy's direction. He leaned over and in one smooth move wrapped his arms around her body, pulling her to his chest.

"Spencer, what are you doing?" she complained.

"I'm gonna give you what you need, sugar, but not out on the patio," he answered, carrying her into the bedroom.

Spencer laid Lucy down on her king-size bed and stripped quickly while she pouted. He pressed his lips onto hers and pulled her black lace panties off at the same time. Lucy turned her back to him, but Spencer didn't give up. He moaned with his hot breath in her ear, creating an overwhelming hunger. Lucy held out as long as she could, then finally guided him carefully to the right spot. Each time Spencer pushed and the tiny space between them disappeared, Lucy let more of her frustration go and focused instead on his love.

7

✳

*H*ours later, Lucy sat in the rocking chair next to the bed and watched Spencer sleep. How could she marry this man? Would he make her happy? A major decision needed to be made and she didn't know how to make it.

Rubbing tired eyes, she thought about their trip to New Roads last year. Pointe Coupee Parish is a beautiful, romantic countryside surrounded by three rivers: the Mississippi on the east, Red River on the north, and the Atchafalaya River out west. Madea and Spencer got along great, and Madea pronounced him a worthy match for her granddaughter. But one evening when Madea left for one of her healing sessions, Lucy wanted to make love, and Spencer refused. She couldn't get him to understand that they were in the house where all of her passions ignited. Where her fantasies had been created. Where angels and demons from her childhood played.

That weekend forced Lucy to finally admit that something was missing, something that she apparently needed to make her life complete. Spencer was a good lover, his touch was soft and his duration long. But he would only make love in the bedroom, calling it the "necessary comforts." He adamantly defended his position whenever they argued, explaining over and over that what they did in bed was make love; anywhere else it was just fucking. And even though she could see his point, Lucy didn't care. She wanted what she wanted and she needed him to give it to her.

Lucy slipped out of the room, tiptoed into the den, and closed the door. Once she found the number she was looking for in her top desk drawer, she dialed and asked to be transferred to Kuba.

"Hello," Kuba sang on the other end of the line.

"Hey," she replied nervously.

A sharp silence touched them both.

"I was hoping you would call again," Kuba finally said.

Lucy shook her head. "You don't even know who I am."

Kuba laughed and the sound set Lucy's soul on fire. "Shame on you, Lucinda, you have no faith in me," he told her.

Lucy tried to slow the flush of arousal that immediately took over. "I didn't think you would remember," she said.

"I willed this call to happen," he continued.

Lucy closed her eyes and slowed her heartbeat. "Keep talking. I just called to hear you talk," she admitted.

"When a woman is loved she can conquer her fears, and you are loved, Lucinda. Your life will always bring you love."

Lucy was amazed at his insight. How did he know that was the issue stuck in her mind? Was it truly love that she and Spencer shared? People with Kuba's kind of power sometimes scared her; shamen, healers, prophets, and diviners who are tied to spirits; watching for signs of good and evil, dealers in truth and falsehood; believers, visionaries, the laying-on of hands; messengers sending and accepting knowledge from the other side.

"How do we know what love really is?" Lucy asked, wondering if he could answer such a question.

Kuba spoke deeply, instinctively, as if he were anticipating her concern. "Love is a newborn baby grasping tightly to your finger. Love is a good friend who lets you cry as long as you want over nothing. Love is passion and kindness, sadness and joy, strength and need."

Lucy didn't speak right away. She wanted to allow the feeling that fluttered inside her to last.

"I don't think I know what I need," she resolved. "Spencer is a good guy in a world where good guys are rare. In many ways, he is exactly what I want, but I don't feel satisfied. I'm missing an inner contentment that I thought true love would bring."

"Is it possible you're missing something that doesn't exist?"

Lucy shrugged her shoulders, but didn't respond verbally.

"Maybe I should read your cards tonight, Lucinda? Maybe the cards can answer some of these questions for you."

Lucy heard the sound of cards shuffling in the background. She held the receiver tightly, noticing a sudden apprehension that tugged at her, making it hard to breathe. "I don't know if we should," she replied.

"It's up to you, Lucinda. We can stop anytime you want and I'll explain what I'm doing as I go along. I think it might help."

It was the rhythm in the way he said her name that made Lucy feel like an enchanted lover. She moved from her desk to the Roma leather recliner, then took a knitted blanket from the back of the chair, pulled her legs up into the seat, and covered them. "Okay," she said. "Go ahead."

"Good," Kuba replied. "I've just finished shuffling the cards and I'm cutting the deck into three separate piles. I'm setting the top third of the pile down on the left side and now the second third down to the farthest left. There are three piles in a row, Lucinda. You must choose one."

Lucy thought for a moment. The number three popped into her head, and she heard Madea talking about how magic emanates from the number three: the magic of birth, woman plus man equals child; for her birthday she would always get three wishes, and almost every religion was based on some sort of eternal trinity. "Three," she told him.

"I'm picking up the third pile of cards and laying them out in an ancient Celtic cross spread. There are four cards in a vertical row on the right side, five cards set up on the left with one in the center and the other four are sitting north, south, east, and west of that center card. The last card I'm laying across and on top of the card in the center."

A sudden rush of air took Lucy's breath away. She struggled to inhale normally again. "Wait!" she yelled out, not understanding the intense fear that gripped her. "I'm not sure I want to do this."

Kuba waited briefly before he responded. "I want you to trust me," he eventually said. "I would never do anything to harm you. Tarot cards are not used for evil. They are simply a way to see your future. Anything we see in your reading tonight you have the power to change."

Lucy glanced around the darkened room. She kissed the small cross dangling from her gold necklace and nodded. "Okay."

"The first card is the covered center card, which will tell us what your past condition is like. I'm turning it over now." Several seconds passed with the tick, tick, tick of a nearby wood-grain grandfather clock. "It is the Queen of Pentacles. The Queen of Pentacles is a product of the earth telling you that a hidden mystery will be shared. Her presence also means that your spiritual insight helps you to learn and love in abundance. Do you understand, Lucinda?"

Lucy let out a deep breath. "I think so."

Kuba continued. "The next card is the crossing card. It will help us to know what external influences are at work concerning your present condition. I'm turning that card over now." The seconds of silence before he spoke seemed like forever. "It is the lovers and it is turned upside down. The lovers card says that one of your most pressing influences right now is your relationship, the union of male and female, but because it was reversed it also suggests that a choice needs to be made or maybe a love will not be returned."

"How can I know which meaning is correct?" Lucy asked, her voice edgy.

"You will have to determine where you are in your current relationship and which explanation is a better fit. The next card may also help to explain. It is called the crowning card and offers advice for current situations. I'm turning it over now. This card is the high priestess. The high priestess represents your intuitive intelligence. What she advises you to do, Lucinda, is tap into your inner feelings, your sixth sense, trust your own wisdom. The answers will come from within."

"But, how am I supposed to know how to do that?" Lucy replied in frustration.

"Be quiet and listen. The answers will come," Kuba said.

Lucy tried to heed his advice. She sat back, was quiet, and listened to more of his interpretations and explanations. The card of the past was the eight of cups, representing Lucy's emotions and personal fulfillment. In combination with the high priestess, the eight of cups was supposed to ultimately bring stability and maybe even tranquility into her life. The card with a hanged man on it called for sacrifice and the need to surrender to a greater cause. Lucy wondered what that sacrifice might be. She was ready to surrender if it meant she would finally have a sense of comfort in her life. Not being able to see a happy and satisfying future with Spencer was tearing her up inside.

"The moon card brings a certain level of faith despite your uncertainties. It allows you to have the courage to make your necessary journey, and at the end of that journey you will be rewarded. Are you with me, Lucinda?" Kuba asked, suddenly realizing how quiet she had become.

"I'm here," Lucy answered. "What rewards are possible?"

"You will decide what they should be. As you move toward the life you want you will receive the rewards you choose."

Lucy braced herself, setting up the next question just right. "What happens if what I want is not what I'm supposed to have?"

"I think that would depend on the circumstances. Can you be more specific?"

"I want to meet you in person, Kuba," Lucy blurted out.

Except for a low hum in the phone line all was quiet. The silence made Lucy want to suck the words back into her mouth. "I know it's a silly request," she added quickly.

"I'm sorry, but it's not appropriate, Lucinda. I have to tell you that this connection we have is very special, but I don't think our meeting would be a good idea."

Lucy squeezed the cross in her left hand. "I understand."

"Now, we have two more very important cards to turn over. Are you ready?"

"Ready."

"The card of self will show us the internal influences that are at work in your current life. I'm turning that card over now. It is the three of swords and it is tied to both conscious and unconscious thoughts and ideas. The three of swords suggests a major conflict is possible and someone will be heartbroken or betrayed."

Lucy pulled the phone away from her ear. This was something she had feared all along. Who would be heartbroken or betrayed? She massaged the muscles in the back of her neck, then held the phone to her ear again.

"This is the last card, Lucinda. It is the card of consequence. This card tells us your future," Kuba said.

Lucy waited, listening for his powerful voice to announce which card it was, but nothing came forth. "What's wrong?" she asked nervously. "Something is wrong, isn't it?"

Kuba took a few more seconds, then in the same calm and protective voice as before, he spoke. "It is the card of death, Lucinda."

It was as if her blood stopped pumping and her lungs no longer held air when she focused on his words. "The card of death. Who's death? When? How?" The questions shot out of Lucy's mouth like bullets. She wasn't afraid of death. Madea had always said that death was just the liberation of one's soul. But since Madea had not been feeling well and she refused to see a doctor, insisting that her own life force would overcome, Lucy couldn't help but be upset.

"Is it Madea?" she asked frantically. "Is she going to die? Is there any way to know?"

"Remain calm, be quiet, and listen," Kuba told her forcefully. "The card of death does not have to mean a physical death. It often metaphorically can relate to a major change, a letting go or the closure of a situation."

His words didn't make Lucy feel any better. Sweat beaded across her forehead and she bit anxiously into her bottom lip trying to reason through her fear. "This card is connected to me, isn't it? My consequences. So, this death has to be related to me in some way. It can't be Madea's death."

"Remember what I said earlier, Lucinda. Anything in the cards can be changed if you believe. We can try something else if you like. It might help to give us a greater insight to all of the cards we've turned over tonight."

Lucy's body shook again from the emotional chill and the fear that surrounded her. She would try anything to understand what it all meant. "Yes, what can we do?"

"I need for you to choose between piles one and two, then I will select one card out of that pile to represent you. We'll use that card to shape your entire reading tonight."

"Okay," Lucy said, clearing her mind. When the number one appeared it was followed by words like *God, unity,* and *winning.* "One," she said immediately. "Pick a card from the first pile."

"Okay, but before we continue, I'd like for you to take several deep breaths with me."

Lucy followed Kuba's instructions and as her breathing slowed along with his, she noticed a slight pull in her chest each time he inhaled. She knew what it was immediately. It was an emotional link moving back and forth between them. She had heard Madea talk about this pull during healing sessions with certain clients. She suddenly remembered Madea's words. The magic was not in the cards, but in the reading of the cards, Lucy had to remind herself. It was she who made the cards real. It was her beliefs that had to fuel the interpretation.

"Lucinda, I'm turning over the top card on the first pile," Kuba continued.

She listened to his breathing and secretly continued to follow him: Inhale, exhale, inhale, exhale. Breathing along with him somehow made her feel closer, more protected; it helped to lull her frightened soul.

"The card is the fool, Lucinda and it is upside down," he said.

"What does that mean?" she asked, distraught.

"Because it is upside down it is a warning that you should not accept anything that happens to you with your usual blind, child-like faith. You need to harness your awareness and use your intuitive energy to protect yourself. Follow your sixth sense, Lucinda. It won't lead you wrong and remember, whenever things get confusing, just be quiet and listen."

Lucy's eyes were suddenly heavy. She had to sever this connection with Kuba. It was draining her spiritually and emotionally. She stood up.

"Lucinda, are you still there?" Kuba asked cautiously. "If you have any questions I would be happy to try and answer them."

Lucy didn't have any questions. Her link to Kuba was inevitable, maybe even necessary and she knew it. She could feel him becoming a powerful force in her life and she wondered if he could feel it, too.

She yawned. She couldn't focus anymore. "I'm going back to bed now, Kuba," she told him in a voice that lacked its usual vibrance. "Thanks and good night."

8

✳

When the Texas oil surge went bust in the early 1980s the state lost jobs by the thousands and many people's lives were devastated. The price of West Texas crude dropped from twenty-five dollars to thirteen dollars in just ten weeks, bringing a major recession to the state. Adel often wondered if anybody paid attention to that crisis. Energy-related industries like oil field equipment, refining, and chemical manufacturing took big hits, some estimated that more than two hundred thousand jobs were lost. But after the chaos subsided and despite talk about economic development and broadening the state's resources, nothing was different.

It had been a week since Adel sent the memo to each vice president: in marketing, international production, transportation, and operations. She requested the files of those employees whose work was below average and could be eliminated. Adel skimmed the three folders that had arrived so far and was surprised when she recognized one.

Susan Harper had been on the chopping block two years ago, now here she was in another layoff pile. Adel cringed. Last time when Susan's file showed up on her desk, Adel decided to come to the rescue like a mother hen covering up her chick. Susan was four months pregnant, and in her depressed, tired, and paranoid state she had missed a number of days and upset many of her co-workers.

The vice president of marketing, Susan's supervisor, was a bigoted Neanderthal who believed that woman belonged at home. He often compounded that ridiculous philosophy by adding, "If they are going to work they should at least fit in. The system should not have to change to accommodate women." If Adel didn't know the man she would never have believed that such a creature could exist in the twenty-first century. She'd heard him bellow more than once: "If a woman wants to work like a man, she should not expect to be treated like a woman." Adel had fought against those kinds of sexist attitudes since she came to the company, so she saw Susan's case as a prime opportunity to carry the banner all the way to the top.

Poor Susan cried so much in Adel's office during that period that her normally tan nose turned a dark, reddish-brown color, matching her frizzled hair. Susan was afraid to lose her job and she had a right to be. She wasn't sure how she would take care of the child she was carrying without a job or a husband. Apparently her husband, the baby's father, had given her an ultimatum on that joyous day when she told him she was expecting. He said she needed to make a choice between him or the baby because he already had two kids from a previous marriage and didn't want another one. According to Susan, he accused her of getting pregnant on purpose because she knew that he wasn't interested in having any more kids. Yet he refused to use a condom because he didn't like the feel of them, so Susan was responsible for keeping up with birth control during their four-year marriage. Her IUD worked for a while, but nothing is one hundred percent.

Adel remembered how Susan haphazardly shrugged her

shoulders that day when asked if she really wanted to have the baby.

"I admire this life inside me," Susan answered. "And in a way, that made the decision between the baby and my husband an easy one to make."

When she refused to get an abortion, Susan said her husband packed up his belongings and left. She had no forwarding address, no phone number, and apparently no help from him in the raising of his child.

Adel's frown turned to a sly smile as she recalled the late-night strategic planning session they'd had. It was the only time she went behind Hunter's back to get what she wanted. The plan made it easy to get the company to back off. Susan was a woman, a pregnant woman, and even though her evaluations were not stellar as an administrative assistant, they were acceptable. First, Adel suggested to Susan that she threaten a lawsuit—not simply against the company, because they were insured and had plenty of lawyers on the payroll, but an individual lawsuit against her Neanderthal supervisor and the CEO of the company, Hunter, too. No matter how the big boys tried to spin it, firing a single mother in her time of need, just before the holidays, would not look good for American Oil.

Adel was confident that her plan would work because she knew Hunter had an enormous ego. He would not allow that kind of negative publicity to be attached to his good name even if he thought he could win the case. She had heard him complain more than once about the news media. Just recently he had balked at the way they flashed the face of one of his buddies all over the front page of the *Houston Post,* bold and incendiary, when he was arrested and charged with embezzlement, but buried the not-guilty verdict in the back of the paper in a weak and pathetic paragraph months later.

Adel shook her head and sighed. Why was Susan's folder back on her desk again? She read the last evaluation and highlighted several statements.

"Work is average, in some cases below average and attendance still a problem," one sentence read. "Needs to focus more on assigned tasks . . ." "At times has an attitude . . ." "Doesn't work well with others." These were only a few of the negatives that jumped out at Adel.

She closed the folder. She had arranged to have Susan moved out of marketing and into operations after everything was resolved mainly because she trusted the supervisor there, Webster Hudson, to be fair. Webster was a man with a good heart. Most of the other vice presidents would have harassed Susan for camaraderie's sake until she quit, but that wasn't his style. This file worried her because if Webster wrote these things down they were probably true.

Leaning back in her chair, Adel swallowed hard. It was back. That queasy feeling in her stomach that made her wonder if she had made a mistake where Webster Hudson was concerned. They had dated briefly before she met Thad. Whenever Adel put everything into perspective, she was forced to admit that her logic might have been a little skewed because Webster was white and Thad was black.

Coming from a middle-class family, Webster had worked his way to undergraduate and graduate engineering degrees. He was raised in a suburb of Houston called Pasadena because his family liked the compromise the location offered. They had access to city amenities and could still enjoy the safety and attractiveness of the suburb. His family chose to substitute the noise, congestion, traffic, and taxes with vegetable gardens, rose bushes, and a big backyard for him and his brothers to play in.

Webster was a kind and decent soul who wanted to take care of Adel. But she, of course, bristled at the thought. She was a strong, passionate feminist and she could take care of herself. Webster was older and more settled. He had been a caring lover who took the time to get to know her as an individual and a friend before suggesting they move to the physical.

Thad had a very different background. He grew up in the fifth ward of Houston, a long way away from the pampered life she knew as a child in the Midwest. The fifth ward was one of the worst areas for gangs, poverty, and crime. Thad would have joined a gang called the Disciples and probably ended up in jail if his Uncle Warren hadn't taken an interest in him. Adel and Thad had gotten physical right away. He was young and passionate, more like the kind of lover she was looking for.

A mutual friend from work had literally pushed them together. Thad was ending a four-year live-in relationship and Adel's divorce had been final for half that time. She was surprised when he talked about living together a few months after they started dating. Adel refused. She wasn't going down the same road as his last girlfriend, playing wife and caretaker, hoping he would someday make it legit. She told him point blank that she wasn't giving nothing up unless he put a ring on her finger and said "I do" in front of both their families and a preacher.

Adel shook off her doubts and buzzed her assistant. "Jane, please set up individual appointments late this afternoon with Susan Harper and Webster Hudson. I'd like to meet with Webster first. And I'm leaving for lunch in about fifteen minutes."

9

*

The wet steam in the sauna spread across the room like an ominous gas, pushing and quivering with heated force. Adel lay with her back against the smooth, wooden bench, sweat trickling down her forehead, while Lucy threw more water on the coals, then sat upright holding her knees to her chest and breathing deeply.

"She doesn't have to be trifling," Adel argued, swiping the towel over her face to pick up the annoying sweat.

Lucy shook her head in disgust. "Adel, sometimes I think you're people-impaired. You want to give everybody the benefit of the doubt, but folks take advantage. They think your kindness is a weakness."

Adel pulled the towel from her face. "I can't believe Susan would do that. If her performance had been so terrible why hasn't Webster said anything?"

"You know, commercials and people are very similar. Both include just a tiny bit of the truth."

Adel turned onto her stomach. "You've gotta believe in somebody sometime, Lucy," she retorted. "I just asked Webster a couple of months ago how were things going and he said fine."

"Webster still cares about you. What do you expect him to say? He doesn't want to mess up his chances in case you dump Thad," Lucy teased.

"Webster don't want me. He probably thinks I'm a flake. Actually, it's probably true. I'm probably the biggest flake in history!"

"Now what are you talking about?" Lucy asked, then picked up a short wooden *ka* stick and applied firm pressure to her wet thighs by rolling it back and forth across her skin.

"When it comes to Thad, sometimes I feel like singing "Always and Forever" and other times I just want to howl at the moon."

"Adel, I have nothing against you keeping Thad around as long as you're realistic about who he is and what he wants out of life. If he can make you happy, more power to the brother, but as far as Webster is concerned, I'm simply saying don't close any doors right now. He's been there for you in a lot of ways."

Adel draped the steaming white towel over her wet stomach. "Give me a little more credit, please. I'm a good student and I admit your course on the art of compromise and negotiation has been invaluable to my career advancement. I'm not sure I could have made it this far in this messed-up industry if I hadn't followed many of your suggestions."

"As long as you're paying attention," Lucy joked, feeling her muscles relax beneath the *ka* stick.

"If you want to worry about something, worry about my mental state if I stay in the oil business, period. Whenever I step into that big, marble lobby and smell the stench of profitability over people, I get sick. I'm eating all the time, gaining weight, and I might even be getting ulcers. My stomach is constantly churning."

"Have you had it checked out by a doctor?"

"No, I'm afraid. What if it's something serious?"

"You can't think like that, you have to think positive."

"The most positive thought I've had lately involves getting the hell out of the oil business!"

"Girl, you'd be crazy to leave that good job. You just need to find a way to reduce the stress. Like this *Chua Ka* movement." Lucy handed her one of the sticks. "These are great. The instructor last month talked about the need to release painful traumas that can build over time by relaxing your muscles. Here, try it."

Adel took one of the *ka* sticks and rubbed it against the back of her neck.

"Not like that," Lucy corrected. She took the *ka* stick and rolled it along the same area for Adel.

"Ummmm, it does feel good," Adel admitted.

"I keep telling you to take better care of yourself. Like a consistent exercise routine. We could do something together."

"I haven't got time right now. There is too much on my plate already."

"I'm serious, Adel. You'll wish you had made the time if you end up in a hospital bed."

"You'd better get serious about your own life, Miss Lucy," Adel argued, consciously changing the subject. "You're not really going to meet this Kuba guy in person, are you?"

"I mentioned it, but he's not ready," Lucy told her. "You know me, though, I usually get what I want."

"You better leave that boy alone. I don't believe in magic, but he scares me."

Lucy leaned closer. "That's the point, Adel, I should be terrified, but I'm not. It is so clear that this powerful link between us is special and it's not going away. Sometimes I wonder if maybe God brought him to me."

Adel tossed more water on the coals and watched the steam rise. "If there is a God, I'm sure he has better things to do than worry about you getting your groove on with some super psychic."

"How else can you explain it?" Lucy asked, closing her eyes

and dropping her head back into the fresh mist. "I've never called one of those lines before. I call and get hooked up with a man who's aura is so strong that I feel he is guiding me to where I need to be."

"And what about Spencer? He loves you, Lucy. A breakup would probably kill him."

"I didn't say I was going to break up with Spencer. But this is not about Spencer. This is about me. It's about my satisfaction and my happiness. If I'm not happy and satisfied with myself, how can Spencer be happy and satisfied with me?"

"Kuba is a psychic. I don't know how you can even think about a relationship with somebody like him, as spooked as you get."

Lucy opened her eyes. "That's exactly the point. I've been running from it all my life. Maybe it's time to stop running and embrace it instead. Look at it from the other side. What if this is the perfect man for me, Adel?"

"Or he could be some loony who will talk you into joining a cult, giving up your worldly possessions, and moving off to a desolate, foreign land to commit suicide."

"Please." Lucy grinned, handing her *ka* stick to Adel. "Here, take this and roll it over my lower back for a minute. Ain't no man, or woman for that matter, gonna ever get me to do something as dumb as that."

Adel sucked her teeth and rolled the stick across Lucy's tense lower back area the way she was instructed. "I hope you're right."

"Of course I'm right."

The smell of steam and heat and sweat mingled together in a soothing balm as both women sat quietly for a moment taking it all in.

"You know, Elaine, my assistant, claims she can play Bid Whist," Lucy finally said.

"Great, now if we can find a fourth person, we can get a monthly game going."

"I can't believe we haven't played since college," Lucy mused.

Adel shook her head. "We were the Bid Whist masters at TSU. I can't believe we graduated in four years, we spent so much time at that table."

"Everybody I ask plays spades."

"I know, and that's such a weak game. They just don't know what they're missing."

"I'll keep asking around. There has to be somebody else in this city who can play some real cards," Lucy said, shrugging.

"I've still got a couple of people to check with, too."

"We should have thought about this a long time ago. We've missed a lot of playing time."

Adel pinned her hair up and prepared to leave. "I still have to figure out what to do about Susan," she said sadly. "What do you think?"

"You will do what you have to do," Lucy replied confidently, then stood up and wrapped the towel around her waist. "If you have to, you will fire her."

10

*

"**W**ebster," Adel said with an outstretched hand. "Thanks for coming."

Webster stepped into Adel's office and took her hand. "No problem. As a matter of fact, I was expecting this call from you. It seems like the only way I get to see you anymore is to create a little havoc in your life." He grinned at the word *havoc*.

Adel smothered the smile that wanted to emerge when she glanced into his blue eyes. "So you know this is about Susan?"

Webster took a seat. "I figured it might be."

"Can you tell me anything else besides what's already in the folder?" Adel asked, leaning against the cabinet across from him.

"She's a nice person, Adel. Her work is okay, but her absences are a problem. There's day care, illness, and other problems that just naturally come along with babies and single working parents. I'm not in favor of getting rid of her, if that's what you're asking. But I had to send you one file that was on the edge in my department and hers is the one."

"So if she's not selected you'd be okay with that?"

"Sure, she can stay. But I'd like for you to talk with her about the absences. She does pretty good for a month or two, then falls back into a pattern."

Adel shifted her legs slowly, forcing his attention to the short tight skirt hugging her big coffee-colored legs. "How do you feel about withdrawing her file altogether?" she asked.

Webster spoke to those shapely legs. "What do you mean?"

"Well, if Hunter sees her name a second time, I'm not sure I can save her again."

"There's nobody else to give up in my department, Adel."

"And that's what I want you to tell Hunter, that you have no one in your department to dump."

Webster marveled at the suggestion. He cared about Adel and was glad that she continued to fight the good fight. He'd seen many folks in her job who'd given up after a year or two of bull-shit. Adel had persisted despite the snide remarks about her qualifications and abilities, the lack of true equal opportunity, and the internal isolation and exclusion that came with the coveted good-old-boy network.

"You've learned a lot about playing the game," he said, glad to be her confidant at the company.

"I learned from a master, and I'll always thank you for that," she responded, glad to know that she still had him in her corner.

"If you add a lunch with me once a month at Polly's, then it's a deal," Webster added, then stood, grinning.

Adel smiled back at him. "Lunch would be great," she said, suddenly walking over and hugging him impulsively.

"I think I miss your hugs most of all," Webster said quietly as they embraced, his breath tickling her neck.

Adel's face went flush and she stepped away, staring down at the blue carpet. She tried to get control of the conflicting feelings. At that moment she truly wondered about the peaceful and se-cure love that Webster offered, and she recognized the difference now. Webster was a solid oak picnic table, weatherproofed so that you could depend on it for many years. With Thad it seemed like she had bought the cheap, cutesy, plastic table that blew over with any big wind.

"Thank you, Webster," Adel said sincerely as they stepped into the reception area.

"You're welcome," Webster answered with a wink.

"Could you call Susan down now?" Adel told her secretary before she floated back into her office.

A few minutes later, Adel was nodding at Susan, who skittishly played with her fingers. She waited for Susan to sit down, then from behind her desk looked directly into Susan's face.

"I'm not sure what's going on," Adel said calmly.

Susan's eyes darted down and back up again. "What did Mr. Hudson say?" she asked, now fidgeting with her bracelet.

"He didn't have to say anything, Susan. Your evaluations tell the whole story. You're missing days, you're still working at minimum efficiency, and you're attitude stinks."

Susan slumped down in the chair. Adel noticed for the first time how tired and sickly she looked.

"I'm doing the best I can, Adel, but you don't know what it's like to raise a baby all by yourself. Very few people around here have a clue. I have to do everything. It's like I can't depend on anybody."

Adel tried to maintain her compassion, yet remain professional. "Look, I know it's difficult and even unfair at times, but American Oil is not going to suffer much longer because you decided to have a baby."

"Men have wives who deal with this kind of stuff. That's why they can't recognize this as a serious problem in the workplace," Susan continued. "I thought you understood."

"I do understand. Maybe you need to get a wife or at least somebody that acts like one," Adel said firmly. "The bottom line, Susan, is if you want to play with the boys you have to play by the rules of their game."

"Even if the rules need to be changed?"

"We can't change them overnight."

"I know, but I was hoping you would consider something else," Susan continued, perking up a little.

"Something like what?" Adel asked curiously.

"I was thinking that maybe the company could set up a day care facility right here in the building. I'm not the only mother with young children. There are at least twenty of us. Some companies are doing that for their employees."

Adel hesitated for a moment. "When are we going to find time to run a day care facility?" she asked, noting that the idea was actually an interesting one.

Susan scooted to the edge of her seat. "You don't have to run it. You can contract it out. You just need to supply the space."

Adel tried to come up with a reason to shoot Susan's idea down, but she couldn't, because she liked it. Her mind clicked immediately to the two large rooms on the fifth floor where a few boxes and old papers were stored. That could easily become a day care facility. If the company offered the space and clientele, maybe they could find a licensed day care owner who would be willing to provide the service.

"Look, you have got to do better or your job will be on the line again, and the lawsuit thing won't work a second time."

Susan smiled and handed her a manila envelope. "I will," she said.

"What's this?" Adel asked, taking the package from her hand.

"It's a proposal from a lady I know who has a very successful day care and wants to open a second. It will give you some idea of what might be necessary to make it happen."

Adel took a deep breath. "I'll look into it," she said, flashing a quick smile.

"Thanks, Adel. I knew you'd understand and I will do better. I promise," Susan added.

Once Susan was out the door, Adel opened the envelope and skimmed the proposal. She got on the phone and called Happy Hearts, connecting with the owner, Liz Griffin, then she set up a meeting with Liz to discuss the details.

11

✳

Happy Hearts was located in Houston's third ward, once known for its famous nightlife. Bluesman Lightnin' Hopkins had played on the sidewalks of Dowling Street for loose change thrown into a bucket, and the Eldorado Ballroom, once a barrelhouse dance hall, still stood on the corner of Elgin and Dowling. Adel was excited when she found out that Liz Griffin was a black woman. Not only would Adel be able to help promote a women's issue with this project, but she could also help someone of her own race to move ahead.

The day care was located in a small, white, two-story house surrounded by a red picket fence next to a deep sea of bluebonnets. The sign in front read HAPPY HEARTS—A CHRISTIAN DAY CARE CENTER. Adel entered the gate and walked around to the backyard following the sounds of children playing.

She stopped to focus on a tiny little girl struggling to sit her bottom down onto a large swing. The girl was probably three years old at the most, with brown curly hair from which red, yellow, and white butterfly barrettes hung loosely. Her chubby little cornbread-colored legs didn't move very well yet, but she was determined to get them to behave. When the wind caught her yellow dress, making it seem as if the matching red and white butterflies were fluttering along the bottom, Adel smiled. She watched as one of the workers lifted the girl up into the seat and gave her a gentle push. Several children noticed the stranger standing at a distance in her sleek, black pantsuit with matching pumps. Some stopped running long enough to stare.

"Miss Kelly," Liz called. She was leaning out of the back door, waving. "Come right in."

Adel turned and followed the hand inside.

"I'm so glad to talk with you about this opportunity. Come on, I'll show you around."

Liz Griffin took Adel on a quick tour of the house. They started in the living room, which served as a large, indoor play area. There were several dollhouses with a diverse collection of Barbies: nurse Barbie, astronaut Barbie, prom Barbie, going-to-a-party Barbie, cheerleader Barbie, and even Olympic Barbie. Balls of all sizes were nestled between puzzles, plastic dinosaurs, and Lego communities. Washable markers, crayons, and activity and coloring books were organized across a large table in the corner.

The kitchen was huge. A wall had been knocked out that once separated the formal dining room area. Two long tables with eight folding chairs on each side sat in the middle of the floor. The only other room downstairs had been transformed into the library and reading room. The story-time area included walls painted with animals, trees, rivers, and children of all races and ethnicities.

The upstairs housed four baby beds in one room, ranging from traditional wood to modern-day metal. Another room sported wall-to-wall air mattresses and a black rocking chair for the older kids' nap time.

"I hope you don't mind this rushed visit, but I'm very excited about the project and wanted to get a better idea of the possibilities," Adel told Liz as they sat in the only other room on the second floor, which served as a small office.

"I'm so happy you called," Liz said. "Day care is something that we've got to take seriously if equality is going to become a reality for women in the workforce."

"I've skimmed the proposal and I want to see if I can help you set up a second facility at American Oil." Adel said directly.

"That would be great. That same proposal was submitted to Community Trust, but they turned our loan application down."

Adel flipped through several pages. "You do understand that low-cost space and a small start-up loan for other necessary resources might be all we're able to offer. And our employees would get first shot at all spaces. Once our needs have been met, then you can offer other companies in the downtown area open spots."

"I understand. My daughter has codirected this facility for the last six years and she's ready to start her own. You saw her downstairs with Gwennie on the swing. We would take care of everything, including licensing and insurance."

Adel vacillated about asking the next question, until she convinced herself that it was necessary. "Mrs. Griffin, I was wondering about the sign out front that says this is a Christian day care center. What exactly does that mean?"

Liz held a look of confusion on her face briefly, then smiled gracefully. "It means that our center has a spiritual core based on God's love," she replied.

"I'm worried how such a designation might affect our employees who are not Christian."

"We don't deny alternative beliefs at Happy Hearts, but we do believe in Christ the savior, and that belief is a fundamental part of our philosophy as we care for our children."

"It's . . . It's not that I don't understand," Adel stammered. "I just would not want to push any parents away who don't want their kids exposed to such beliefs."

"I'm not sure what I can do about that, Mrs. Kelly. We spend eight hours a day with these children, often more time than their own parents, so we take our responsibility to help raise them very seriously. We don't follow a religious curriculum here, if that's what you're worried about. It doesn't matter if God is called Allah or Jehovah or Goddess. We've been blessed by a holy love and we like to pass those blessings on."

Adel nodded, then dropped her gaze and skimmed over a couple of pages of the proposal.

Liz eventually broke the silence. "As far as our philosophy goes, day care involves much more than watching a child and keeping them safe. We include educating them in preparation for school, training them to function effectively in society, and helping them to learn and grow as positive human beings. We may not be able to satisfy every one of your employees, but I guarantee that those who place their children with us will be very happy."

Adel complimented Liz on her facility and took the proposal home to read through it thoroughly. As she drove, her mind was rushing through all of the pegs that would need to be put in place to make this thing happen. She was motivated because this was the kind of significant change she had hoped to make at American Oil when she accepted the vice presidency position.

The little girl in the bright yellow dress, Gwennie, continued to linger in Adel's mind. Adel smiled broadly. If anyone would have told her twenty years ago that she would see her thirty-fifth birthday without at least two or three crumb snatchers pulling at her and whining "Mommy," she would have had them locked up. She was supposed to have a husband and at least three kids like stairsteps by now.

Adel tightened her grip on the steering wheel. Why was she working so hard if it wasn't to have a family? When Thad came into her life it was as if the God that everyone talks about knew exactly what she needed and gave him to her. She had hoped that kids would come the same way, as a gift from God to be cherished.

Last year she and Thad found a lost little boy at the mall. He was crying for his mother and sucking desperately on a purple bubble gum lollipop. Thad lifted the boy up easily as if his forty or fifty pounds were only ten. He sat the boy on his shoulders, and they walked all over that mall looking for a mother who was probably frantic about her missing child until they finally found the security office and an announcement was made. Adel reminisced at a stop sign about staying with that little boy until his mother arrived.

That day in the middle of a crowded mall, where boyfriends and girlfriends, parents and grandparents, husbands and wives, friends and lovers strolled in and out of chain stores, Adel thought most carefully about the miracle of having a child. Both Thad and his brother had defied the stereotype that all black men from the inner city have illegitimate kids. Both were over forty and neither had taken that path. But now Adel was ready for motherhood. She hadn't swallowed a birth control pill since the day she said "I do."

12

✳

Birch Tallan, the director of the Austin center, waited anxiously for Lucy first thing Thursday morning. He had driven for two and a half hours, working himself into a frenzy. He was ready to give Lucy the little piece of his mind that he had left. She had stepped over the line with her probation slip and proposal suggesting that he was incompetent in his job. Birch glanced at his Stanford class ring and mulled over his accomplishments. He'd graduated in the top ten percent of his class, was in the 1995 *Who's Who of the Fitness World*, and he had won a number of intense competitions such as the USA Weightlifting Championship and Mr. Texas Fitness three times.

Birch jumped out of his seat when Lucy entered the reception area. "I need to talk with you!" he yelled and started across the room. "This proposal is designed to get rid of me and I'm not going to allow you to do it that easily," he fumed, waving the pages in the air.

"Excuse me?" Lucy asked, wishing she could either scream back at him or totally ignore his ignorance.

"When I signed on, I was told I could run the center as I saw fit! I have done a damn good job and made a lot of profit for this company," Birch told her.

Lucy took a deep breath and slid the key in her office door. "The center is currently not at the appropriate level of profitability and that means you cannot continue with business as usual, Birch. Something has to change," she told him as the door swung open and she stepped inside.

Birch followed, still ranting and raving. "I can't successfully do half the stuff in this proposal at my center. I'm in Austin, Lucy, not Houston or Dallas."

"How do you know you can't do it if you haven't even tried?" Lucy asked, her voice slightly elevated.

"Because I know the people. I know the community and they are not interested in *Chua Ka* or Pilates or any of that other spa movement mess you want to shove down their throats. My members are primarily men and they want weight equipment and personal training."

Lucy exhaled and stared. "Well, if that's true, Birch, we have a major problem. Looking Good Fitness Centers are more than basic workout gyms. When you expand to include other approaches and techniques to wellness, you also expand your potential clientele and your profit margin."

Birch tossed the proposal onto her desk and the pages flew everywhere. "If you want to fire me why don't you just go ahead and do it? You've made it clear from the beginning that you don't like the way I run the center and you don't like me."

Lucy tried to maintain her composure. She was not prepared to deal with him this morning and she wasn't as good in these kinds of situations when she had to wing it. The man was out of line and she knew if she didn't get control right now they could never work together until the end of his probation period.

She had promptly sized up his cocky attitude the first time she met him. It was obvious that he didn't like the fact that a black woman with a degree from a historically black college was his superior. He was so arrogant that day that she wanted to fire him on the spot. She had flown to Austin to officially introduce herself when she became regional manager, and ended up standing at the counter for about thirty minutes waiting for him to emerge out of the glass cubicle he called his office.

From where she stood Lucy could hear that he was engaged in a personal conversation. She frowned, watching him strut and cluck around the room like the only rooster in the henhouse. When he finally ended his discussion with the macho declaration: "If you loved me, you'd do this for me. It's only money," her feminist antenna went up. Eventually he made his way over to Lucy, but didn't speak. He simply handed her a job application and strolled away.

Lucy thought about that first impression and walked confidently back around to the front of the desk. She stood before him looking into his twisted face. "Let's get something straight," she said firmly. "I don't give a damn about you, Birch, one way or another. As regional manager it is my job to make sure each center meets its profit margin. When we added the spa component to the Houston Centers our profits shot up twenty percent. More people, especially women, have joined the facility because they can get a massage or mud bath or pedicure after a good workout. Your center has not met its profit expectation in months."

Birch shifted his eyes upward to indicate his irritation and Lucy tightened her stare.

"The situation here is very simple. You don't have to follow any of the suggestions in my proposal, but make sure you understand this: you will bring the profit level up twenty-five percent at your center in the next three months or you will be terminated!"

Birch's face went fire-engine red and his eyes burned hatred. Lucy was not afraid he would do anything violent, but she did recognize the seriousness of the situation. No matter what, she knew she couldn't let him know that he scared her. She stood rigidly in front of the six-foot-tall, body-building frame, watching the dark eyes dash back and forth. Lucy refused to blink or turn away first, so they challenged each other until Birch finally grunted, stepped backward, and stormed out of her office.

Lucy collapsed into the chair behind her desk, silently thanking James Jeffers for teaching her twenty-eight years ago not to show fear to her enemies. It was hard to think back on how the kids in New Roads thought she was weird and constantly teased her. They did it not because of anything she had done, but because she was guilty by association. They didn't know what her grandmother actually did as a healer. They feared Madea and attacked Lucy because she was Madea's grandchild.

There was a permanent file in Lucy's head that held the chants and screams she'd endured while growing up. "Your grandma is a voodoo queen." "Lucy, Lucy she's a flake, sleeps at night with her pet snake." "Don't touch Lucy, she's got the voodoo hoodoo."

At first she let their taunting and teasing impact her relationship with her grandmother. She decided that she would not like Madea either and refused to let her get too close. But less than a year later Lucy finally realized that her grandmother's power was amazing and that's when things in her life started to make sense again.

Annaple Mayeaux, better known in Pointe Coupee Parish as Madea, had been a healer most of her life, connecting with people through the spirit. One of the first lessons Madea taught Lucy involved balance. She explained that there was good and bad existing in every soul, and that for every problem God put on earth he provided a solution. It was a difficult concept for Lucy to accept because she didn't care about balance. She didn't know what balance was. Her life was not balanced. Her mother and father were dead and she had been snatched away from everything and everybody she loved and dumped into this strange place that some people called the Bayou Wonderland.

Lucy didn't know why her classmates hated her, but she knew there was no balance in it. The day when James Jeffers pulled her long, soft brown hair and told her she was cursed because she was Madea's granddaughter, she cried and tried to run away. James and his buddies caught her and pushed her to the ground. They took turns kicking dirt at her, hawking gobs of spit on her mauve cotton dress, and laughing until a passing adult made them stop and helped her get home.

She didn't plan to tell Madea what had happened because she believed it was Madea's fault in the first place, but when Lucy stomped up on the porch, breathing hard and wiping at tear-stained eyes, all it took was one glance into her grandmother's warm, loving face and it all poured out. She fell into those waiting arms and they rocked back and forth together until the tears stopped.

That evening Madea made a gris-gris for Lucy's protection against such incidents in the future. Lucy remembered feeling a fascination that was wrapped in apprehension throughout the ritual.

Madea took a small red flannel bag and sprinkled it with protection oil. Then she carefully chose seven internal items for the bag including several strands of Lucy's hair to identify the bag as hers; a tiny piece of coral, which is one of the strongest protection stones; a silver crucifix for faith; a half-inch piece of iron for strength; a tablespoon of five-finger grass to keep Lucy from the harm of any five fingers; a light blue piece of cloth for peace and tranquility, and a tiny medal of St. Michael, the Archangel who would next time protect her from such evil. When the bag was complete they lit a white candle and prayed.

Lucy imitated Madea. She cupped her hands together, closed her eyes, and repeated the prayer of protection: "Lord Jesus Christ, who tells us to ask and we shall receive, we now ask that You grant this prayer in honor of Your patron Saint Michael. Please protect Lucy from those who would hurt her and guard her spirit from damage. Bless this gris-gris bag that it may radiate Your power and Your love always. You have given Your angels charge to keep us worthy of Your blessings, so in Jesus's name we ask this prayer dear Lord. Amen."

Lucy carried that bag to school with her the next day. When James rushed into her face on the playground she didn't move, she didn't cower, she didn't cry. She looked at him with the power of Moses, the strength of Daniel, and the faith of David. James backed off, along with his buddies, and she was never bothered by anybody else again.

13

*

Digging into the bottom of her purse, Lucy pulled out the tattered red bag. Over the years it became a precious part of learning to love the uniqueness of her life with Madea.

New Roads was originally named St. Mary's until the Bayou Sara Ferry Road was constructed in 1848. With about five thousand residents, sixty percent of them black, it was a tiny place compared to Chicago, where Lucy had been born. The residents of New Roads were a proud group of people. They boasted over their hospital, Pointe Coupee General, one of the few in the area; and the weekly newspaper, *The Pointe Coupee Banner*, was a prominent community tabloid. They loved to talk about the False River Air Park that was supposed to be an airport, but never had any scheduled flights in or out. And they praised the mayor for his brilliant idea to use the air park for the Fourth of July fireworks show that got bigger and better each year.

The park was also used as a makeshift stadium twice a year to host the traveling black rodeo. Local townsfolk would get swept up by the roping, bareback riding, and bronc busting events. They'd wear their cowboy boots and hats with silver spurs and red bandannas. Lucy had heard many years ago that James Jeffers actually joined the rodeo in his junior year to get away from home in the same way that kids run away with the circus.

Lucy's mother, Julienne, was Madea's only child, born of a brown-sugar Creole man named Sonny Alexander. Sonny's words were butter and his touch was warm toasted bread. Through her visions Madea saw the ending of their romance the minute she touched his perfectly formed body and her heart absorbed those translucent green eyes. But it somehow didn't matter that he was only going to be around for a little while. It didn't matter that he cared for Madea, but he cared more for himself and his family name. And it didn't matter that he was the one man who would ever know Madea intimately in her lifetime.

Sonny was a descendant of African, French, and Spanish ancestries. The Alexanders were one of the oldest families in Louisiana, but they had never claimed Julienne or Lucinda, who was named for Sonny's own mother and grandmother. Madea could not be accepted in Sonny's Creole family because he was considered *sorti de la cuisse de Jupiter,* a delicacy from the thigh of Jupiter.

With Madea's Cousatta Indian and African slave background she could never be part of the society crowd. They both knew that their physical bond couldn't last forever, yet they spent long, torrid nights tangled together, dreaming of that elusive goal. They ultimately shaped a love that would spiritually last forever and physically be enough.

Lucy had not been able to shake her worry about Madea, especially since the tarot cards saw death. She was trying to believe that the vision was not a physical one, yet the possibility that it might be was frightening. She had already called Madea two times since the reading, but had not gotten straight answers to her questions in either conversation.

She picked up the phone to try again. "Madea," Lucy said when her grandmother answered after the third ring. "I need the truth. Madea, is anything wrong?"

Madea laughed at her granddaughter's effort to take control. She knew Lucy was a headstrong but compassionate child who could not be hurt by fate. "The truth. You want the truth, baby. The truth is I'm an old woman with lots of aches and pains, but nothing that will take me away from you anytime soon."

"I want you to come see me next month, Madea. I'll send a ticket. You've only been to Houston once in the last five years," Lucy continued.

"I can't leave New Roads right now, Lucy Marie. There is too much going on in this old town, too many people who depend on me."

"I wish you'd think more about yourself and less about other people," Lucy complained.

"You don't mean that, sweetheart. Taking care of others is the same as taking care of myself and you know that."

"So, I guess I have to come visit you."

"I'd like that. I'd like that a lot. You know you're my heart and you're welcome anytime."

Lucy didn't want to go back to New Roads, but her fear shaped the words she spoke. "I'll come and see you for Marie Saint day, Madea. I'll cook you a feast of healthy food. My collard greens now have turkey in them instead of ham and my macaroni and cheese is cooked in skim milk to cut the fat. I bet you can't tell the difference."

Madea frowned on the other end of the line. "You make it sound delicious, baby, but I'm afraid my experienced taste buds may not be pleased."

"You'll try it though, won't you?" Lucy pleaded. "Different can be better."

"I'll try it." Madea gave in.

"Do you need anything before I get there?" Lucy asked, knowing her grandmother wouldn't tell her even if she did need something.

"I'm fine, you just take good care of yourself."

When Lucy hung up the phone she thought again about her grandfather. She had only met Sonny Alexander once. He was passing through New Roads when she was fourteen years old. He had lost most of his teeth and hair, but not the twinkle in his eye that Lucy could tell was the spark of love he still carried for his Madea. He stayed one night, which, now that Lucy thought back on it, was one of the most joyful nights she remembered in that house, but it soon changed to a muted sadness that filled their lives in the months to follow.

Two weeks after his visit, Madea got the news that Sonny had passed away. She took it hard, but only Lucy could tell how hard. On the outside Madea kept up a strong front. Her main project that month was to help Mrs. Henry control her arthritis by teaching her to listen to her body. Mrs. Henry first had to learn to move into herself to create an inner space where she could connect with the problem. Then an image that was wise and loving had to be imagined. It should be an image of someone or something that she believed could help her with the pain. Mrs. Henry imagined a divining rod like her father had used to find water for a well. She could see it clearly—a long, forked branch made of hazel wood. She followed it through her bloodstream and it led her to a clot that was forming in her lower right leg. Once she told Madea about the clot, Madea mixed up a concoction to flush it away using grated lemon peel, sassafras leaves, eucalyptus root, and white rose oil made from flowers gathered after the morning dew had dried.

It was only after Mrs. Henry was feeling better that Madea pulled the telegram from Sonny's sister in New Orleans out of her top dresser drawer and cried uncontrollably. Lucy envied the wonderful memories that her grandmother had eventually turned into precious stories. She wanted those kinds of memories and those kinds of stories to tell someday. She wanted to know that kind of unconditional love.

14

*

The phone beckoned to Lucy, but she completed some filing and shuffled a few papers on her desk instead, trying to resist. She sat and gazed out the window for a while, nursing the frantic urge to call Spencer and tell him that she loved him, tell him that she needed him, tell him that she would marry him. When the phone buzzed, Lucy jumped, then picked it up.

"I'm going home now," her receptionist, Elaine, told her on the other end.

"Okay, I'll see you tomorrow," Lucy responded automatically. She didn't hang up the phone, instead she focused on the keypad and dialed.

"Hello." Spencer's voice startled Lucy since she'd expected to get his machine.

"Hi," she whispered.

"Hey, baby, I was just thinking about you."

Lucy couldn't help but smile. "What were you thinking?" she asked.

"I was thinking that we need to get away this weekend. Go somewhere to be alone. I want to talk about our future. I want to be so good to you that by the end of the weekend you will say, 'Yes, Spencer, my love, I'll marry you and have your babies.' " He chuckled once the words were out.

"That's what you were thinking, huh?" Lucy teased.

Spencer laughed. "I'd like to have at least ten kids with you."

"You've been doing some serious thinking."

"And what do you think about my thinking?"

Lucy squeezed her eyes together tightly to stop the tears from forming. "I like your thinking, except for the part about the ten kids. Maybe three. But I'd love to get away with you this weekend."

"So, I'll plan the trip and you simply prepare yourself to be pampered." Spencer told her.

"As long as you let me know in advance what type of clothes to pack. You know I hate to get somewhere and not be dressed right."

"I'll let you know. Love you."

Lucy wiped her nose, then whispered after he had hung up, "I love you, too."

She started to drop the phone in its cradle, but something stopped her. After hesitating a few moments she dialed another number. She asked for Kuba's extension and waited as the line connected.

"Kuba here." The voice on the other end licked her ear.

"Hi, Kuba," she whimpered.

"Hello to you," he replied excitedly.

Lucy almost hung up the phone. This was not a sane thing that she was doing. Spencer was a good man who loved her, so why was Kuba on the other end of the line?

"Lucinda, I sense a tension. Is everything all right?"

Lucy couldn't explain it the way she wanted to, so she said nothing. She sat and held the phone next to her ear, wondering how it would feel for Kuba to hold her in his arms.

Kuba continued when he didn't get a response. "I want to tell you a story, Lucinda. Are you with me?"

Lucy shifted the phone to the opposite ear. "I'm listening," she answered in a low tone.

"It is written that in Africa, early one spring, a gazelle called Pullo and a frog called Churu became good friends, but very competitive friends. One day Pullo goaded Churu into racing him, knowing that he had an unfair advantage with his long, sleek gazelle legs. Churu didn't want to race, but he finally gave in and after he lost, he grew very angry. He thought for a long time about how he could get back at Pullo, and several weeks later he challenged Pullo to a test of his own.

"Churu bet that he and his wife could visit the Lord and return. Pullo didn't believe it, but after much chiding he decided to see for himself. He followed Churu's instructions and showed up at the frog's house that night. He checked to see that Churu and his wife were inside. Then he watched as Churu set fire to the house and continued to watch as it burned to ashes. Once the fire was out, friends and neighbors looked for Mr. and Mrs. Frog, but they never found any trace of them. Pullo mourned for his friend. He didn't want to see him dead. He felt bad that he had beat him in the unfair race and he was sorry that he didn't treat him better when he was alive.

"Six months later the dry season ended and the rains came. One day Pullo ambled down to the spot where the frog's house had been to get a cool drink from the stream. He had wished many times that he could see Churu again and on this day he got his wish. Churu and his wife were happily singing and rebuilding their home.

" 'You have come back,' Pullo exclaimed with genuine happiness.

" 'Yes, it was wonderful in Heaven and we were blessed by God with three beautiful children while we were there,' Churu gloated, pointing to each child. 'I win our bet because I have been to visit with the Lord, and that is something that you cannot do.'

"Even though Pullo was happy that his friend was alive, he became very jealous again. Pullo and his wife had not had any children despite how hard they had tried, and he had to be just as important to the Lord as Churu. Pullo went home and told his wife what happened. Then after she had gone to bed he prayed that God would give him the same good fortune as Churu and he set the walls of their house on fire. When Churu learned that Pullo and his wife were burned to death, he was very sad. He regretted that he did not explain to his friend how frogs always sleep inside the earth during the dry season and wake when the rains come."

It was suddenly quiet as Lucy waited for Kuba to continue and Kuba waited for Lucy to respond.

"And what does that story say to me?" Lucy asked.

"It should say, Lucinda, that it is not good to keep secrets from your friends."

Lucy held on to the receiver as if it were a life vest keeping her head above water. What was it about this man that drew her to him? The attachment was so strong that she didn't feel she had the strength to break away. For the first time, Lucy believed that she was feeling the kind of love seen in movies, heard about in songs, and read in romance novels. The emotion in his voice made her heart beat faster, his suggestive laugh forced her temperature to rise, and the compassion he offered satisfied her needy soul.

"Kuba, do you remember telling me during my first call that I need a certain kind of love?" she asked.

"I do," he replied.

"What happens if that love comes from a person who is not available?"

The intense silence served as a catalyst to pull her closer until finally, he spoke. "If the person is not available the love cannot manifest itself."

"Then I don't know what to do," Lucy told him.

Kuba spoke with a cautious tone. "Why do you think this love is not available?"

Lucy wiped the sweat from the bridge of her nose, but didn't respond.

"I want to tell you something, Lucinda." Kuba continued. "Something that should not be said."

Lucy waited, breathing in and out along with him.

"More than anything else on earth, I want this love that you need to be mine."

Lucy's head jerked forward and her heart pumped vibrantly. He had said out loud exactly what she was thinking.

"I want you to want me, Lucinda, but I am afraid that you are not ready to give up your current lover. And you should never leave one relationship simply because another has presented itself."

Lucy's soul suddenly opened up. Of course it was him; who else could it be? "It is you, Kuba," she explained. "You have to know it's you. You've touched my soul and created a yearning that won't go away."

"I also feel it, Lucinda. And it's stronger than any other link I've ever had with anyone, but I'm not sure if it's love. I've chanted your name over moonstone, orrisroot, and juniper berries, trying to see what might be the result of such a union, but the vision doesn't come. I'm afraid that the result may not be what we want it to be."

She was quiet, listening to her own heart beat. It was as if his spirit filled the emptiness inside her like a mythic fireball burning brightly. "At least we have to try," she urged.

"I am willing to try, Lucinda. But I don't want to hurt you."

Lucy kissed the cross that swung from the chain around her neck. "You won't hurt me. I know you won't. When can we meet?" she asked, anxiously shoving the fear back down into a deep cavern in her soul.

The tone of Kuba's voice now raised goose bumps on Lucy's uncovered arms. "I feel like I'm holding you right now, Lucinda. Can you feel yourself tucked away in my arms, my spirit soothing your troubled heart?"

Lucy nodded without a verbal response and Kuba understood.

"Listen to this," he continued.

She listened and thought she recognized the sound of a toy train moving around in the room. "Is it a train?" she asked.

"Yes. As a child building model trains was my favorite thing to do. Do you like trains, Lucinda?"

Lucy concentrated for a moment on the rhythmic sound. "Trains are nice," she replied.

"Then I have the perfect spot. We will meet on the Texas Limited. It's right here in Houston. I love the motion of the train and I know that you will love it, too."

Lucy caught something strange in his words. "You're in Houston?" she asked, bewildered.

"I'll meet you Saturday morning at eight-thirty at Eureka Depot in the Heights. The train is called the New York Central 61."

"Are you going to answer my question, Kuba?" she asked.

"Yes, I'm in Houston, Lucinda," he answered.

"How can you be in Houston?" she wondered out loud.

"I'm in Houston, because it was not an accident that you called me. I've been searching for you for a long time and I knew the moment I heard your voice that my search had ended."

Lucy held her breath. She focused on the tightness in her head and chest. She had been right all along. This was destined.

"How will we know each other?" she asked.

"We will know," he replied, and hung up.

Lucy leaped from her chair savoring the heightened sense of

euphoria. There were three days until Saturday and she had a lot to do. Then the smile disappeared as she noticed the sun slowly setting outside her window, hiding a blue-gray sky. Lucy suddenly panicked. How could she go away with Spencer this weekend and meet Kuba on Saturday, too?

15

*

Adel rushed into the house, stopping briefly to listen for sounds of her husband. She only heard the swish of the central air as it kicked in, the whirl of the ceiling fan in the living room, and the hum of the refrigerator. He wasn't home. She threw her briefcase across the dining room table in disappointment. It was nine o'clock at night. Was it too much to ask that her husband be at home?

She dragged herself into the bedroom and kicked off her shoes, not surprised that their marital bliss had quickly turned to this marital bewilderment. Thad had swooped into Adel's life like a rare and beautiful eagle. He moved her, pleased her, filled her, and inspired her. During their courtship, every now and then she would catch a little discord in his tone of voice or he would abruptly end a telephone conversation, but she rationalized that everyone had those kinds of moments.

It was not until Adel woke up that fresh spring morning almost a year into their relationship and realized that she was serious about Thad that a jealous trickle dripped down her spine. She suddenly wondered if those strange and distant actions could be tied to another woman, possibly to his previous woman. At one point, these thoughts became so overwhelming that she hired a detective who had worked with American Oil on several projects to follow Thad for a while. After two weeks and five thousand dollars there was no trace of an affair.

That same trickle again brought doubt and distrust on their wedding day, when Thad disappeared for two hours right after he said "I do." He kissed his bride, took her to their downtown hotel room to change, and didn't come back. His older brother, Max, eventually escorted her to the reception, corroborating Thad's story about some problem with the tickets for their honeymoon at the travel agency and his sorry car overheating twice. But to this day Thad had never explained what happened to Adel's satisfaction, and whenever she tried to question him about it an ugly argument would flare and Thad would stomp out of the house and disappear again.

It had been so long since they had spent a whole evening alone together that Adel found herself questioning Thad's faithfulness for the third time. She wanted to trust him, but why else would a man never get home before ten at night? Especially since he doesn't have an actual job. His computer project was something that he could work on anytime. Unfortunately, the most logical explanation was another woman. Adel blinked back tears just as the phone rang.

"Hello," she said dryly.

Thad spoke quickly. "Hey, Del. How are you, baby?"

Adel took a deep breath and dropped across the bed on her stomach. "Hey, where are you?"

"My damn car broke down over on Hillcroft and Holmes Road. I'm at the Seven Eleven on the corner. Can you come pick me up?"

Adel sighed and sat up. "Yeah, I guess," she replied, holding at bay the rage she really felt inside.

"Is something wrong?" he asked, noting the somber tone in her usually chipper voice.

She didn't respond to the question. "I'll be there in about thirty minutes."

"Thanks, baby."

Adel changed from her work clothes into a sweatsuit and tennis shoes. She adjusted her bra, which was feeling too tight lately, then loosened the drawstring around her waistline, which was obviously thicker.

As she backed her car out of the garage, Adel cursed Thad and the sorry jalopy that he loved. Who cared that it was a 1967 Chevy Malibu? It didn't run half the time, and wasn't that the more important issue? As a matter of fact, she decided at that very moment that she would co-sign, maybe even buy the man a new car if necessary, because this was the last time she was going to pick him up off some street corner. She turned onto 610 North Loop, followed it to the Southwest Freeway, and exited on Hillcroft.

As Adel passed various street signs—Bellaire, Beachnut, Bellfort—she instantly recognized the area. She hesitated at one stoplight too long and the cars behind her honked their dissatisfaction. This was the neighborhood where Thad had lived with his ex-girlfriend, Melany. Their condo in Sugarland was only a few blocks over. Adel knew this was the area because of the address, map, and twenty or more pictures she had been given by the detective.

She had also driven to the house a few times and sat out in front until Melany came home because she had questions that needed to be answered. Who was this woman that Thad had once loved? What did she look like? Why did he love her? Wasn't it natural to be curious about this woman who had spent four years with the man that she loved and was now married to?

The investigator's report had included an extensive profile. Melany was a bank teller. She grew up in Dallas, Texas, the youngest of three kids and earned an associate arts degree from Houston Community College. Adel flashed back to the pictures of Melany embracing a man at her front door. The detective had gotten close-ups as the man walked back to his car, so she knew it wasn't Thad. She assumed it was the guy who had eventually caused their breakup, the man that Melany loved now.

By the time Adel pulled up next to Thad's car she was fuming. How could he think she was so dumb that she wouldn't know what was up? Hanging in the streets and hanging with his ex-girlfriend were two entirely different things. And to be honest, she was fed up with both. She refused to accept this kind of crap from his tired ass any longer.

"Boy, am I glad to see my baby," Thad said as soon as she pulled into the gas station driveway and hopped out of the car.

He held out his arms, but Adel didn't move into them. Her eyes purposely searched the area to make sure that Melany or some other suspicious-looking bimbo was not around.

"What's going on?" Thad asked, noticing her peculiar actions.

"You must think I'm stupid," Adel hissed at him.

Thad threw his hands into the air and shook his head. "Now what are you talking about?"

"I'm not stupid, Thad. I know Melany lives over here!" Adel screamed. She rolled her eyes and jumped back into her car. Thad rushed over to the passenger's seat and got inside.

"Would you stop acting crazy and talk to me?" he huffed, snatching the keys from her trembling hand.

Adel's eyes narrowed. "I can't believe I got up out of my bed to come and get your sorry ass and you've probably been down here screwing Melany." She grabbed the keys back, jammed them into the ignition, and started the car.

Thad watched her in amazement. "What? Screwing Melany? Who told you that?"

Adel flipped the car into drive and stepped on the gas. "She lives a couple of blocks from here, Thad. Nobody had to tell me anything; I'm an intelligent human being."

"Well, you're not acting very intelligent right now because I have been nowhere near Melany since we split. If you'd stop and think for a minute you'd also remember that Max lives over on Guessner. That's where I'm coming from."

"So why the hell didn't you call Max and get his ass up to bring you home?" she asked as she entered the freeway.

"Because as I was about to leave he had a visitor and I figured he'd be getting busy about now."

"And I'm just pathetic old Adel, sitting around the house waiting on your call, right?"

"Stop it, Del! You know I don't feel like that. If you didn't want to come and get me you should have said so. I could have called a cab or something."

Adel banged both palms against the steering wheel several times. Thad was so good at turning shit around to his advantage. He knew she would never leave him stranded anywhere. He could have called a cab in the first place, but he liked this game of Show-me-how-much-you-will-do-for-me-because-you-love-me. He knew she had every right to be upset, but instead of being sorry, he was twisting things around like she was the one with a problem and he was somehow the one being wronged.

"This is not about coming to get you, Thad, and you know it," Adel finally spit out. "It's not even about tonight. It's everything. Why can't you ever be at home when I get there? Once in a while it would be nice to come home to you, to come home to my husband in our house. Why do you always have to be out in the damn street?"

"Slow down, please," Thad said, patting her right leg to get her to ease up off the gas pedal. "I don't understand. You never get home before eight or nine yourself, so why am I supposed to be sitting at home waiting on you?"

"Maybe I'd come home earlier if you were there. Maybe I don't come home because I don't want to sit up in that big house by myself all the time."

"So tell me that, dammit!" Thad hollered. "Instead of accusing me of some bullshit like sleeping with Melany. If I wanted

Melany I wouldn't have left her and I wouldn't have married you."

Adel tried to calm herself down. She sucked in deep breaths and pulled her shoulder blades up to relax them. This was the man she hoped to spend her life with, but they had to communicate better if that was going to happen.

"I want a normal life, Thad," she continued more calmly. "I'm ready to start a family with you, the man I love, and I can't deal with all this drama."

"Drama? Del, I hate to tell you this, but you're the one creating the drama. You want a baby, okay, let's have a baby. I'm sure Phoenix can handle that," he said, motioning to the bulge in the front of his pants.

Adel smirked. "It's not that easy. We need to make sure we're ready to be parents. I want my child to have a good life, the best possible life."

"You don't think I'd be a good father? Because I *know* you'd be a great mother."

Adel shrugged. "I don't know what to think, Thad. We need to make a commitment to this if we're going to do it. That means your 'I need to be free' mentality has got to go."

Thad glanced at Adel as she veered into the right lane just before their exit, but he didn't speak. He was collecting his words carefully, repeating them over and over in his mind.

"So now you're just going to ignore me?" Adel asked flippantly.

Thad still did not answer, so Adel stopped talking too and they drove the rest of the way home engulfed in an awkward silence. As the car moved their eyes darted about, looking at the street lights, the moon, the stars, the passing houses, the sudden rain on the windshield—everything except each other. When Adel finally pulled into the garage, Thad hopped out of the car and cornered her before she could get into the house.

"Why did you marry me, Del?" he asked.

Adel made a face at his question. "Because I love you, why else?" she replied.

"And who was I when you chose to love me?"

"What are you getting at, Thad?" Adel asked, trying to walk around him. He shifted his weight to block her path again.

"Who was I, Del, who am I?" he continued.

Adel took a step back because she knew the speech that was coming by heart. But she didn't plan to listen, not tonight. This fantasy world he was living in was about to come to an end. You don't get married and still expect to be free.

Thad continued. "I've never been a homebody. I like to go out and be around people. If you wanted a homebody you should have hooked up with Lucy's old man. Oh, sorry, I forgot, you complain about him, too. Sometimes I wonder if you even know what you want."

Adel put her hand on her hip and leaned back. "I know what I want and I didn't want Lucy's old man, I wanted you," she said.

"And that's who you got, Del, me!"

"Sometimes, it doesn't seem like I've got you at all, Thad, at least not all of you," she told him.

Thad let out a deep sigh and rubbed his temples before responding. "I don't even know what that means, Del. What I do know is that I love you and if you're ready to have a baby, I'm all for it. I know how you career women are, so I wasn't going to push the issue. But understand this. If you think having a baby is going to make me into someone I'm not, if you think the pitter-patter of little feet around the house will make me stay home, then you need to think again and you need to think long and hard."

Thad shoved the door open and stormed into the house. He headed straight to the bedroom, undressed, and fell asleep not long after his head hit the pillow.

Adel marched into the den and turned on the television for background noise. She dropped down on the couch and crossed her arms over her chest. If Thad thought she was going to have a baby and be stuck at home raising it alone while he's out in the streets hanging and swanging, he was nuts. Adel gritted her teeth and tried to release some of the building anger. She couldn't believe that the man had the nerve to say have a baby, just don't expect me to be around to help you take care of it.

Her thoughts wandered back to a reoccurring question that she had first pondered in junior high school. The new career counselor visited every homeroom one year, jump-starting students' thoughts about what kind of life they wanted to lead. Tommy Walden, the boy who sat next to her and whom she'd had had a secret crush on for months, said he wanted an ordinary life. She wondered what that meant. What was an ordinary life?

She remembered hoping that her mother and father's lives were not ordinary, because she wasn't sure she wanted to be like them. If they had an ordinary life, it meant that she couldn't marry Tommy. Not that anything was wrong with her parents' lives or that she didn't like who her parents were or how they had raised her. She just knew she wanted something different, something more. She didn't plan to be an ordinary mother and give up her job to raise a child. And it was obvious that Thad wasn't planning to be an ordinary father. He apparently couldn't stay out of the streets long enough to spend time with his own wife, let alone his child.

When she had asked her mother about ordinary people and ordinary lives in their crowded kitchen one day while making buttermilk fried chicken and banana bread pudding, her mother explained that ordinary was what it looked like on the outside. She added that nobody really cared about the storms people go through on the inside, they only worry that the ship gets home safely.

A commercial break ended and Adel glanced up at the television when she heard a choir singing "His Eye Is on the Sparrow." She caught only the end of the religious passage that flashed boldly on the screen over a field of waving bluebonnets. ". . . behold, all things are become new."

Adel had an urge to read the entire passage, so she grabbed a pen and scribbled the citation, II Corinthians 5:17, on a blank corner of the newspaper. She pulled Thad's Bible, a gift from his parents, from the top shelf of the hall closet, slipped it out of its case, and found the spot. "Therefore if any man be in Christ, he is a new creature: old things are passed away; behold, all things are become new."

As she curled up on the couch and closed her eyes, Adel softly repeated the verse out loud several times. She wasn't sure why that passage touched her the way it did at that moment, but she was glad to find some peace, even if it was only temporary.

16

✳

Many of the huge glass and steel buildings in the Houston downtown area belonged to oil companies. Gulf, Texaco, Shell, and American Oil were just a few that boasted an annual revenue of more than one billion dollars each. As Adel sat at a small cozy table in the corner of Polly's restaurant and waited for her lunch date to arrive, she thought about all of that money and where it went. It seemed odd to her that she needed to fire people to improve the company's profit margin.

Webster had called to say he was going to be a little late, so she'd chosen to meet him at Polly's. She couldn't stay another minute in that depressing building. When Webster hurried into the restaurant, she waved him over to the table.

"Hi, sorry," he said, leaning over to kiss her on the cheek.

"It's okay," she replied. "I just got here."

Webster sat down, quickly taking in her mocha lips and amber eyes. "You look beautiful, as usual," he said.

Adel blushed. She had consciously worn her short red Donna Karan suit to get his attention. It felt good to know that her efforts were not in vain.

She almost didn't wear the outfit this morning because she couldn't button the waistband of the skirt. She finally had to find a needle and thread and move the button over so that she could close it. Adel couldn't believe she was gaining weight. She had been a size twelve for as long as she could remember. She had been forced to accept large, rounded breasts that blossomed on her fourteenth birthday and ample hips that spread and filled in a year later.

Adel knew Lucy would blame her expanding waistline on age and a sedentary lifestyle. She was always trying to get Adel over to the gym to work out. Many times Adel made plans to do it, but she rarely followed through. She justified her lack of motivation with the idea that she just wasn't as vain as Lucy. She wasn't worried about looking like some unrealistic model in a magazine. She was healthy and happy.

Her physical examination four months ago had confirmed that her blood pressure and cholesterol were fine and her heart, lungs, kidneys, and other vital organs were working within normal capacity. She had even asked the doctor about having kids and been given an A-plus for her body's condition at thirty-five. The doctor went so far as to compliment Adel's health by saying that he had seen younger women in much worse shape because of years of smoking, drinking, and abusing their bodies.

"Would you like to order your drinks now?" the waiter asked, standing over them.

Webster spoke first. "Yes, I'll have a draft, and what would you like?"

"A Diet Pepsi," Adel replied, and the waiter rushed away.

"So how is life treating you?" Webster jumped right in.

"I'm okay, I guess. Things are a little shaky on the marriage front, but we're hanging in."

Webster stared as if he could see right through her. "I hope you're happy, Adel, because you deserve to be happy."

Adel shifted her eyes to her napkin before she said anything.

"I am happy most of the time," she finally responded. "Nothing in life is one hundred percent."

Webster noticed her uneasiness. Even though he wanted to tell her that he was still there for her if she needed him, he didn't know how to say it, so he changed the subject. "I got a call from Hunter about my memo," he said.

Adel twisted her bottom in the chair to get more comfortable. She was thankful for Webster's sensitivity. Thad would never have picked up the signal. "I know, I got a call, too. Were you surprised?"

"Not really. I've been here long enough to know how it works."

"I appreciate you taking the flak for this one and I know Susan is thankful, too. I wish we could find another way to salvage the profit margin."

"There are other ways, but it would mean that my colleagues would have to get up out of their padded-leather seats and do some real work."

Adel and Webster smiled knowingly at each other.

Adel shook her head. "Too much of a sacrifice, huh?"

"Jesus himself would have to return to earth," Webster teased.

"I'm not even sure Jesus could change things," Adel added pessimistically.

They both laughed, then sat quiet and content for a while until Adel broke the silence between them.

"I'm exploring an idea that I think has great potential, but I'm not sure how the company will feel about it."

"Well, tell me about this great idea and I'll give you my colleagues' potential perspective."

Adel hesitated. "It's still in the early stages."

"Tell me anyway, maybe I can help somehow."

"I think we should create a day care facility in our building. It was really Susan's idea, but it makes a lot of sense. If the job offered day care, mothers and fathers wouldn't have to be late dropping the kids off or leave early to pick them up or hassle over lunch checking on them."

Webster cocked his head to the side. "It is a good idea, but who would run it and where would we put it?" he asked.

"I've already talked to a woman who's been in the day care business for ten years. She's interested in starting a second center. She would take care of licensing, insurance, employees, and all other operations. I'm looking at those two empty rooms on the fifth floor. I plan to talk to our lawyers about setting up a discounted lease, and our employees would get first shot at the twelve or fifteen available openings."

Webster's eyebrows raised. "It's a very good idea, Adel, but there's a problem."

Adel tensed her shoulders. "What problem?"

"Hunter and the other vice presidents are turning that space into a fitness center for upper-level employees."

Adel's mouth fell open. "You're kidding."

"I think they've gotten the bids for equipment and everything. They're even talking about hiring a trainer to come in two or three times a week. You didn't see the memo last month?"

Adel's spirits dropped. "It's probably in one of those piles on my desk."

"Well, yours is the better idea. Maybe you can get them to change their plans."

"Yeah, right . . . give up their luxury weight room for top executives to help low-level employees like mothers with babies. You know just like I do how well that idea will go over."

The waiter brought their drinks and they ordered lunch.

"Look, don't give up. You've had a lot of success in steering Hunter in the right direction. Put your best plan together and have some faith," Webster encouraged her.

Adel curved her lips into a smile and tried to stop the negative thoughts that were swelling inside her head. It *was* a great idea and maybe somehow she could make it work. Webster was right. She had to have faith.

17

✳

*T*here are different types of auras that can radiate from a person's body. In her lifetime so far, Lucy had seen two of them. She first saw a halo emanating from the head of her cousin Kenil when they were both eight years old. As he played an antique goat skin drum called the *bamboula* at a family gathering in Baton Rouge she watched the halo grow bright, then dim, and bright again. No one knew except Madea, Kenil, and her that Kenil was going to die soon. Lucy and Kenil talked for hours that weekend about everything because both understood that there wasn't much time. The night he died, Lucy sat under a darkened moon on her grandmother's front porch watching Kenil's star. At the same time that the cancer consumed his last breath Lucy swore that she saw his star fall from the sky.

Another kind of aura is called an aureola. It is a colored light that surrounds the head or the entire body, and Lucy was used to seeing this aura because it flowed from her Madea all the time. Madea had a unique energy that scattered whenever she laughed through her rainbow spirit. Lucy would often watch people, feet stumbling, eyes glazing over, as Madea's laughter would capture them momentarily, then set them free.

Standing in front of Kuba on Saturday morning, Lucy knew she was looking at a third kind of aura. This was the most powerful aura of all. Kuba's brilliant glory was a combination of both the halo and the aureola linked together. She stood mesmerized by the multicolored energy field hugging his broad, muscular frame. There were layers of red, blue, yellow, and violet waves tangled together. Lucy tried to remember what the colors meant. Red could be both positive and negative. It was a powerful hue that often led to some kind of achievement, yet it could also suggest a selfish or egotistical nature. The blue ring was large and vibrant, illuminating a positive soul. Abundant creativity and intelligence came from the yellow ring, and violet, the most prominent color surrounding Kuba, announced his supreme spiritual base.

Madea had trained Lucy to intuitively recognize a person's spirit as a way to quickly assess their soul. A lot of people had this power, but very few knew how to use it effectively. When a spirit was negative Lucy could tell through an instant dislike that overwhelmed her. If the spirit was positive she could tell by a distinct pleasure that its presence could create. Lucy sensed that Kuba's spirit was so light and so wonderful it could probably lift her up off the ground and into the air.

She moved closer, noticing something else almost hidden inside the colored rays. She could barely make it out, but it was a series of visceral shapes similar to several triangles linked together. This symbol she instinctively connected with some kind of security or protection.

Kuba held out his hand and Lucy took it, allowing him to pull her up and onto the platform of the train. His touch was mystical, and even though a surge of radiant energy sent a shockwave through her body, she did not let go. She absorbed the metaphysical charge deep within, allowing their spiritual chakras to expand and their souls to meet gracefully.

"I'm glad you came," Kuba said softly, never taking his eyes from Lucy's beaming face.

"I had to come," she told him. "I had to know."

As they stood for a brief moment, face-to-face in the morning breeze, the force of Kuba's soul merging with her own was like the vibrant swirl of cool vanilla ice cream mixing with heated chocolate syrup.

Kuba led Lucy to a seat in the parlor-style observation car at the rear of the train. "This car was built after World War Two," he explained as they sat down in an empty section. "Would you like something to drink?"

Lucy simply nodded because there were no words. She couldn't form a complete sentence if she wanted to. As soon as Kuba left to get the drinks, she tried to focus. She had to get her heartbeat under control, stop her knees from shaking, and clear the muddled thoughts in her head. When the train slowly inched forward, Lucy couldn't help but listen to the steel wheels turn: *shooooo, shooooo, shooooo, shooooo, shooooo, shooooo.*

She thought about Madea and what she might advise her to do in this kind of situation. Madea would probably say follow the light that is brightest because that light is the beginning of all happiness.

So when Kuba returned, Lucy took a moment to admire his bright light. Vivid, laughing eyes made her shiver, a broad heaving chest pulled her close like a magnet, and smooth, walnut skin wrapped around an intense spirit soothed her frazzled soul.

"Each of the cars on this train has a history of its own," Kuba continued as he sat down beside her. "Like the Silver Stirrup, which was built in 1948 with one of the first vista-domes, and the Silver Queen, made in 1957, was the first train to use oil-fired heat rather than steam."

"Are you nervous, Kuba?" Lucy asked, taking his hand in hers.

Kuba looked into her eyes with an intensity that she couldn't ignore. "No, not nervous, but excited and happy."

Lucy smiled. "I'm nervous and very few people in this world can make me nervous."

Kuba absorbed her words like water on a cotton towel. "And why are you nervous, Lucinda? You have enough power of your own to know that I'm not going to hurt you. You should know that this is God's will."

"I guess I just can't believe I'm here and you're real," she responded. "Do you know how long I've prayed for someone like you to come into my life?"

Kuba leaned over and whispered in her ear. "As long as I've prayed for someone like you to come into mine. I am real, Lucinda, I'm as real as you want me to be." Kuba took off a silver ankh that he wore on a chain around his neck and slid it over Lucy's head. "Would you believe me if I told you that this ankh can be the key to the rest of your life?" he asked.

Lucy nodded. "If you tell me, I'll believe it," she replied honestly.

Kuba slowly kissed the ankh, then pressed it against her shapely lips. "See these markings?" he asked after pulling it away. "They are Egyptian hieroglyphics that represent life. This circle on top shows us eternity. Touch it," he requested.

Lucy gently took the ankh from his hand and held it in her palm.

"Now, listen to the energy that the symbol attracts."

Lucy closed her eyes, cleared her mind, and waited. Seconds later she heard hundreds of voices, low at first then getting louder and louder. Kuba laid his hand across her heart and Lucy jumped when his fingers brushed against her skin, magnifying her desire.

"I hear it," she told him.

"That's life," Kuba repeated. "Now kiss it," he instructed.

Lucy did as she was told and felt a sudden magical force filter into her bloodstream. Her whole body tingled with electricity and she was frightened, but stimulated at the same time. "What, what is it?" she stammered, dropping the ankh.

Kuba raised his hand. "Don't let it go," he ordered. "It's love, God's pure love."

Lucy scooped the ankh back into her hand and promptly felt the chill again. She noticed that the train was moving faster now: *shooo, shooo, shooo, shooo, shooo, shooo, shooo, shooo, shooo, shooo.*

Her heart pulsated and her mind yearned to hear Kuba speak again because the silence was unbearable. She turned to look at his face and with each glance felt more and more sure that the Greek philosophers had to be right. How else could she explain the love that surrounded them almost immediately? How else could she describe this feeling that they had been separated at birth? How else could she believe that only now would their union make the world complete?

"Your aura is even more powerful than I imagined over the phone," Lucy finally said out loud.

"When you're ready, Lucinda, I will help you to develop the power of your own aura. You have spent so much time running that there is no stability, no direction."

His tangled dreadlocks fell loosely across his face and onto his shoulders. Lucy gently stroked the unruly locks. "I'm ready to stop running," she told him.

Kuba smiled. "So you will," he answered. "And you will learn how powerful you are now that we've found each other."

Lucy glanced out of the window, watching trees and fields pass by. She felt the need to tell Kuba so many things, but held it inside. Madea was the only one who had ever understood what she wanted. And now here was this man offering her everything she had ever dreamed of, everything she had ever prayed for.

When Kuba finally turned and pressed his lips firmly against hers, Lucy released her soul and let it speak for her. She allowed it to tell him all that he wanted to know. His fiery tongue searched her mouth for hidden treasure and she gave him everything she had. Lucy realized that she had been searching most of her life for this connection, for this man.

Shoo, shoo, shoo, shoo, shoo, shoo, shoo, shoo, shoo, shoo, shoo, shoo, shoo, shoo, shoo, shoo. The train was rolling faster now and Lucy's heart rolled right along with it.

18

✳

From the moment Kuba took her hand and pulled her up onto the train, Lucy knew that she would follow him anywhere. When she straddled his motorcycle there was no doubt or fear. She tightened her arms around his waist and laid her head against his warm back. Their breathing was in tandem, inhale, exhale, inhale, exhale, no longer two bodies, but one.

It was in the comfort of Kuba's sanctuary hours later where love truly took hold. He whispered a Latin proverb: "Love comes by looking," as he slowly undressed Lucy and took in all of her. He massaged each uncovered limb, igniting the flames that were buried deep inside.

They knelt together in front of the mahogany coffee table that served as an ancestral altar. Lucy knew many of the symbols from a similar worship space at Madea's house. A clean, white cotton sheet draped the table and one white candle stood on each corner in the back. A large gold cross lay in the center surrounded by white carnations. Seven tiny glasses filled with blessed water were set in a semicircle next to the pictures of seven ancestors: Chaka Zulu, Zora Neale Hurston, Marcus Garvey, Nat Turner,

Malcolm X, Martin Luther King, and the picture of what looked like a young slave boy in chains. Long sticks of incense burned over brown wooden holders, next to a white Bible.

Lucy took in every element of Kuba's gorgeous, mahogany body. She was turned on by the perfectly sculpted arms and legs. His stomach, although not as chiseled as a six-pack, was close enough, and his manhood was unquestionable. She stopped when she got to his long, polished fingernails.

"Your nails are longer than mine," she told him jokingly, while studying each finger carefully.

Kuba looked down at his hands, then at hers. "I cut them only at special times because of my religion."

"What religion is that?" she asked, already guessing the answer.

"Voodoo," he responded.

Lucy leaned back, not because she was surprised, but because she hadn't thought this thing through enough to add that part of him into the equation. Of course a man who is psychic with a combined halo and aureole would practice voodoo, what else? It probably should have made him off-limits, but instead she became even more intrigued and moved up close again.

Lucy learned quite a bit about voodoo growing up with Madea. Her grandmother had drilled in the fact that there was a big difference between voodoo and hoodoo. Voodoo, as Madea defined it, was a bona fide religion brought across the ocean by West Africans who were sold into slavery in the West Indies, Haiti, and America. The people in that African region saw nature and spirit as the same, so they created a life that would honor and respect those beliefs. Nature's herbs were mixed and blended to make remedies for daily health needs. Charms, chants, and rituals were developed to mediate life and protect souls. Since God stayed very busy with matters of extreme importance such as the earth and sky and water, supreme dieties called *orisa* or *loas* were identified to relay human messages to the Lord when necessary.

Voodoo, Madea had insisted, was not about demonic forces or Devil worship. It was the connection of present-day souls with ancestral spirits from the past. Since slaves were not allowed to gather except under the umbrella of Christianity, African gods and goddesses were connected to Catholic saints. Dambala became St. Patrick because Dambala appeared through a series of snake-like movements and St. Patrick was known for chasing the snakes from Ireland. Ezili was tied to the Virgin Mary as a beautiful and graceful mulatto who represented the heart. And Shango, the God of War, was a mirror image of St. Barbara, the patron saint of all warriors.

Hoodoo, Madea went on to explain, was all about superstition, involving spells cast to make someone love you or a curse to hurt someone you don't like. These were exaggerated media horrors constantly fed to the American public to promote mass hysteria. Most people didn't see the separation between the two as clearly as Madea did.

"In voodoo, fingernails can be used in potions and charms, so they are rarely cut. An enemy could take hold of your soul through your fingernails," Kuba explained.

Lucy slid her arms around his neck. "You couldn't possibly have any enemies," she told him.

Kuba followed suit, wrapping his arms around her small waist. "I hope not."

Lucy thought for a moment how romantic it would be if she could get Kuba to cut his nails for her like Sampson cut off his hair for Delilah. It was not until much later, when the carefully manicured tips scraped gently across the nipples of her bare breasts, that Lucy decided it really didn't matter.

At the front of the altar, a mixture of herbs and stones were tossed inside a glass bowl half filled with water. Lucy paid attention to Kuba's choices. The herbs included sweet basil and juniper berries to elicit passion, eucalyptus and golden seal to assure good health, vervain leaves for success, and ginger root as protection. They were joined by sacred stones like the golden amber of life, a fluid moonstone stimulating love, and a blue topaz, her favorite, to calm the emotions and alleviate stress.

Kuba sucked her lips and nose and eyes and neck and ears. "I want you to be with me in mind, body, and spirit," he told her before moving on to each new area. "I want us to love each other endlessly."

Lucy agreed, fully aware of how their auras sang a harmonious song. "That's what I want, too. I need you in my life, Kuba," she added, just before their lips meshed together more forcefully.

Lucy slid her tongue down Kuba's chest and into his belly button, until he vibrated with intensity. When he couldn't take it any longer, he motioned for her to lay back against the oriental carpet and pulled a large, white blanket from the back of the couch to cover her body.

"If I start a love ritual will you finish it with me?" he asked, pausing until he knew her answer was yes.

The hesitation in Lucy's mind served only to heighten the urgency in her body. She nodded her affirmation, believing that it was possible to see the stars if you accepted the darkness, and she now longed to follow Kuba's light straight up into the clouds.

"I will begin the chant and you join in as soon as you're ready," Kuba told her.

As he placed a large, red candle on the table and lit its flame, Lucy glanced at her surroundings. She took note of several large wicker baskets stacked in one corner, heard wind chimes playing incessantly with the breeze outside the window, and felt an odd chill that whipped its way across her body and wrapped around her heart. She wanted to sit up, but couldn't move until Kuba leaned over and brushed his lips against her hardened nipples, reigniting the passion.

As he lit the two white candles on the back of the altar, Lucy closed her eyes and prepared herself for the ecstasy that would soon come. She wished to know this man intimately. She craved his tenderness, warmth, and power inside of her. Destiny had led her to Kuba, to this moment, and it was exactly where she wanted to be.

Kuba started to chant: "This light of love is a burning fire, to spark our deepest soul's desire, each day our devoted fire burns true, and strengthens the love from me to you."

He repeated the chant while using a pair of scissors to cut a small lock from his hair and Lucy's. She watched as he took a red paper heart, twisted the pieces of hair together, and taped them to it.

"This light of love is a burning fire, to spark our deepest soul's desire, each day our devoted fire burns true, and strengthens the love from me to you."

He laid the heart on the altar and sprinkled wet juniper berries, orrisroot, and sweet basil all over it.

"This light of love is a burning fire, to spark our deepest soul's desire, each day our devoted fire burns true, and strengthens the love from me to you."

He tipped the red candle over and let the melted wax fall onto the pure lover's heart. Tears of joy flooded Lucy's eyes when he uncovered her body and dropped delicate pools of wax on her breasts, stomach, and thighs. Kuba kissed the tears away while whispering the chant again. "This light of love is a burning fire, to spark our deepest soul's desire, each day our devoted fire burns true, and strengthens the love from me to you."

They kissed passionately, holding and caressing each other. Through the power of his touch, Kuba produced a sensual energy that flowed freely from his body to hers, and that heated touch seared their souls together.

Lucy repeated the chant along with him. "This light of love is a burning fire, to spark our deepest soul's desire, each day our devoted fire burns true, and strengthens the love from me to you."

An hour later, she stopped to reflect on Kuba's true power as they lay next to each other trembling from contentment, without penetration, without intercourse.

Laying her head on his chest, they chanted together: "This light of love is a burning fire, to spark our deepest soul's desire, each day our devoted fire burns true, and strengthens the love from me to you."

19

✳

The message on Lucy's voice mail the next morning instructed her to get to the Texas Medical Center as soon as she could. Spencer's voice was frantic as he explained quickly that his mother had had a heart attack and was at the Texas Heart Institute.

Lucy took a shower and dressed slowly. She wasn't sure what she should do. She regretted leaving that message on Spencer's answering machine Friday night backing out of their weekend. She'd lied and said she needed to pay a surprise visit to the Austin center because of some problems that had been reported there.

Spencer needed her now and she liked Mrs. Gray, but she didn't want to face this thing so soon. How could she comfort Spencer when the memory of Kuba's love was still so fresh? The tarot card's prediction of death popped into her mind and she knew now what it meant. The relationship that she had hoped would last a lifetime had to end.

Lucy practiced telling Spencer it was over on the way to the hospital. Maybe she would be straightforward and just tell him the truth. "Spencer, there's someone else and I can't stay with you."

Maybe he didn't have to know that there was somebody else. Maybe she could heap all of the blame on herself. "Spencer, we've been through a lot together, but you deserve somebody who can totally commit to you. I'm just not the one."

What if she stopped answering his calls and avoided him until he got the message? No, she wasn't cruel enough to carry that one out. Lucy shook her head vigorously. This was such a bad time to hurt him like this. Maybe she should just wait. He needed to focus on his mother right now. Yes, that's what she would do, wait until things got better.

Parking in the first empty spot, Lucy rushed into the six-story building, trying to summon all of the courage she could find to face Spencer. With Kuba in her life now there was no room for anyone else. He was everywhere—his spirit feeding her soul, his love occupying her heart, his energy surging through her blood-stream, and his laughter shaping her thoughts. He had miracu-lously spread his protective aura to include her, eliminating doubts and erasing fears. Lucy felt so satisfied and happy at that moment that if she were to burst, her spirit would probably spread tiny pieces of joy throughout the world.

Stopping at a beat-up vending machine, she looked for hot tea or hot chocolate, something warm to calm her nerves. Lucy was really procrastinating. She needed a little more time, so she stole a few more minutes in the restroom checking her hair and makeup, then she stopped in the hallway, tying her shoe strings tighter before she finally reached Mrs. Gray's room.

Standing right outside the door, Lucy kissed the silver ankh that now hung around her neck in place of her usual cross to draw strength from the thousands of voices. Studying it closely, she wondered if it was some kind of aphrodisiac; a symbol blessed by a lover's spell from the goddess Aphrodite, the mother of erot-ica. How else could she explain experiencing this new intense and wonderful love with Kuba, a love that didn't involve actually making love?

After taking several long, lingering breaths, Lucy seized a moment of strength and opened the door. She stepped inside the room, shrugging off the worry that tapped on her shoulder. There was very little time to look from Mrs. Gray asleep on the bed to Spencer half asleep in the nearby chair before he saw her and leaped up, sweeping her into his arms. Lucy's worries rapidly vanished like raindrops on a hot July sidewalk. She stood molded inside Spencer's massive chest. She returned his firm embrace instinctively.

Spencer led Lucy out of the room and into the hallway so they could talk without waking his mother. He talked fast, telling her all about the emergency bypass operation and how the doctor emerged from the operating room a few hours ago to tell him that her prognosis was a fairly good one.

"I didn't know what to do," he explained. "Mom was on the floor when I got to her house this morning. I don't know how long she'd been there. I called 911 and prayed. I was so scared, Lucy. I'm glad you're finally here, baby. I needed you here."

When Lucy saw the tears tumble down his face, her eyes watered, too. They walked over to a nearby couch together and sat holding each other without words. She had never seen Spencer cry before; until now she wasn't sure that he could. He lay his head in her lap and she tightened her arms around him.

The hospital lobby brought back painful memories of the last time Lucy sat in the midst of sickness. This lobby was very similar to the lobby in the hospital where her mother died. For the most part it was the same: sturdy white walls built to last for many years, sparkling clean floors holding the terrified footsteps of loved ones, and bright sunshine filling windows with the outside where heaven beckoned.

Her father had been killed instantly by the impact of the truck, but her mother fought to hold on. She struggled for six exhausting days. During that time Lucy was only allowed into her hospital room once. She recalled waiting in the lobby area for the nurse to come and get her. She knew something was wrong, but wasn't sure how bad it might be. When the nurse took her hand she closed her eyes and followed because she was afraid to see her mother in a place like that. She imagined that tubes would be attached to practically every part of her body. She thought about the movies, where children were always brave in such situations, but she didn't know how they did it and she didn't think that she could do it.

Lucy didn't open her eyes until they were inside the room and the nurse let go of her hand. She was pleasantly surprised to see her mother sitting up, arms spread wide waiting for a big hug, a final hug. Lucy ran to the bed and, with the help of the nurse, positioned herself beside her mother for more than an hour. They sang "This Little Light of Mine" and "Jesus Loves Me" maybe a hundred times, she didn't keep count. And her mother laughed at her silly faces and corny jokes. "What time is it when an elephant sits on your bike? Time to get a new bike." "Why did the turkey cross the road? To prove he wasn't a chicken."

They played games. Games with their fingers. "This is the house and this is the steeple, open the doors and greet all the people." Games with their hands. "Patty cake, patty cake, baker's man, bake me a cake as fast as you can. Roll it and pat it and mark with a B, then put it in the oven for baby and me."

And games with their hearts. "I love you," her mother had said, patting her heart. "Remember that Mommy and Daddy will always be with you in here."

Lucy hadn't thought about that day in a such long time. When her mother's soul entered heaven later that night, Lucy knew instinctively that her father was waiting. She panicked when she realized that the memories were beginning to fade. She couldn't remember the color of her mother's eyes or the curve of her fingers.

Softly sliding her hand up and down Spencer's back, Lucy felt his breath filtering in and out along with hers and knew that their spirits were settling into the old union as if nothing were different. She sat amazed by the magnitude of Spencer's love. It was not the passionate, explosive connection that Kuba summoned. But it was powerful in its own right. It reminded her of the first buds that survived an early spring frost, resisting defeat, refusing to die.

"It's okay, baby," she whispered sincerely. "I'm here."

20

✳

Adel's heart mourned every time she had to witness an oil spill and the destruction that it caused to the earth's environment. Hunter had called first thing that morning. He wanted all of the vice presidents on the company's private jet by nine. American Oil promoted environmental consciousness, so they would always lend a hand when such accidents occurred. When Adel first began working for the company there was an oil well explosion in the Gulf of Mexico. Galveston and South Padre Island were hit hard by the Ixtoc I explosion in 1979 and hundreds of Kemp's Ridley sea turtles washed up dead on shore in Brownsville, Texas. The oil slick drifted more than five hundred miles before the well was successfully capped off.

Now it was happening all over again. Adel cautiously walked along Galveston Beach, noting the pockets of shiny black oil that had settled around rocks, leaves, and branches. She lifted up one of the rocks and watched the oil seep into the ground, poisoning the organisms that lived below. Cleanup crews were already on the scene using skimmers to remove the oil from the surface, placing booms around sensitive areas, and preparing high-powered water hoses to scour the beaches. This well-defined routine had been established to remove as much of the oil as possible, but unfortunately most of the damage had already been done.

Adel stopped to watch a portable television monitor where a marine biologist in Brownsville reported that dead turtles were already washing up on shore. One that he had recently dissected showed high levels of oil in its tissue and digestive tract. Newly hatched turtles that were exposed would also be a major concern. The biologist cautioned viewers that the genetic systems of these creatures would be infected in a number of ways: some of the effects could be seen immediately and others might not manifest themselves for generations to come.

Hunter had already taken his place in front of the local camera crews, ready to pledge his assistance in support of the clean-up effort. Adel thought it was all such a crock. The Houston port was one of the country's busiest, and there were constant oil leakage problems that never got this kind of media attention. Oil that leaked from the various barges had already had a serious impact on the fishing, shrimping, and tourist industries in Texas, yet nothing much was said.

Everybody closed their eyes and pretended that all was right with the world. Scientists had found that many types of birds in the region were showing signs of impaired walking or unstable flying, and a number of different plants were growing odd-shaped leaves or broke easily from brittle stems, but nobody seemed to care.

"How many people can we put on this?" Hunter asked as he walked up behind Adel.

"Not many," she replied. "Remember we're about to fire three or four people and that's going to make us pretty limited."

"Well, it may mean smaller bonuses this Christmas, but maybe we should reduce that number. We can let two people go and assign two others to work with this effort."

Adel didn't respond right away. She stood and watched the cleanup crew tugging at hoses and sifting through sand. "You know, Hunter, we need to talk," she finally said. "This whole situation is making me ill and I'm not sure how much longer I can take it."

"Me too," Hunter interrupted. "When I look around at the destruction of such beauty I feel like crying. It is such a sad day for us all. Hey, I should probably say that next time the cameras are rolling, maybe even go ahead and cry a little. It would be great for community relations, don't you think?"

Adel stared at him for a moment and several responses lined up in her mind, but she didn't voice any of them. All she could do was bite her tongue, shake her head, and walk away. She should have known his decisions were all about public relations. Hunter didn't really care what oil companies were doing to the environment. She couldn't believe his cynicism. The ill feeling she was talking about was because she was sick of this business-as-usual routine. The ill feeling she was talking about was from watching him strut ridiculously around the beach like he'd just shot a ten under par on the golf course. The ill feeling she was talking about was from her stomach, which was all tied up like she was going to be sick.

It didn't matter that scientists were busy trying to determine the size of the spill, what kind of oil it was, and of course how the timing factor would play itself out so that the potential for damage could be minimized. All that mattered to Hunter was community relations and what kind of positive publicity American Oil could milk from the disaster.

Adel hiked over to Webster, stood beside him, pointing. "Can you believe his arrogance?" she asked.

Webster nodded his understanding. "He's doing what he does best. Taking his image to the next level."

Adel kicked at a small pool of oil in the sand. "How can people continue to live when they don't see the world getting any better? What hope do we have for a positive future?"

"We've got to have faith," Webster assured her. "Faith that life will prevail over all circumstances."

Adel closed her eyes and willed back the pain that spread through her body. The churning in her stomach connected with the ache in her soul. "What is faith and how do I get some?" she finally asked. "Because I'm not sure I can even make it through today, let alone next week or next year."

Webster smiled and put his arm firmly around her shoulders. "Faith is trusting that good will always win over evil," he explained.

Adel smirked. "You can't prove that in today's society. Everywhere I look evil seems to be in control and good is getting kicked in the butt."

"That's because you're focusing on the evil and not the good."

"Now you're just playing with semantics."

"No, I'm telling you the truth. Look at the debate over greenhouse warming. Some scientists say that the warming is within the bounds of our climate's natural fluctuation pattern, and others warn that there is evidence of global warming trends that could ultimately destroy everything."

Adel cocked her head to the side. "And how is that good?" she asked.

Webster frowned for a second. "I guess that was a bad example, because I believe we probably are destroying the earth. It's pretty clear when you take into account the extensive number of hurricanes and droughts along with soaring temperatures."

"See, even you can't tell me what to do to get through this," Adel teased.

"I can tell you one thing," Webster continued. "With little faith you can get into heaven, but with great faith heaven will come to you. Do you go to church, Adel?" he asked out of the blue.

"Not really," she answered, then noticed that she felt a pang of guilt after admitting it. "My family wasn't very religious."

"I'm Catholic," Webster responded automatically. "I attend St. Mary's over on West University. I'd like for you to come sometime."

"I just might take you up on that offer."

Webster nodded his approval. "I hope so."

Adel continued nervously, "I've been thinking a lot about God and religion lately. I don't know why."

"And what are your thoughts about God and religion?"

"Nothing specific. It's strange. Like this feeling I got the other night that I was somehow suspended in space. I couldn't go backward and I couldn't move forward. I was stuck in a kind of limbo. It was what I think purgatory must be like. I knew I was supposed to do something, but I didn't know what."

Webster leaned forward, obviously intrigued. "Was it something you *wanted* to do?" he asked.

"I don't know." Adel shrugged. "Lately, I've been wondering who I am and what my purpose is here on earth."

"You have to know that you're a wonderful human being and an important part of American Oil."

"Do I?"

"I hope you do. And if you don't, I know it, Hunter knows it, Susan knows it, and so do many others."

Adel wanted to respond, but her entire body suddenly shook in a kind of spasm and she started to fall to the ground.

Webster caught her. "Are you all right?" he asked, leading her over to a large rock so she could sit down for a minute.

She threw up on the side of the rock, holding her stomach through a series of cramping pains.

"You're sick? Can I get you something?" Webster asked, handing her his handkerchief.

"I've been feeling like something was going on for a couple of weeks now, but I blamed it on being tired."

"I'll get you some water," Webster said, rushing to an emergency table set up on the left side of one of the fire trucks.

Adel looked across the gulf and envisioned herself sailing out past the horizon. She took a moment to enjoy the serene, steady wind that would push her over the waves. It was the first time she had thought about sailing since college. Levin Foster, a well-off Rice University student, taught Adel to sail. He almost convinced her that they would sail away together some day. His family owned a lot of real estate in Houston, including a couple of restaurants, a hotel, and a mall. Levin promised her that whether or not his family approved he would love her forever.

They spent a lot of time out on the water to get away from the stares and jeers that their interracial relationship provoked from others. They dreamed about life's possibilities, until Levin's father told him to end it and he obeyed. Adel called him every day for almost a week until the operator told her the number had been disconnected and the new number was unlisted. It wasn't that she wanted him back. She wanted an explanation. She deserved a proper good-bye.

Adel laughed when she remembered seeing Levin many years later sitting in his black Saab in front of Foleys at the Galleria Mall. She knew it was him even with the hair loss and the wire-rimmed glasses hanging off his thin nose. She still wasn't sure why she did it, but she walked right over to the open window, leaned inside, said "Remember me?" then spit in his face.

Closing her eyes, Adel saw herself tying off the sails, freeing up the mooring lines, lifting the head sails at the bow, and floating away with the breeze. No contradictory job to perform, no husband to compromise with, no nausea, just the wide blue sea and the huge yellow sun to comfort her.

"You want to talk about it?" Webster asked as he handed her the bottle of water.

Adel took the water, thanked Webster, drank a large swallow, and wondered if Levin's rejection so many years ago was part of the reason why she had not chosen Webster.

She needed to talk about what was going on in her life with someone, but not Webster. "I don't think so," she finally replied. "But thank you for everything."

21

On the flight home to Brownsville, a few days later, Adel tried to sleep, but she tossed and turned instead. She kept thinking about faith and God. Faith is the trusting in good over evil, Webster had said. She believed that. Floating in an airplane high up in the sky, admiring the beautiful shades of blue, mauve, and gray outside her window, Adel had to have faith. She had to have faith to be way up there among large fluffy clouds that scattered and bounced like unused cotton balls. Everyone on the airplane had to have some kind of faith.

As she listened to the rush of the engines twisting around the hiss of air vents, Adel found herself analyzing a familiar argument between her mother and father. Robinson, as everybody called her father, and Alice, the middle name that her mother went by, would sit in front of the television after dinner to debate current events.

One of her father's favorite arguments was how slave masters had used religion to trick Africans into accepting slavery as well as their inferiority. He didn't listen when her mother would explain that slaves turned that limitation around and used religion for communication and spiritual unity. He would simply growl his disbelief and suggest that slaves worried too much about being eligible for the good life in heaven and not enough about changing their terrible life on earth.

Her mother would wrinkle her nose in frustration and mumble that he was talking stupid. "How could black people have ever gotten out of slavery if that were true?" she would ask.

Adel could see her father's lips curling downward as he continued to complain about the white images of Jesus that still hung on black church walls and how religion in the twentieth century was primarily about money. Her mother, not ready to move on, would counter with the idea that Africans *never* accepted their situation, but used religion to find ways to escape and force change.

Neither would give in to the other's argument. Both would walk away convinced that their point of view was right and someday their significant other would have to wake up and see the light.

The plane veered left and Adel felt the wing shift upward. When the nose dropped slightly, it caused her stomach to tighten and roll. She held on to the barf bag, then yawned, trying to force her ears to pop and release the pressure. What was this obsession with God that seemed to be hovering over her lately? Religion had taken on so many forms, traditions, movements, sects, and cults that she had no idea how to figure it all out or why she felt she needed to try.

She leaned her head back on the seat. How can human beings these days be sure of anything? There was a group on television last week arguing that society is moving toward science at the expense of what the Bible teaches. They said that even though it is possible to do heart transplants, create drugs, and clone things, maybe we shouldn't. On a number of levels Adel had to agree with their logic. Just because we can do it, doesn't make it right. But on the other hand, what was society supposed to do, remain in the Dark Ages? Should we have stayed in caves and continued using sticks and stones for protection?

Adel felt the floor vibrate as the plane rocked up and down over strong gushes of wind. Fear grabbed hold of her for just a few seconds. She jumped up as the plane plowed through the heated air, walked down the narrow aisle, and slipped into an empty seat next to a nun in full habit that she had noticed earlier.

The nun didn't look up from her computer right away.

"I'm sorry to disturb you, Sister, but can we talk for a minute?" Adel asked in a whisper.

The nun looked up and smiled slightly. She closed out a file and turned off her laptop.

"I'm sorry to bother you. I'm not even sure if this question has an answer," Adel admitted.

The nun nodded. "Ask it and we'll see," she said softly.

"How do we know for sure if God is in control of our destiny, you know, ordering our steps and stuff, or if He's sitting back and judging the choices we make on our own?"

The nun's eyes lit up as if she understood the question exactly, then she spoke. "Well, first you must understand that this response is based on my experience and knowledge. You could ask a hundred different people and get a hundred different answers." She stopped and shifted her body sideways. "For me it depends on where you are in your faith."

Adel leaned forward as the word *faith* smacked her in the face for the third time that week. "I'm sorry, but I don't know what that means," she confessed.

"Let me try to explain. There are people who have given themselves to God and recognize His guidance in every part of their lives. And there are others who are still seeking God's love, and as a result they are limited in their interaction with Him. So when they make choices, those choices probably don't take his wisdom into consideration."

Adel's eyes brightened. "Okay. I think I get that," she said as another question formed in her mind. "So, I've been noticing lately that strange things keep happening to me. Questions about

God and religion seem to be everywhere. Does that mean He's trying to guide me in some way?"

"Do you lead a God-centered life?"

Adel lowered her head. "Probably not, it's more self-centered."

The nun patted her hand gently. "Well, it is still a possibility, because sometimes God doesn't wait for you to come to Him. Sometimes He will take the initiative and reveal Himself to you."

"Is there any way to know if that's what's happening?"

"Just listen and He will guide you."

Adel thanked the nun and returned to her seat just as the plane dipped inside a pocket of massive clouds on its way back down to earth. She stared out the window surrounded by a surreal brightness. It was that same temporary peace from a few weeks ago that slowly and deliberately moved through her soul. As a pervasive force of awareness stilled her body, Adel smiled, contemplating miracles.

There were more than one hundred people sitting inside tons of massive steel far up in the sky, yet the plane didn't fall crashing to the ground. That had to be a miracle. And when the sun's rays briefly broke through the cumulus patches and greeted her with an inviting sparkle, she held her breath, admiring what she thought could have been a wink of approval from God.

22

*

Halloween was one of Lucy's favorite days of the year. Only Valentine's Day and her birthday were more important to her. It was the one day where spiritual and physical worlds collided and the one night where everything was acceptable and anything was possible.

In early Celtic culture Halloween was created as a day to honor the dead, a time to help evil souls earn redemption. Decades later, Pope Gregory IV tried to discourage those ideas. Since *hallow* actually meant holy man or saint, he renamed the day All Saints' Eve. But by then it was too late and the spirits were not about to relinquish control of the one day that they had laid claim on.

Lucy called in sick to stay with Spencer for a few days until his mother recovered. She chauffeured him to and from the hospital, sat by his mother's bed with him, and made sure he ate and got some rest. But she had gotten very little rest herself. Kuba's aura was searching for her. She could sense it whenever she closed her eyes. She wanted to be with him too and the guilt was tearing her apart. Spencer slept every night with his arms wrapped tightly around her body as if he knew how badly she wanted to get away.

Lucy purposely did not contact Kuba to let him know what was going on. Even though she wanted to see him again, Spencer needed her now. So she stayed, feeling like a candle that couldn't burn fast enough. When she couldn't stand it any longer she snuck away to call and agreed to meet Kuba on Halloween at a séance that he was hosting.

She talked Adel into going with her for moral support. The plan was to return to the hospital as soon as the séance was over, but she knew she had very little willpower where Kuba was concerned, so Adel would have to keep her focused.

Rubbing her nose to ease the strong smell of ammonia mixed with cut flowers and dust in the hospital room, Lucy had already pulled her hand away from Spencer's twice. She looked down and he was holding on again. Her palm had become sweaty and her fingers were cramped. She stood up, motioning toward the door. Spencer followed.

"You're not leaving, are you?" he asked with concern.

"I need to go home and take care of some things. I'll be back later," she assured him.

"Don't leave, Lucy. I need you here with me," Spencer pleaded.

"I've got to get some work done, Spencer," she explained. "I'm not leaving you. I'll be back."

She reached out to kiss him lightly on the lips, but he pulled away and paced up and down the floor. "Lucy," he said, almost as an afterthought, "can you give me an answer about the marriage?"

Lucy tried not to let her weariness show, but this was not the time for that discussion. She wished she could tell him the real reason she had postponed her answer so long. But how could she tell him that nobody she knew was happily married? Women cooked and cleaned when they preferred not to so that they could be considered good wives, men tried to accept responsibilities despite the fact that they were not ready to give up their carefree lives in the streets.

Both Thad and Lane were insensitive and selfish men. Adel ignored it, but Lucy knew she couldn't accept that kind of garbage from anybody. She used to listen carefully when the old timers in New Roads would say, "You can't keep trouble from coming, but you damn sure don't have to invite it in and let it stay awhile."

What was the point of marrying somebody so that the two of you could be miserable trying to change each other? That was what she didn't understand about the so-called "sacred bond." Most couples didn't come together prepared to accept each other's flaws, they came ready to fight for change.

"We can't get into this right now, Spencer. There are too many other more important things going on."

"I disagree," he shot back, a little more forceful than before. "Because of what's happening in my life right now, our future is very important to me."

Lucy rubbed the back of her throbbing neck. "Well, I can't think about it at this moment. I'm too burned out. I'll see you later, baby."

"What do you mean you can't think about it? I've waited for months now, Lucy, and you still haven't told me anything. Do you know how that makes me feel?" he yelled.

Lucy looked quickly up and down the hall and made a gesture suggesting that he lower his voice. "I just don't know yet, Spencer. I'm not ready to accept the marriage routine. I don't want to hurt you, but I can't tell you I'll marry you right now."

Spencer stopped pacing. He looked curiously into her eyes. "Do you love me, Lucy?" he asked.

Lucy hesitated, watching the color drain from his face with each passing moment. "Yes, I love you, Spencer, but there are other issues to be considered here."

"Issues like what? If you love me and I love you what other issues are there?"

"You need to focus on your mother now, she needs you," Lucy answered in a sharp tone.

"If you don't want to marry me, why don't you just say so! At least I'll know and I can move on!"

"I don't know what I want, Spencer, and I can't tell you what you want to hear."

"What if we didn't have any more time, Lucy? What if the world were going to end tomorrow and this is the only chance we get? Would you marry me—yes or no?"

"Don't force me to make this decision, Spencer. Let me work things through and give you an answer when I can see more clearly."

Spencer shook his head. "You either love me or not. You either want to marry me or you don't. Bottom line, Lucy."

Lucy refused to respond to his ultimatum. "I'll see you later, Spencer," she said, turning to walk away.

"Lucy," he called softly behind her.

Lucy turned back around. For a moment when she looked into his distressed face she wanted to run into his arms and tell him things would be back to normal soon, but that would be a lie.

Spencer lifted his head to look straight into her eyes before he spoke. "If you come back, Lucy, come back with an answer."

23

✳

Lucy stopped at the convenience store on the corner, then spent the evening handing out candy to neighborhood children dressed as witches, goblins, superheroes, cartoon characters, ghosts, and everything in between. They skipped and hopped and jumped and ran from house to house with parents close behind. They would stand in her doorway and receive their treats after they had offered assorted tricks.

As promised, Adel picked Lucy up at eleven o'clock and they drove to Kuba's house. Despite the darkness, when they pulled up to the small house in Missouri City they couldn't help but admire the beauty of the four-seasoned porch. Next to it, thick ivy leaves covered every square inch of a wooden gazebo, with lightly colored blossoms scattered here and there. The only furniture on the porch was a long wooden swing that hung from the ceiling by shiny brass chains. Lucy knocked on the door, but it was already ajar so they entered.

In the hallway the first thing Adel noticed was a large Star of David that had been etched into the floor. She knew that symbol because Lucy had once talked about how Madea used it to help a man who believed he was possessed by demons. A series of metal circles strung like loops along the wall also stood out.

"What do those mean?" Adel whispered to Lucy and pointed.

Lucy leaned close to Adel's ear, then answered. "Many people believe life is determined by circles, the circle of the sun, for example. There is also a myth that the bad spirits cannot enter a circle, so it might be some sort of protection."

Just as Lucy turned in the direction from which they heard Carribean music being played, they were greeted by Kuba's celestial aura. He kissed Lucy's lips quickly and held out his right hand to Adel. Adel stood in awe for a moment. There was an uncomfortable shock from his handshake and she didn't like the way his dark eyes seemed to penetrate her personal thoughts. They followed Kuba into the den, where a woman was sitting alone at a large black lacquer table.

"I can't believe I let you talk me into this," Adel whispered, elbowing Lucy uneasily.

"It'll be fun," Lucy replied, secretly wishing Adel's doubts away. They sat down in two of the empty seats, nodding at the other woman. When she smiled back, Lucy thought she saw two long, pointed eyeteeth resembling vampire fangs, probably a prank for the evening.

Kuba made introductions once they were seated. "Shaela, this is Lucinda and her friend Adel. Lucinda, Adel, this is Shaela. Shaela works with me at the psychic hotline," he explained. "How about something to drink, ladies?"

"Just water, please," Lucy told him.

"Me, too," Adel added.

Kuba headed for the kitchen. "Another black cherry soda for you, Shaela?" he called over his shoulder.

She nodded. "Bring it on."

"So you're the famed Lucinda that Kuba has been raving about lately," Shaela said caustically.

"I hope so," Lucy answered, looking carefully around the room.

"What brings you out on Halloween?" Shaela asked.

"Kuba invited me." Lucy answered, suddenly noticing a thin, dark green aura encircling Shaela's head. She immediately recognized it as a ring of envy. Her instincts told her that Kuba had been with this woman in a personal way.

Shaela picked up a nut off the table. "Do you know what this chestnut is for?" she asked, allowing the fang-looking teeth to show again, but just barely.

Lucy shrugged. "No," she said.

Shaela taunted them. "If you want someone's soul to come back and visit you on Halloween you must leave a chestnut on the table."

Adel looked at Lucy and Lucy looked back, then Lucy glanced over toward the doorway, hoping Kuba would return soon.

Shaela released a sinister laugh that barely made it out of her throat. "Does that scare you?" She continued speaking directly to Lucy.

"It depends if they are good souls or evil souls," Lucy replied, as nonchalantly as she could manage.

"We won't know until they get here."

"Then, yes, it scares me," Lucy admitted.

"Good, you're smart to be scared," Shaela added, rolling her eyes up into her head. "People think that death is final, but it's not. Death only means the end of your body, unless you're a zombie, but the spiritual soul continues on forever."

Kuba entered the room with three glasses and set them on the table. "Don't start talking about zombies, Shaela. You know that's not what real voodoo is about. That's only the voodoo you see in the movies," he clarified. Then he lectured to Lucy and Adel. "We practice voodoo as a ritual to offer prayers for assistance, praise, guidance, knowledge, and gratitude to our ancestors."

"If you say so," Shaela mumbled under her breath.

The doorbell rang and Kuba left to answer it. Lucy took a sip of her water, frowned, and swallowed.

Shaela watched her closely. "Kuba always puts salt in his water as protection on Halloween."

"I wish he would have warned me," Lucy complained, pushing the glass away.

"Protection from what?" Adel finally got up the nerve to ask.

"From the demons who walk with us tonight," Shaela hissed.

Adel pushed her glass of water off to the side too and frowned. Suddenly Kuba returned with an older man. The man had a bald head and a graying beard. He was tall, about six-foot-three, with bulging biceps. Adel and Lucy's eyes both opened wide when they saw the thick, seven foot snake that dangled around his neck like a piece of jewelry.

"Ashon, this is Lucinda and Adel, and you know Shaela," Kuba said.

Ashon approached, but stopped suddenly. He stood and stared intensely past Lucy to Adel, his eyes boring into her skin. "You don't believe," he spit out.

Adel squirmed in her seat. "I don't know," she grumbled.

Ashon stroked the albino python as he spoke. "You will believe after tonight," he promised, then the python lifted its head and slowly moved as if it were coming toward her.

Adel leaped out of her chair and headed for the front door. "I don't think I can stay," she said to nobody in particular.

"Come on, Adel, don't leave now," Lucy urged. "If it were a dangerous snake he wouldn't have it hanging around his neck."

Adel surveyed the room, which was decorated like a bad horror film, and shivered. "I can't stay here, Lucy," she repeated. "Are you coming?"

Lucy spun around to Kuba and back to Adel. Part of her was also a little scared and wanted to leave, but part of her had to stay. The stronger part won out.

"I can't leave," she told Adel. "Not now."

"Fine," Adel said, hurrying down the hall and out the door.

Lucy tried to follow, to at least see Adel to the car and make sure she was okay, but her feet wouldn't budge. It was as if everything was put in pause mode until Kuba stepped behind her chair, bent over, and kissed her left cheek.

"Thank you for staying," he said. Then he sat next to Lucy in Adel's empty chair and took her hand in his.

Lucy took a deep breath in an effort to let go of the fear.

"Tonight we travel with the ancestors," Ashon proclaimed while taking his seat at the head of the table. "Let's begin."

Lucy studied each face as the group held hands. Shaela's round cocoa-brown face featured large eyes and thick eyebrows. She looked like a sister from the Islands. Ashon reminded her of the actor Ving Rhames with a beard. He controlled a powerful voice that gave him a natural sense of authority. She searched Kuba's face, finding no flaws, from the pencil-thin mustache over his top lip to the exquisitely looped earlobes that held shiny gold posts.

African drumbeats pulsated softly in the background and candles flickered around the room as Ashon started a prayer to the ancestors.

"Ancestors." Ashon spoke in a deep bass tone. "We come tonight to offer our humble hearts. Please remove all negative energy in this room and replace it with the positive light that is you. We are here to uplift your spirit. We are here to speak to you."

Lucy didn't know much about ghosts and séances. Madea didn't deal with them, at least not the way that Kuba and his friends were carrying on. She had heard many of the same stories that all children hear about ghosts from the past that haunt a specific place and ghosts from the present who warn of impending danger. She knew better than to believe in poltergeists that come to earth to take away the living, or evil spirits that suck little girls into television oblivion.

"Come ancestors: Arise, Speak, Heal. We ask tonight for Lwa Agwe to serve as our mediator." Ashon dipped his hand in Adel's glass of water and sprinkled some of it across the table. "Come, Lwa Agwe, the spirit of water, the spirit of the sea. Arise, Speak, Heal," Ashon continued.

The drumbeat stopped suddenly, and Ashon's head snapped back. He raised his body up from the chair in slow motion and the drumbeat started again. In the barely lit shadows Ashon seemed to grow much taller than when he first entered the room. Lucy held on to Kuba's hand, never taking her eyes off the large swaying snake in front of her.

"I come," Ashon spoke in a voice that was not his own.

"Who are you?" Kuba asked, taking Ashon's hand and guiding him back into his seat.

"I am the man-child, Makandal."

Shaela held tightly to Ashon's other hand, nodding as if she understood.

"Tell us what we should know," Kuba said.

Ashon's eyes under his eyelids were jetting back and forth in REM state. His chest heaved up and down as if he labored to breathe. "In the hills of Bois-Caiman that night we chose freedom and from that moment on we no more be slaves."

"You survived?"

"Through powerful spirits, poisons, talismans, and prayer we survived and continued to rebel in the souls of Boukman, Toussaint, and Jean-Jacques. We survived until Haiti was free."

"Can you guide us through our trials and tribulations?"

"The head cannot hear until the heart can listen."

"Has your heart found peace?"

Ashon nodded. "There is peace for the child."

"Who is the child?" Kuba asked.

Ashon or the spirit within him didn't answer, but his neck snapped back again and he sat very still. Lucy watched, fascinated, as the fuzzy apparition of a young boy no more than fifteen or sixteen appeared to float luminously from Ashon's body. She couldn't help but think that it was just like those images she had seen in the movies. The boy's tall and lanky body was covered with tattered clothes and his bushy head of hair caught blobs of light reflecting from the wall. She zeroed in on his face and saw that he could have been a much younger version of Ashon or Kuba. Maybe he was one of their ancestors. The ragged boy turned around, never acknowledging that he knew anyone else was in the room. He strolled away until his transparent form literally vaporized into the air.

Lucy was not sure what to think. She sat there trying to rationalize what she had just seen. The trance and the boy seemed very believable. There were many stories about such occurrences in Pointe Coupee Parish. It was not even the first time she had seen a ghost. Kenil's spirit had visited her a number of times, not long after his death, to ease her sadness.

She closed her eyes and silently prayed that God would protect her from harm, but when she tried to open them, she couldn't. As she struggled with her own will, two angels suddenly appeared. One offered a warm and secure nature, sporting calm silvery wings: the other flaunted a bright and exciting essence, flexing golden wings. Both reached for her as if wanting her to make a choice. It was obvious to Lucy that each angel represented the two men in her life. She was supposed to make a decision as to which path she would walk; which life she would lead. But she couldn't choose. She didn't want to pick one over the other, not at that moment. Her eyes opened automatically when she felt Kuba stand up and release her hand.

"Are you okay?" he asked.

She nodded, then looked at Ashon, who remained still, eyes closed, portions of the snake resting comfortably around his neck and on the table. Shaela was mumbling inaudible words as she rocked back and forth in her chair.

"He'll be out for hours," Kuba explained before she could ask.

"Is she okay?" Lucy asked, standing up beside him.

"She's fine. She talks with spirits all the time. She sees them everywhere, like the boy we saw tonight."

Lucy looked surprised. "You saw him, too?"

"Yes. And as you can see they're not harmful. They come to help us understand something or to ask for our help."

Shaela rose from the table and walked out the door, still talking to the spirits.

"Follow me," Kuba said, taking Lucy's hand.

She wanted to open her mouth and tell Kuba that she needed to go, but instead she followed him outside and into the wooden gazebo. While he lit a round, purple candle and sprinkled lavender oil, Lucy closed her eyes again. The angels were still there; waiting, reaching. When she held out her hand and touched the angel with blazing golden wings they both disappeared.

Lucy welcomed the strong, carnal feelings that suddenly claimed her.

"How can I love you, pretty lady?" Kuba asked, pressing his fingers against her breasts.

"Any way you want to, beautiful man," Lucy answered, reaching for his belt buckle.

Kuba stopped her, holding her hands up to his mouth and nuzzling them with his wet, lucious lips.

Using only the tips of his fingers, he manipulated those long nails to sensually stimulate her body without removing her clothes.

"Ummmm," Lucy moaned with an excitement that was almost unbearable. His touch penetrated the cotton cloth that covered her, creating an intense heat within her soul. Like a magician, Kuba satisfied her every need while they stood entangled in the center of the thick ivy leaves.

"This light of love is a burning fire, to spark our deepest soul's desire, each day our devoted fire burns true, and strengthens the love from me to you," they chanted together.

24

✳

Adel paced back and forth outside Kuba's house, first up and down the sidewalk, then out in the street beside the car. She was hoping that Lucy would follow her, but it didn't happen. Lucy was hooked real good like a fish on a line, and the struggle to break free only served to strengthen the hold.

Adel had sensed that something was wrong the minute she stepped into that house: the Star of David, the circles, that man's accusation, and that snake. She thought about going back inside and dragging Lucy out. Instead she opened the car door and dropped into the driver's seat. Lucy was a grown woman and if she wanted to spend the evening with a bunch of lunatics holding a séance, that was her business. Adel glanced over at the house again, then started the car and drove off.

She had originally planned to go home, but after driving around for a while she found herself not far from where Spencer lived. Adel was convinced that something was wrong with this Kuba person and if Lucy wouldn't listen to her, maybe Spencer could get through.

Once she made it to Spencer's street, she turned into the driveway and cut the car off. Adel hesitated, not getting out immediately. Maybe she shouldn't tell Spencer about Kuba. Lucy didn't look afraid. She wanted to stay there with him and she had the right to make her own decision.

She stared at the house in front of her. It was dark inside. Spencer was probably asleep. She checked her watch and groaned when she saw it was already two in the morning. Spencer's mother's illness had taken so much out of him, she probably shouldn't bother him with this. But what if Lucy was really in trouble? Adel's mind shifted back and forth for a while until she finally decided that Lucy might need help.

The car door opened almost at the same time as the front door of the house. Spencer stepped down onto the front step in his robe.

"Adel?" he called, straining to see in the darkness.

"Hey, Spencer," she yelled back and walked toward him.

Spencer motioned for her to come into the house as he spoke. "What's going on? Is something wrong?" he asked.

"Umm, I'm not sure," Adel told him nervously.

"Is this about Lucy? Is she okay?" he continued as they stood awkwardly in the foyer. "I thought it was her car outside."

"Can I have a glass of water, first please?" Adel stalled, wondering again if she was doing the right thing.

Spencer slipped into the kitchen and she followed. He filled a glass from the faucet and handed it to her.

"Now, tell me what this is about."

Adel took a sip of the water before she spoke. "Spencer, I don't know for sure, but Lucy might need help."

Spencer's body tensed up. "What kind of help? Where is she? What's wrong?"

Adel started to cry as the words tumbled out: "We went to a séance tonight at this guy Kuba's house and it was real strange. There was a woman talking about bringing back the dead and a man with a huge snake on his neck. I left, but she wouldn't leave with me."

"Do you know this guy, does she know him?"

"It sounds silly, but we met him on one of those psychic hot-lines. Lucy has been calling him for a while and I'm worried that he's filling her head with a lot of nonsense."

Spencer instructed Adel to take a seat while he went into the bedroom and threw on a pair of blue jeans and a T-shirt. Minutes later he was rushing out the door and pulling her behind him.

She directed Spencer to Kuba's house and they parked across the street. As they walked up into the yard there were no sounds inside or out. Adel prayed that Lucy was okay and that bringing Spencer wasn't a big mistake. The door was standing wide open, so Adel rushed in and Spencer trailed her. They moved slowly toward the den, where she had left Lucy, Kuba, Shaela, Ashon, and the snake. The room was empty.

They continued down the hall cautiously, checking the kitchen and an empty bedroom. Just as they reached the bathroom door Lucy stepped out, fully dressed, makeup refreshed and every hair in place. She jumped when she saw Spencer standing in front of her.

"What are you doing here?" she asked, shooting a sideways glare at Adel.

"I came to see if you were okay. Adel was worried that something was wrong."

"Everything's fine," Lucy maintained.

"I thought you had some work to do tonight," Spencer said accusingly.

Before Lucy could answer, Kuba came out of his sanctuary with only his pants on. The sweat on his bare chest glistened like diamonds on black cheesecloth.

Lucy tried to play it off. "Spencer, this is Kuba," she said, more coolly than she'd expected. "Kuba, Spencer."

Spencer nodded his acknowledgment and Kuba smiled.

"Since you're apparently okay and you felt the need to lie to me, I'll just go on back home," Spencer barked before turning to leave. Lucy cut her eyes at Adel, who stood uneasily in the hall-way.

"Spencer, wait," she said, pursuing him as he stormed out the front door.

"You don't have to say anything, Lucy," he told her when she caught up with him. "I get it, I understand now."

"But I want to say something," she replied. "I didn't want you to find out like this. I was going to tell you."

"When?" he huffed.

"Your mother got sick, Spencer, and I didn't want to add to the pressure. I know I should have said something, but I care about you and I was trying to do the right thing."

"You care about me." Spencer laughed loudly. "What happened to a few days ago when you loved me?"

"I do love you, Spencer. I realized that in the hospital when you held me in your arms."

"It must be a strange kind of love, since you're over here doing who knows what with somebody else tonight."

"Spencer, please."

"Do you love this guy, Lucy?"

"It's a different kind of love than the one we have. I know that's not what you want to hear, but it's the truth. You and Kuba are two different people and you bring two different kinds of love into my life."

"Well, you can't continue to see us both. Your life is going to have to make do with one love or the other."

"We've already been through this, I can't decide now. It's just not possible."

"That's not really true, is it, Lucy? Because not deciding is actually the same as making a choice, as far as I'm concerned. I'm outta here."

Lucy tried to think of something else to say, but she was out of words. "I'll call you in a couple of days, once you've had time to cool off."

Spencer snatched the car door open before he replied. "You're right, Lucy, we have been through this before. And as I told you earlier, don't call unless you're ready to make a choice and that choice is me." He hopped into the car, started the engine, and almost drove off until he remembered Adel.

Lucy stomped back into the house, practically knocking Adel over. "What the hell is wrong with you? Why would you bring him here?" she screamed.

"I thought you were in trouble. I was worried," Adel cried.

"Well, thank you very much for all your help," Lucy said bitterly.

"Look don't blame it on me because you're playing two men and got caught. I'm sorry I tried to help your ass, but you don't have to worry about me ever doing it again," Adel snapped back and ran out the door.

"Great!" Lucy hissed, taking a deep breath.

Kuba stood in the shadows of the hallway waiting patiently for his turn. When Lucy felt his protective aura reach out she went to him immediately and marveled at how quickly he calmed her spirit. Her heart fell rhythmically in sync with his.

"It's okay, pretty lady, you have me and everything is going to be fine," he sang sweetly in her ear.

"You promise?" she asked.

"I promise," he answered.

25

*

Adel parked in a visitor's spot since a large tractor-trailer truck was blocking her usual space behind the American Oil building. She got out of the car and walked around to the back of the truck to see what was going on. What she saw took her breath away. The truck was full of exercise equipment. Two men hustled out of the building's back door with an empty dolly and walked up into the truck bed. One guy leaned the dolly against the wall, then both men grabbed opposite ends of an exercise bike and carried it down the ramp and inside.

Adel entered the building in a daze, rushing toward Hunter's office. A frown began taking over her face as she realized she was probably too late. She should have approached him last week about the day care idea right after she and Liz finalized the proposal. She nodded at Hunter's secretary, but didn't stop, rounding the corner to his office door. She reached to open it, then stopped when she heard him yelling. She leaned her ear closer to the door and listened to the conversation inside.

"Look, I don't really care how you do it, but you need to fix this!" Hunter shouted.

It was quiet for a while until he spoke again. "I'm not going down by myself on this one. Everybody had a part in this thing and everybody is going to share in the heat."

Since Adel could only hear Hunter's voice she assumed he was on the phone. There was another long silence.

"Maybe if we just stay cool and let the trade commission poke around like they want to, it will blow over. They won't find anything because there is nothing to find, right?"

Adel heard the sound of Hunter blowing his nose, followed by a couple of soft coughs. "Fine, fine. Call me back if you hear anything else."

She waited for a minute or two, not wanting Hunter to suspect that she had overheard the discussion, then she knocked.

"Come in," he said.

Adel entered the office and sat down abruptly.

"Adel, how's the layoff report coming?" Hunter asked distractedly.

Adel nodded her head. "Fine, but I need to discuss something else with you."

He got up, walked around to his second guest chair, and sat beside her. "Okay, go ahead," he urged.

"Well. . . . " She hesitated. "I saw the truck outside unloading exercise equipment. I was working on another project for those rooms on the fifth floor."

Hunter scowled. "What project?"

"A proposal to turn those rooms into a day care center for the parents in our company who are struggling with child care."

Hunter looked baffled. "What? A day care? We've already bought the equipment and the contractors started putting in the whirlpool and sauna first thing this morning."

"I'm sorry, Hunter, but I think a day care center is much more important than an executive spa. You can't keep stepping on the little people if you want this company to grow and prosper."

Hunter's body language made it obvious that this was not a

topic he was interested in tackling now or in the future. He crossed his arms and stuck out his chest. "I don't agree. This spa will help our employees to become healthier. It will bring more allegiance to the management team. Perks, that's what it's all about, Adel. Of course, we'll open the facility up during certain times of the week and weekend for all employees to enjoy. So everybody wins!"

Adel was not ready to let go. "Is there any other place that we could put a day care center?" she asked desperately.

Hunter shrugged. "To be honest, Adel, I don't see where that's our responsibility. We pay our employees a good wage so that they can afford quality day care and we even give them six weeks' paid leave in case of a family emergency to care for a child or elder. We do plenty in that area already."

Adel rolled her eyes. She couldn't believe he had the nerve to throw that six-week leave in her face. If she hadn't fought him and the other vice presidential cronies for that benefit it would never have happened. As it was, there were so many burning hoops to jump through that employees didn't even bother to apply for the compensation half the time. They'd rather take an unpaid leave and be free of corporate hassle.

"Hunter, I believe in this proposal and I need for you to seriously consider it. If we're going to move American Oil into the future concerning equal employee environment, especially where women are concerned, this is the direction we need to move in."

Hunter shrugged and crossed his legs. "I'm sorry, but that space is already designated, Adel. You can leave me a copy of the proposal, but I don't know what I can do," he added, then stood up to signal an end to the discussion.

Adel took the cue and stood as well.

"You know, Adel, that is the one concern I have about you as a future CEO. It's okay to have a heart, but yours is much too big. You could run a business into the ground just by giving it all away."

Adel let out an ironic chuckle. "You know what? Forget it, Hunter, just forget it," she snarled and started for the door.

"Hey, wait a minute," Hunter said.

Adel stopped, her heart sinking as she waited to hear what other stupid thing he had to say.

"There's another matter that we should discuss since you're here," he told her, then motioned vigorously for her to sit back down.

Adel did so reluctantly.

"We've gotten two subpoenas from the Federal Trade Commission, asking a bunch of questions about the increased gas prices this past summer."

Adel couldn't hide her surprise. "Is it a full-fledged investigation?" she asked.

"Looks like it. Here are the forms they sent. They need to be filled out. I'd appreciate it if you would handle the task personally."

Adel stood back up. "Why me?" she asked.

Hunter softened the tone of his voice. "Because I know how thorough and fair you are and I wouldn't trust anyone else on my staff to handle something as sensitive as this."

He handed her the papers from his desk and she snatched them out of his hand.

"They're asking for the usual information about our transportation services, marketing, pricing, and supply," Hunter added. "If I can help you, let me know. I'll tell the other VPs to cooperate as well."

"So what do they think is going on?"

"I don't know. They just want to make sure that when prices skyrocketed last summer, especially in the Midwest, it wasn't because all the oil companies had gotten together and jacked them up on purpose."

Adel cocked her head to the side. "Did they?"

Hunter's head jerked around as if he were surprised by the question. "What? I know you must be kidding," he choked out.

Adel looked at him scornfully and shook her head. "Who else got copies of these?" she asked.

Hunter sauntered to the other side of his desk before responding. "I think all of the other oil companies got them, along with some pipelines, blend plants, and terminals. The director of the Petroleum Council is trying to get to the bottom of it for us."

Adel quickly skimmed through a couple of pages to pretend she was interested.

Hunter sat down. "It's so ridiculous for them to think that we don't have anything else to do but sit around and create diabolical plans to dupe the public out of a few more pennies at the gas pump," he complained.

"If I remember right it was a lot more than a few pennies, Hunter. People in Chicago were paying two dollars and fifty cents a gallon at one point," she corrected him.

"Just fill out the forms and get them back to my office by the end of the week."

"And what about the day care idea?" Adel asked, giving it one last try.

Hunter put on his glasses and peeped over the top at her. "Adel, I know you want to help folks. That's fine and good, but right now this company is swimming in shit and I need to focus on trying to get us out of the toilet."

26

✳

Adel woke up wondering how she could have been so blind for so long. In two months she had added nine pounds to her already healthy frame, she was barfing up most of what she ate, and she felt emotionally drained most of the time with mood swings that spiked and dipped like a shaky stock market. The first step was to call in sick, then she made an appointment with her gynecologist, and finally a leisurely walk down to the drugstore on the corner to get a home pregnancy test.

Strolling in the brisk morning air, Adel laughed out loud when she shivered in the fifty-degree weather. It proved that she was now fully acclimated to Texas. Back in Missouri, fifty degrees in November would have been a warm blessing. In Houston it was considered a frigid curse.

Adel was instantly excited about the possibility that she was expecting. If the tests were positive she would fight harder for that day care for her own sake as well as Susan's. She entered the store and found the correct aisle right away, then studied the diverse brands. Not sure which was better, she recognized the package with plus and minus signs from TV commercials and grabbed the box. In line at the checkout counter, she watched an elderly man pay for a carton of cigarettes and a half-gallon of milk. Behind her was a young girl whose arms were filled with baby products.

"Are you excited?" the young girl, who didn't look more than twelve years old, asked. She stepped up closer behind Adel and gestured toward the pregnancy test.

"A little," Adel answered. "A little nervous, too."

"You shouldn't be nervous. They're real easy to use," the girl continued. "Just pee on the stick. The hardest part is getting the stick in the right spot so you can soak it through."

Adel's brow wrinkled. "How do you know so much about it?" she asked.

"I've got a baby, six months old, at home. And before that I had a couple of misses."

Adel tried to get the look of surprise off her face. "How old are you?" she had to ask.

"Fifteen," the girl answered shyly.

"You're just a baby yourself. Did you want to have a baby?"

"Yeah, Brian and me decided to make a baby together a couple of years ago. We knew he'd be beautiful and he is. Look." The girl pulled out a small photo book and flashed several pictures at Adel. "It took almost a year before it finally happened. If I didn't want to get pregnant it would have happened the first time like with my cousin Tayna."

"He's precious," Adel whispered.

"Do you want to have a baby?" the girl asked.

Adel nodded and smiled. "It took me a while, but I think I'm ready now."

Cocking her head to the side, the girl spoke again. "So, why did it take so long? Was something wrong?"

Adel had to laugh when she realized she was having this conversation with a fifteen-year-old stranger. She couldn't imagine wanting a baby at fifteen, let alone having one. One of her major goals was *not* to get caught in that trap when she was a teenager, but so many young girls today were jumping into the hole willingly. She and most of her friends planned to have careers first, then husbands and babies last.

"What did your mother say about you and Brian trying to make a baby? Where was she?" Adel asked bluntly.

The girl shrugged. "She didn't have nothing to say about it. She was too busy getting busy herself to worry about me."

Adel looked past the young girl. She wasn't living in the inner city in poverty. This was an affluent neighborhood, so her family could probably afford to send her to college. But what would make a child of fifteen *want* to have a baby instead of getting out and living life first? Adel sighed, recognizing that those were her values and dreams and she couldn't force them on anyone else. For this little girl a baby probably meant unconditional love, her womanhood trophy, a badge of honor, or maybe even a life worth living.

The cashier grabbed Adel's box and slid it over the scanner. "That's fourteen forty-nine, please," she informed her.

Adel pulled a twenty-dollar bill out of her pocket, handed it over, then slipped the change back into the same pocket.

"You take care of yourself and your baby," Adel said to the girl as she headed to the front of the drugstore.

"I will," the girl replied, hoisting a jumbo pack of Pampers and several cans of formula onto the counter. "Hey!" she called before Adel had gotten through the sliding doors.

Adel twisted back around.

"Good luck."

Grinning all the way home, Adel thought about how she would make that small room next to the master bedroom into the baby's room. She looked around at the brilliant sunlit colors of the sky. Every year she was amazed that the trees still had their leaves and the grass was still beautifully green in November.

A boy would be great. Maybe Thad would be so proud and

happy with a son that he would stop running the streets for his sake. But a girl could also have a positive effect, because many men got a kick out of spoiling daddy's girl.

The young girl's wisdom proved true fifteen minutes later as Adel was trying to figure out how to sit on the toilet stool and hold the stick under her in just the right spot. She tried to squat without touching the rim, then she had to hold herself steady with her left hand while reaching between her legs with her right hand to position the stick correctly. At one point when she lost her balance and tilted over too far, everything shifted and pee streamed down the side of the toilet bowl and onto the floor.

The wait for the results went by quickly because Adel spent the time cleaning up the mess she'd made. She washed the rim of the toilet, the surrounding floor tiles, and finally her hands. As she worked, she thought about names for the baby. It had to be something that sounded good. A name that was regal like Martin Luther King, James Weldon Johnson, or Maya Angelou. Possibly a name with an African flare like Aleela, Kamali, or Onani. When she traveled to Nigeria several years ago for American Oil, she was told that African children had two names, one that reflected the experience of the moment of birth and the other representing the family's expectations or hopes for the child's future. A young African girl who followed her around named Adamma came to mind. Adamma meant "beautiful one" in Nigerian. It was a name she liked a lot.

When the time was up Adel hurried back into the bathroom. Her heart skipped when she saw the blue plus sign on the plastic stick. Looking down at her stomach, she released treasured tears and thanked God for His miracle.

Now that she had good news, Adel spent a couple of hours idly sitting in the room that would become the nursery. It would be easy to move the luggage, boxes, extra comforters, and pillows. The bed and dresser would go against the right wall and a wooden rocking horse like she loved as a child would wait patiently on the left of the room until the baby was old enough to ride. She smelled the tuna mushroom casserole that baked in the oven. It was Thad's favorite. She wanted the aroma to fill the house and welcome him home.

When his car pulled into the driveway late that night, Adel had already put the casserole in the refrigerator and gone to bed. She heard the front door open and close, followed by the sounds of someone stumbling through the hallway.

"Del," Thad called in a slurred voice.

Adel immediately got up and went to him.

"Del," he called louder.

"Thad, what's wrong with you?" she asked as she emerged from the bedroom and almost collided into him. She could smell the stench of liquor on his hot breath.

"Are you drunk?" she asked, very surprised. She had never seen him drunk before.

He slumped against the wall. "Yep," he replied. "I think I am."

When he clutched his stomach as if he was going to throw up, Adel quickly guided him into the bathroom. He dropped down on his hands and knees and vomited, missing the opening the first time. Adel pushed his head over the rim and held it there for the second and third bouts.

"I feel like I'm going to die," he groaned.

Adel was confused. "Why would you drink like this?" she asked.

Thad coughed through his explanation. "Max and I had a contest at his house."

Adel's brow wrinkled. "A contest?"

"This was a day from hell for me. I know you can't understand since your life is so perfect, but I just wanted to unwind."

"And drinking until you're sick and puking was the method of choice?"

Thad took a deep breath. "I felt fine until now."

Adel sighed wearily. "So just tell me what happened today."

Thad cleared his throat. "They turned down my loan for the car." He flopped down on the floor with his back up against the bathtub waiting for the room to stop spinning. "My investors are getting cold feet, and the guy I paid to do my web page totally screwed it up. Is that enough or do you want to hear more?"

"Let me get you some water," Adel said, reaching for a paper cup and running the cold water in the sink.

Thad frowned. "I don't want any water. I can't swallow anything right now."

"Here," Adel said, tipping his head back and pouring the water into his mouth. "Drink it anyway, it will help you feel better."

Thad choked down several swallows and moaned. Then he leaned over the stool and vomited again.

"Del, I think I need to go to the hospital. I could be dying," Thad complained as he lay on the floor rolled up into a ball.

"You're not dying," Adel told him. "You've probably already thrown most of it up. I don't know why you would let your brother goad you into such a childish game."

"I beat him. I took twelve shots to his eleven."

Adel held a washcloth under the cold water, wrung it out, and wiped at Thad's forehead and mouth. "Whoopie. You were the sucker who won." She exhaled loudly.

"Max never has been able to beat me at anything," he bragged.

"I know, baby," Adel murmured, cleaning up the mess.

When Thad doubled over again, Adel sat on the edge of the tub next to him. She waited until the worst was over, then helped him out of his clothes and into the shower. After she had wrapped the white fluffy towel around his body and led him into bed, a frightening thought pierced her mind. She wondered how in the world she would take care of two kids.

27

*

Lucy picked up the phone to call her best friend, then slammed it back down. How the hell could Adel do something like that to her? Adel knew damn well that bringing Spencer to Kuba's house would be a disaster.

She paced around the house, angry and hurt. She wanted to tell Adel what was going on with Kuba. How the man could set her soul on fire with a simple touch. She needed to talk about the situation with Spencer, since she hadn't been able to smooth things over. And she'd like to catch her up on what was happening in the Austin center, maybe get some advice on what to do about Birch. Lucy didn't have anyone else to talk to, at least no one that she wanted to talk to. She thought about Madea's words, "To be without a friend is a serious form of poverty." Adel had always been her sounding board, her confidante, her friend. Lucy picked up the receiver again and stared for a moment at the numbers on the keypad, then hung it up.

The pages from the folder on soy products lay scattered across the table in front of her. She slid the papers together and picked the pile up. Not that she was particularly interested in soy at the moment, but she needed something to do to get her mind off how she had lost control of her life. The thing with Kuba was moving too fast, she wasn't ready to let Spencer go yet, and her best friend might not be her best friend anymore.

On the way to the living room she ambled over to smell the pot of marigolds that had replaced last week's daisies. Last week when she was happy the daisies reflected the smile of God, but the marigolds were more suited to this week's sadness. The golden hue was supposed to help soothe her sweet sorrows of love.

In her living room, soy folder in hand, Lucy turned on the TV for a moment, avoiding the task in front of her. She caught bits and pieces of a TV biography on Shirley MacLaine that had already started. She admired Shirley because she was not afraid to talk about her spiritual beliefs, even to naysayers like the journalist who was interviewing her at that moment. While she described a reccurring dream where a gorilla was chasing her, a dream that was obviously causing her a lot of pain, the interviewer sat up straight in his chair with a stupid smirk on his face.

Lucy knew exactly the kind of dream it was because she had had a similar one for years. The only difference was that she never knew who was chasing her. She couldn't remember details, but at least two days a week Lucy woke up bone-tired from running all night in her dreams.

When a commercial came on, she opened the soy folder on her lap and liked what she saw immediately. The first page was a flyer that explained the health benefits of soy, including protection against heart attacks and strokes. Lately she had tried taking an aspirin or two every other day to help the blood flow, but maybe soy could also help. Another page explained how soy could assist in the alleviation of side effects from menopause. The fact that certain cancer risks might be reduced was what actually sold her on soy products. Since Lucy turned thirty-five, every ache or pain was attributed to a growing cancer somewhere in her body that would eventually kill her.

The fight with Adel weighed heavy on her mind again. It couldn't be a permanent riff. Things could never get that bad between them. It had only been a couple of weeks, but usually one of them would have apologized by now. Lucy knew she should be the one to initiate contact; after all, Adel was only trying to help. She thought she was protecting her and that's what being a friend is all about. But damn, how could she have brought Spencer of all people to Kuba's house? Somewhere the bells and whistles had to go off.

Her attention shifted back to the television when Shirley's biography confirmed that she believed in life after death. Lucy and Madea had talked a lot about the spirit and the soul and about what might become of them once the physical body was gone. Lucy was convinced that they both lived on in some way.

She had once read some literature from an early religious group called the Rosicrucians that confirmed her idea. The group's symbol was a rose crucified in the center of a cross. They were powerful teachers of magic and mysticism in the seventeenth and eighteenth centuries. Based on the Rosicrucian belief about purgatory, Lucy had decided to rethink her definitions of Heaven and Hell. They believed that Earth was actually Hell and the goal for every soul was to eventually get back into Heaven. The more sins a person had, the longer it would take them to work off those sins in purgatory. The process was described as the soul getting lighter and lighter every time a sin was released and as that soul got lighter it would float up higher and higher until it ultimately reached the pearly gates.

Lucy jotted down a note on the front of the folder to order several of the soy products that were advertised—oil, chips, cheese, and maybe some milk for the health bar—as soon as she got to work on Monday morning. She would also check out the yogurt and something called natto, a fermented and cooked whole soybean that was supposed to be easier to digest.

She leaned closer to the television, listening along with the reporter about Shirley's trek over a 484-mile trail that began in

France and ended in Spain. It was an energy-building quest, Shirley explained, that had helped her to clarify her purpose in life. The reporter's eyes rolled up in his head when she went on to say that she had walked the same trail as a Moorish girl in a past life twelve hundred years before.

Lucy wanted to reach into the screen and smack that negativity out of him. She hated it when people put down other folks' beliefs. He didn't have to believe it himself, but he was a journalist. His job was to present the information and let his viewers decide for themselves what might be true and what might not.

Her mind jumped again. The only other time things had been this tense between her and Adel was when Adel's ex-husband, Lane, decided he would return after Adel first put him out. Lucy couldn't believe she allowed his trifling, lying behind back into her house.

She tried to stay out of it. Lucy listened and consoled only, but then her best friend showed up late one night crying because Lane had come in drunk and took what he wanted, justifying his actions by saying she was still his wife. Lucy never told Adel, but she put a spell on Lane that night. It was the only time she tried to use hoodoo on her own.

The first step was to purchase a beef tongue and split the center of it. After writing Lane's name on a piece of paper nine times, she slid the paper into the slit in the tongue. Various spices were sprinkled over it as she repeated the curse to push Lane away from Adel. Adding balmony root, cruel man of the woods, yohimbee, and pepperwort, she closed the opening with nine straight pins, roasted the tongue, and chopped it up. Finally she invited Adel and Lane to dinner, mixing the beef tongue thoroughly into Lane's plate of lasagna.

Lucy wasn't sure what she did wrong, but the next day Lane got really sick. He was spitting up blood, so the doctor ordered him to stay in bed. Poor Adel was stuck waiting on his majesty like a slave for three weeks. Lucy was about to call Madea and confess, until Lane got up one day, said he was feeling better, packed his bags, and left.

Shirley MacLaine concluded in her interview that "seeking truth" was her goal in life. She totally ignored the man's ignorance and Lucy drew her hands together to applaud.

Lucy made another note to look into Qigong, a Chinese meditative practice that Shirley said cultivates the life force. Apparently she practiced it every day and she definitely looked good for her age. Lucy figured she could promote Qigong classes at the spa as the stuff that gives Shirley MacLaine her stride and clients would flock to them.

The reporter asked one final question as the program was about to end. He wanted to know if Shirley had been able to determine the message of her gorilla dream. She smiled before she responded. Lucy had to laugh because it was such a wicked smile. Then Shirley told the reporter that the purpose of the dream was to force her to face her fears. That made perfect sense to Lucy because she needed to do the same thing.

Adel woke up sick, she knew it was the baby rebelling against her pepperoni pizza dinner. She picked up the phone to dial Lucy, but changed her mind when she remembered their last encounter at Kuba's house.

She still didn't believe Lucy could turn on her like that over some man. They had always been together, always taken care of each other. She only did what she thought was right. She didn't know who Kuba was, with his snake-toting and vampire-looking friends. If Lucy couldn't understand that she acted out of love and friendship, then this Kuba person was more dangerous than she thought.

Adel glanced at the clock. She was going to be late for her doctor's appointment. She grabbed a pair of jeans, but couldn't button them and there was no time to iron anything else. Sorting through a laundry basket of clean clothes that she had not had time to put away yet, she pulled out an oversized sweatshirt to cover it and decided she would buy a few pairs of more comfortable pants with elastic waistlines after her appointment.

Outside her doctor's office Adel put the car in park and jetted into the building. She gave her name to the receptionist and sat down to fill out the forms she was handed. They wanted an update of basic information: name, current address, insurance carrier. Some of it she didn't know, like when she had had chicken pox. She started to leave it blank, then changed her mind and pulled out her cell phone.

"Hey, Mom," she said when she heard her mother's voice on the other end of the line.

"Hi, baby. How are you?" her mother asked.

"I'm good. What about you and Daddy?"

"We're doing okay. Except he's been talking about getting some of that Viagra mess. I told him he'd better find somebody else to bother because I'm not interested."

"Mom!" Adel said, exasperated. "That's way too much information."

"Well, you're grown now. You and Thad are still enjoying those early years when the gettin' is good. But I'ma tell you, in this period of life the best part is when you and your husband have moved beyond those sexual games that men and women play. You can actually be friends and spend time together without all that other mess."

There was a click on the line. "Hello, hello, who is this woman on the phone telling all of our business to?"

"Hi Daddy," Adel said with a grin.

"Hey, baby. Don't listen to that garbage your mama is talking. She knows she would love it if my engine were purring a little bit louder. Ain't that right, sugar?"

"You need to get on away from here with that crap," her mother teased.

Adel could hear them wrestling in the background.

"Hello," Adel said with a chuckle. "This call is in the middle of the day, folks."

It was quiet for a couple of seconds. Then her father laughed long and loud. "I'm going to let you two finish talking about nothing," he joked.

"Thanks, Daddy, love you."

Once they heard the click of the other line the more serious conversation started. "Why *are* you calling in the middle of the day?" her mother asked. "Is everything okay?"

"Yeah, I'm fine. I'm in the doctor's office. I think I'm pregnant."

"Oh baby, how wonderful. Here I am going on about your old horny daddy and you have great news like that to tell us."

"Don't worry about it, Mom."

"So, you probably have morning sickness bad. Are your clothes getting too little yet? And there should be a brown spot more like an oval than a circle on the right side of your neck."

Adel pulled out a compact and peered into the mirror at the side of her neck, but couldn't see anything.

"I took one of those home pregnancy tests and it was positive, so I'm here to have it confirmed."

"Should I get a ticket and come down? Do you need anything?"

"No, Mom, maybe a little later when the time is closer. I'll let you know."

"I'm due for some time away from your father and this would be a great excuse."

Adel laughed. "No, it's okay, Mom. I'm in the waiting room and they're going to call my name any minute. I need to know when I had the chicken pox."

"Sweetie, you were six. Remember your cousin Renatta got them from some friend at school first and you had stayed all night with her, so you broke out, too."

"Adel Kelly," the nurse called from inside the swinging door.

"Thanks, Mom. I've got to go, they just called my name."

"Call back tonight and let me know what happens," her mother added.

"I will, love you," Adel said before closing the phone and dropping it into her purse. She followed the nurse into the back waiting room and prepared for the doctor to come in. While waiting, she stepped behind the door and took a quick look in the mirror. Now she saw it: a small, brown oval spot on the right side of her neck.

28

*

Adel opened her eyes and looked at the empty left side of the bed. The clock read 7:30 and Thad was already gone. When her pregnancy was confirmed yesterday morning she had hoped to finally tell him the good news. She closed her eyes and tried to go back to sleep, shifting and twisting her body every few minutes to get more comfortable. Sleeping on her stomach was her favorite position, but now that there was a baby in there it was the most uncomfortable one.

She lay staring at the streaks of sunlight that hit the burgundy comforter, then faded away. Thad's Bible sat on the bed because she'd been reading it before she fell asleep earlier. She turned on the light and picked it up, and her eyes fixed on the same verse where she left off.

"Be still and know that I am God." She read it out loud several times. It was in the Forty-Sixth Psalm, which she was familiar with, but had never paid much attention to. She slid down to her knees on the side of the bed, bowed her head, cupped her hands and concentrated on each word one by one. "Be—still—and—know—that—I—am—God."

Adel struggled in the silence listening for the answers to her questions. Who was He? What did He want from her? How could she get her life back in order? Where was happiness? Where was peace? What could be done about the greed and corruption in the world? She was still not sure why this sudden religious focus, but if God wanted her to listen He needed to speak loud and clear. She waited almost twenty minutes for God's answers. Nothing came, so she crawled back up into the bed and wrestled herself back to sleep.

When she woke again Thad was snoring softly beside her. She got up and brushed her teeth, then sat at the kitchen table skimming through the mail from the day before. A promotion for a local Seventh Day Adventist church caught her attention. It offered three possibilities for looking at life. You could focus on how things appeared to be, on how things actually were, or on making things the way you wanted them to be. When she thought about it, Adel had to admit that things right now appeared to be pretty bad. The company day care idea would probably never get off the ground. Her pregnancy had been confirmed, yet she had not told Thad because she was afraid of his reaction. And she and Lucy had not spoken to each other since that Halloween mess.

Maybe she should focus on making things the way she wanted them to be. While munching on a piece of dry toast and hoping to keep it down, she decided to concentrate on other ways to make the day care idea work. Then it suddenly dawned on her that Thad never said he didn't want a baby, as a matter of fact he'd said the opposite. She smiled. Lucy was her girl. They had been through much worse together. This too in time would pass.

Adel closed her eyes and bowed her head, thanking God for sending her the answers she needed. She had been focusing on the wrong things. She was worried about stuff that couldn't make a difference because it was in the past. What she had to do now was focus on the stuff that she could do something about.

Adel stretched, then opened her morning Pepsi and took a big swallow. She thought about the baby and how much her life was about to change.

It had been wonderful to have her mother at home all the time when she was growing up. Whatever she needed, her mother supplied. If she cut her hand or bruised her knee it was her mother who kissed it and put the Band-Aid on. She frowned, thinking about how she wouldn't be able to do that.

Adel had read articles and skimmed books from the experts about raising a child and she was totally confused. While one article assured mothers that it didn't matter if children were with a parent or a day care provider as long as they were loved, another warned that children in day care tended to have more difficulties in decision-making than those who stayed at home with a parent. One book suggested that you should never force kids to eat anything they don't want, including vegetables, but another one said a well-balanced meal is crucial for a child's health and well being.

Adel read through the morning newspaper, stopping at a large headline: RACIAL PROFILING DEEMED OKAY. She shook her head in disgust. What about bringing a baby into this world, a black baby, maybe a baby boy who would be fair game for the hypocrisy and ignorance that seemed to be spreading rampantly? She read with disbelief that the Supreme Court had ruled it was okay for the police to stop a black person while driving if they suspected them for drug possession simply based on their race. Yet somehow this same Supreme Court ruled that it was not okay to help a black child get an education through affirmative action because it was based on their race. Adel shook her head again and tossed that section of the paper in the trash.

When the doorbell rang, she was annoyed. She wasn't expecting company and didn't really want to be bothered. She planned to lounge around the house in her pajamas all day. She wanted to strategize about how she could save her day care project, figure out the best way to tell Thad about the baby, and set up a make-up party with Lucy. She threw on her robe and went to the front door.

"Yes?" she said irritably to the thin middle-aged white woman and chubby young black man standing outside.

"Hi. We're with the Jehovah's Witnesses and we're canvassing your neighborhood today to tell residents about God's promise."

"I'm sorry, but I'm too busy right now," Adel said rudely while attempting to shut the door.

"Excuse me, but we have a very simple message, then we won't bother you anymore," the woman pleaded.

Adel frowned, but softened up a little when she noticed that the woman's soft eyes reminded her of a good friend of her mother's. "What is it?" she asked.

The woman pulled out a clipboard with a piece of paper on it. On the paper was the image of a butterfly covered in various shades of gray.

"If you would please simply lay your hand on top of this butterfly," the woman instructed.

Adel looked skeptically at the two people, but she did it and instantly, bright, beautiful colors spread through the butterfly's wings. "That's a neat trick," Adel told them, unimpressed. "So what do you want?"

"It's not really a trick," the young man jumped in to explain. "The image responds to the warmth in your hand, and the sadness reflected in the gray turns into the happiness of the rainbow of colors."

"And the point is?" Adel tried again, dropping her hand to her hip.

The woman spoke animately. "Our message today is simply that your touch is all the world needs to become beautiful again. Everyone longs for a hug or a kiss or a pat on the back to make their lives special. You have that special touch; Jesus had it, we all have it, and we all must use it. That's what we're trying to say today and we thank you for your time," she concluded.

Adel laughed so hard as they turned to walk away that they had to flip back around and stare for a moment. "Okay, okay, I get it, God," Adel hollered, looking up into the sky. She swung the door wide open. "Please, please, come on in," she said.

The man and woman glanced at each other doubtfully. They were obviously surprised, but intrigued at the same time. They smiled and proceeded into the living room in front of Adel.

"You want some orange juice, water, or a Pepsi?" Adel asked. "Have a seat."

"No, thank you," they replied, then sat down on the couch.

Adel grabbed her warm can of soda off the kitchen table and joined them in the living room. "Boy, did you guys pick the wrong house today," she warned. "I have a lot of questions that need answers."

29

*

When Lucy examined the Austin reports for November she had no other choice but to send Birch his walking papers. The numbers were down. She understood that the holidays were not a good time for fitness spas. Most people were more interested in eating, drinking, and enjoying life than worrying about calories and their bodies, but every other outlet in Texas had at least maintained their numbers.

Lucy dreaded dealing with that crazy man, but what else could she do? He was not going to go quietly. A new manager would need to be found as soon as possible, so that she wouldn't have to spend too much time in Austin cleaning up the mess. Birch's assistant would probably be first in line as long as she didn't have the same brazen mentality. Lucy had only met the woman once, so she wasn't sure what to expect.

While typing the letter of dismissal, Lucy almost felt bad about the tiny sliver of joy that was buried deep beneath the surface. She concentrated on how much better things would be when everything was all over and he was finally gone.

Dear Mr. Tallan,

As we have discussed on several occasions, the profits of
the Austin Looking Good Fitness Center have not improved
during your four-month period of probation, and therefore
we will no longer need your services as manager.

I will arrive in Austin on Monday, November 16th, to
assess the facility and begin the search for your replacement.
In the meantime, you should clear all of your personal items
out of the building and consider Sunday, November 15th,
your final day as an employee of Looking Good Fitness
Centers.

If you have questions or need additional information
please don't hesitate to contact me.

Sincerely,
Lucinda Merriweather
Regional Director

After faxing the letter to the personal fax machine in Birch's
office, with copies to corporate headquarters and legal, Lucy prepared herself for the fireworks that were sure to come. She wasn't
actually worried. She had already spoken to legal several weeks
ago to make sure that Birch didn't have a chance in court. They
assured her that he didn't. Over the past four months Lucy had
gathered two thick folders of documentation concerning problems with the center and her thwarted efforts to work with Birch
toward a solution.

On Monday morning when Lucy strolled into the Austin fitness center expecting a fight, ready for it, there wasn't one. Birch
was not in the building and as best she could tell his personal
things had been removed from his office. The shelves were
cleared of his first- and second-place trophies, the walls no longer
displayed his macho posters of women training in G-strings, and
the desk drawers were empty.

As Lucy stood and looked out the window, thankful for one less battle, she heard a soft knock at the door, then it squeaked open. She turned to see the assistant manager, Dana Cassidy, walking toward her, right on time for their meeting.

Lucy extended her right hand. "Hello, Dana," she said.

"Hi," Dana replied nervously.

Lucy started to talk as they both sat down. "I want to answer any questions you have concerning Birch and the facility because if we're going to work together we must be honest with each other."

"I kind of know most of it," Dana said in a pleasant, but cautious tone. "Birch wasn't one for keeping secrets."

Lucy smiled, trying to help her feel at ease. "Okay, then tell me what you know, so I can tell you what parts are true and what parts are fantasy."

Dana chuckled. "Well, Birch was very upset the last few months. He kept complaining that you were trying to drive him out, but I also know that sales and memberships are down. That has to be part of the problem."

"Did he share with you a copy of my proposal with strategies to improve things?"

"No, he treated it like a joke. He waved it around in the air saying stuff like, 'Welcome all homos to the new sissy spa.' Then he and his buddies would laugh about gays and lesbians taking over if he implemented anything in it."

Lucy sat dumbfounded, listening to Dana's account. The man was truly an idiot. If somebody gave him a penny for his thoughts he would have to give them change.

"So you didn't get a chance to read my report?"

"I did read it, but I had to pull it out of his office trash can and copy it after he had gone home."

Lucy smiled. "Well, thank you for making that effort. How do you feel about my suggestions?"

Dana shrugged. "Uhmm. . . . " She hesitated.

"Go ahead and be honest," Lucy pushed. "We've both got to be honest if we are going to work together."

"Well, I think some of them could work right away, but others we might need to wait on until we have pulled in a different kind of clientele."

"Can you give me some specific examples?"

"Like the yoga and other spiritual classes might be a hard sell to our current members, but I think a sauna and massage facility could work if we promoted them correctly."

Lucy leaned forward. "Can I ask you a personal question?" she asked.

Dana nodded.

"How in the world did you work with that man and his unbelievable arrogance?"

Dana was smiling now.

"It was harder on some days than others, but in any business there are assholes you have to get along with. I can do what needs to be done to succeed."

Lucy stood up and offered her hand again. "Well, Dana, why don't you show me around the place and let's talk about some of the strategies you think we can implement as quickly as possible. I'd like to see this center increase its profit margin in the next six months."

Dana stood up, but didn't move toward the door. "Can I ask you a question?" she asked, now timid again.

"Sure," Lucy answered.

"What are my chances of getting the director's position here?"

Lucy sighed. The girl was definitely not one of Birch's stooges. It was obvious that she had ambition and Lucy liked women with ambition.

"Well, I've looked at your resume and your credentials are solid. You've been in the second spot for more than a year, so I'd say your chances are very good. Of course, we'll have to go through a normal search process, but in the meantime, help me get this place moving in the right direction and I promise you that your application will be given top consideration."

Dana bobbed her head gratefully as Lucy spoke. "Just one more thing," she added.

Lucy wiped a piece of lint from her jacket lapel and waited for Dana to continue.

"Birch said in front of me and several other people too that if you fired him, he could have you killed just by snapping his fingers."

Lucy's head jerked back and her forehead wrinkled. She had never imagined that he talked about killing her. "Do you think he was blowing off steam or was it something that you feel he might try to carry out?" she asked, more out of curiosity than fear.

Dana swallowed. "All I know is that he has a gun and he used to brag about how well he could shoot it. He and his buddies' favorite pastime, outside of the gym, was going out to some shooting range to practice."

Lucy decided to ignore his threat for the moment. "Thanks for your concern, Dana, but Birch is not that demented. My impression is that he liked to run his mouth and show off. Those kind of folks rarely follow through."

Dana's face was now more relaxed. She had said what she needed to say. She turned to leave the room with Lucy close behind.

The tour of the facility was eye-opening. Lucy could barely get past the front lobby on her visits with Birch, not that she'd tried very hard, and now she understood why profits were so low. It was basically a he-man's dream in both clientele and ambience.

The sweat-soaked towels, chipped tile, dingy walls, and a low level of light reminded her of a *Rocky* movie. The only thing missing was the boxing ring; but a grubby-looking punching bag actually hung in one of the corners.

While Dana was busy pointing out the area where she thought the sauna and whirlpool should go, Lucy's mind raced. She had meant what she said to Dana about Birch just showing off. She didn't believe he was insane enough to try to kill her, but to be on the safe side she would practice caution over the next few days. She wouldn't stay in the building alone, especially at night, and she would park under a streetlamp in the parking lot, as close as possible to the building.

The transition went more smoothly than Lucy had imagined, until the end of the week when a strange box arrived first thing Friday morning. It didn't have a return label, but Lucy's sixth sense instantly confirmed that it was from Birch. It was almost as if she could smell his macho scent radiating from the cardboard. The box was addressed to her, but she didn't open it. She had to assume that it might be a bomb or something else harmful, so the police were called, and they took the incident very seriously. The bomb squad showed up, clearing the entire building.

Dana told the investigating officer everything she knew. A delivery guy had brought the package early that morning and left it outside the front door. She had never seen him before, but she admitted that she didn't know any of the delivery people because Birch usually took care of those things.

After a bomb expert carefully pulled the thin, brown paper away from the box, he opened it slowly and peeked inside. He breathed a huge sigh of relief when he saw it wasn't a bomb at all. He tipped the box over to get a better look, realizing too late that fresh and dried dog turds were falling onto the top of the desk. The bomb expert called the investigating officer, who told Lucy and Dana it was safe to return to the office. Lucy grimaced when she saw and smelled the mess. What a stupid and childish thing to do! The bomb expert made a final check inside the box and found a ripped newspaper article still tucked inside. He reached in with metal tongs and pulled the clipping out.

With her nose turned up, Lucy used several pieces of paper to swipe the turds into the trash can, then she tied up the plastic bag to minimize the smell and wiped at several spots on the desk with a spit-soaked Kleenex. When she was finished, the bomb squad officer handed her the article, which was now protected by clear plastic.

"Have you seen this before?" he asked.

Lucy read the first paragraph and shook her head. The article was about a woman who had been found dead in Bray's Bayou a week ago. Authorities suspected foul play and had few leads concerning the killer. That part had been highlighted with a yellow marker.

"Do you have the address of the person that you think sent this?" the investigating officer asked.

"It should be in the file," Dana answered and left to retrieve Birch's folder.

"Do you think he's really dangerous?" Lucy wanted to know.

The investigating officer cocked her head to the side. "You should realize, Ms. Merriweather, that we will probably not be able to pin any of this on him. I doubt if there are fingerprints and he probably has an airtight alibi."

Lucy shuddered. "Maybe this is just his chickenshit way of trying to scare me," she mumbled.

"You do need to be careful. Anything is possible nowadays," she advised, then began packing up her materials to leave.

When Lucy left the center that night, the sky was black. She could barely see the moon. Dana waved as she crossed the street and headed for her bus stop. Lucy walked quickly over to her car door, but hesitated when a sudden sensation of danger surrounded her. First, she noticed that the light was not shining down on her car as it should have been. On closer inspection she saw there were fragments of glass all over the ground below. It looked like the light had been purposely broken out.

While she fumbled with the keys in her pocket, footsteps approached slowly from behind. Lucy dropped the keys on the ground and cursed herself for acting like one of those silly women in horror shows that always get killed by the monster. She picked up the keys and balled her right hand into a fist around the longest, adjusting the point so that it stuck outward. She figured she would use it as a weapon. If Birch or any of his sorry friends really tried to hurt her, they would, at least, lose an eye, because that was exactly where she planned to take aim.

Lucy listened to the footsteps getting closer, then counted to three, spun around, and thrust the key out in front of her. "Touch me, motherfucker, and you die!" she shouted in her toughest voice.

Kuba stepped back, surprised. "Wait a minute," he said, throwing his arms in the air. "It's me. I'm sorry, I didn't know you felt this way about surprises."

Lucy was never so happy to see anyone in all her life. She rushed into his arms, letting the tears of relief cover her face.

"Hey, hey now. What's the matter with my baby?" Kuba asked with concern.

"This guy I fired is threatening me. I think he just wants to scare me, but I don't know," Lucy lamented.

Kuba cupped her face in his hands and tilted her chin upward. "Trust me, pretty lady," he said confidently. "No one will harm a hair on your beautiful head. I can promise you that."

Lucy tried to smile. "What are you doing here?" she asked.

"Something told me that you needed me," he answered.

"But how did you find me?"

"You left the message that you'd be working at the Austin center this weekend, so I found the address in the phone book then got on my motorcycle."

Lucy hugged her hero, enjoying a few moments protected in his arms. "I tried not to let him get to me," she finally confessed. "But I guess I'm not as strong as I thought I was."

"You are one of the strongest women I know, Lucinda," Kuba assured her. "And about that I don't have to lie."

When he escorted her back to her hotel room, Lucy hoped this time that they could make real love. As they undressed and slid between the cool sheets together, she inhaled the strong smell of lavender that brought her desires forward. At that moment, she wanted to feel him so deep inside her that nobody could tell where she ended and he began. She held him close, trying to guide him down her path of longing, but Kuba managed her passion with a mastery that had to be supernatural. With magical hands and lips and thighs, he brought everything out in a way that made intercourse seem shallow and maybe even unnecessary. When it was all over, Lucy was content and grateful to lie in Kuba's strong, loving arms.

This was the man she had wished for. He understood her so completely that it boggled the mind. This man was her fantasy come to life. She had surrendered her aggressive, sexual nature to his powerful self-control and it felt good. Lucy grinned. If he could make her feel like this with the touch of his hand or the caress of his lips, true ecstasy, when it did come, had to be heaven.

30

*

That Saturday when Lucy arrived home she received terrible news. Spencer's mother had died. Lucy had called Spencer before she left for Austin to apologize again, but she got his answering machine. She knew that it was over, but it was hard to let go. She shivered when it hit her that she was actually glad to have this reason, as terrible as it was, to see Spencer and be with him again.

Lucy thought for a second that maybe she was losing her mind. It was as if she were a character in a movie. What was going on as real life didn't make sense, but in the movies it was perfectly normal. In real life, for Lucy to want both men was wrong, but audiences paid big money to see these kinds of personal conflicts play themselves out and guess about which love might prevail.

She went straight to Spencer's house and used her key to get in when he didn't answer the doorbell. She found him in his bedroom with his head hidden under the covers. She wasn't surprised. This was his usual retreat when he was depressed.

"Spencer," Lucy whispered as she entered the room.

He didn't move. So she stood over the bed and pulled the cover down from his face.

"Spencer, baby," Lucy said again, this time touching him softly on the shoulder.

Spencer opened his eyes; they were red and swollen. He glanced at her, then turned his head into the pillow. The television was blasting a college basketball game on one of the ESPN channels. Lucy picked up the remote and turned the volume down.

When she lifted the covers and discovered that Spencer had on all of his clothes, including his shoes, it was as if they had never argued or separated. She pulled off his shoes, crawled up into the bed beside him, and slipped her arms around his body. She didn't say another word. She just held him to let him know that she was there for him.

Hours later Lucy threw a quick meal together. The boxed macaroni and cheese, green beans, and broiled steak emitted delicious smells in a room that originally reeked of sweat socks and tennis shoes. She set the tray of food next to the bed.

"I know you must be hungry," she said, not expecting an answer. "Come on and eat."

Spencer rolled over and leaned up on his elbow. "You don't have to stay and baby me, Lucy. I'll be fine," he barked.

Lucy responded with little emotion. "I'll go if you want me to, Spencer, but I'd like to help."

He took a bite from of the steak, which, had already been cut into small pieces for him, without a reply. He hadn't realized how hungry he was until that first bite entered his throat and fell into his empty stomach.

"What do you want to do about the funeral?" Lucy asked guardedly.

Spencer shoved another forkful of food into his mouth. "I haven't been able to think about it," he said.

"Maybe I can work on that for you," she offered. "Did you call your aunt Wanda?"

"Yeah, it'll take a couple of days for her to get here."

"I can stay around until she comes if it's okay."

Spencer glared at her. "I don't know if that's a good idea. I don't feel like being strong right now."

"What do you mean?" Lucy asked. "You don't have to be strong around me."

"You know what I mean. I've lost everything, Lucy, and I'm not ready to deal with all of it at once."

Lucy frowned. She had no idea what he was talking about. "You haven't lost everything, Spencer. You still have your business, you still have your life, your future."

He shrugged, finishing off the macaroni and cheese.

Lucy sat down beside him on the bed. "Look, I know how hard this is. I can't tell you that the sick feeling in the pit of your stomach will ever go away, but I can tell you that you'll learn to live with it."

Spencer set the plate of food back on the tray and stared past her. His eyes focused on the trace of sunlight that beamed through a tree outside the window. "When I said everything, Lucy, I was talking about more than losing Mom. I was talking about losing you, too. I thought we were going to spend our lives together. What happened to that dream?"

Lucy hated the twinge of apprehension that seeped into her heart along with his question. This was a conversation that needed to happen, but she wasn't ready for it. She didn't know what to tell him to make him understand. "I thought that too, Spencer," she eventually replied. "And I honestly don't know what happened."

He took her hand and caressed it gently. "Do you really believe it's too late for us?"

Lucy pulled her hand away. "Spencer, I don't know," she answered in anguish. "Can we just deal with one issue at a time?"

Spencer's eyes seemed to sink deep into their sockets. He grabbed the remote and turned the volume on the basketball game back up. Then he picked up his plate and finished the meal, watching the final minutes of the game tick by.

Lucy spent the week helping Spencer get his mother's things in order. Neither of them brought up the subject of their relationship again. He called relatives and friends while she took care of the arrangements for the funeral. It wasn't a difficult task since they found, among his mother's papers, a prepaid burial service that included the plot and headstone next to Spencer's father.

The hardest part was going into Mrs. Gray's closet and picking out something for her to wear. Lucy took her time, separating each hanger and carefully assessing every piece. She wasn't sure what she was looking for, but somehow she knew the right outfit the minute she saw it. It was a blue linen V-neck top with a matching skirt that Mrs. Gray looked gorgeous in the first day they met.

She remembered that day well. Lucy tried to be quiet, ladylike, and respectful, but that didn't last, it couldn't. Madea had labeled her "a free spirit" not long after she moved to Louisiana. Lucy never pretended as a child, and she hated superficial attitudes or actions. Mrs. Gray saw through her well-engineered front in no time. She asked Lucy to drop the charade, and from that moment on they shared an uncommon bond despite the distance that hovered between them.

That distance was not of their making, but they had both come to accept it. It was created by an overbearing son and boyfriend who held both women up to a certain standard, making it difficult for them to be themselves. Spencer loved the ideal, so they in turn acted out his fantasy.

Lucy handled most of the details until the day before the funeral when Mrs. Gray's sister, Wanda, swooped in and took over. Lucy didn't mind, she was actually glad to have some time to think. She needed to deal with what was happening. She had been so busy trying to keep Spencer positive that she hadn't been able to process the loss for herself. There was a hole inside Lucy's chest that not only represented a sadness for the loss of Mrs. Gray, but for Spencer and the end of their relationship, too.

The overcast November day was perfect for the somber occasion it hosted. As they stood at the solemn grave site and listened to the prayers of Reverend Tailor, Lucy let the tears go without warning. Spencer wrapped his arms around her and accepted the fact that it was her time to be comforted. She cried not only for Mrs. Gray, but for her own mother and father all over again. Lucy was taught that it was okay to cry, so she wasn't used to holding things in. She cried all the time as a way to help the pain pass on by. Madea told her that it didn't make sense for people to hold on to hurt or pain or anger. She encouraged Lucy to let it out, to purge her system.

The subject of death was never a sad one for Madea. It was only a physical letting go. She had helped Lucy learn to rejoice in the spiritual presence that she would always feel with those she loved. There was no need to be afraid, because the spirits of her loved ones would remain within her. At her high school and college graduations, Lucy carried her parents' spiritual forces up onto the stage. When she was afraid as a child in the middle of the night she would envision her father's enduring spirit as her protector driving the demons away. And her mother's carefree spirit escorted her to every party or dance she had ever attended, urging her to buy a certain dress, nudging her to accept a certain boy's invitation, and inspiring her to live life to the fullest.

After the service, Spencer's aunt Wanda bustled around the house making sure that the food was plentiful and everyone was served. Lucy was ordered to sit down and rest herself and she followed those orders thankfully. She plopped down on a couch in a corner of the house and watched Spencer mingle, forcing a smile whenever he could. She loved to look at him, especially his eyes. They were a radiant brown, accented by long, thick eyelashes and a well-groomed mustache. Lucy thought Spencer's eyes were the highlight of his mature and sexy demeanor.

"She was a nice lady," Adel said, speaking over Lucy's head.

Surprised, Lucy glanced up. "Yeah, she was," she echoed.

Adel shuffled her feet. "You still upset with me?"

Lucy shrugged. "Not really."

Adel smiled briefly. "Can I sit down?"

"Sure," Lucy replied, scooting over to make room.

Adel spoke first, making an attempt to lighten the moment. "I'm sorry I stuck my big nose in your business, Lucy, but I've been doing it for so long it's real hard to stop."

Lucy smirked. "We're both guilty of that; look how many times I've dogged out your husbands," she tossed back.

"So, are you okay?" Adel asked, switching back to the subject at hand.

Lucy thought for a moment. "I guess. How about you?"

"Pretty good, I think," Adel answered. She sat further into the couch to rest her back.

Lucy frowned. "What do you mean you think?"

"Well," Adel continued, unbuttoning her jacket so Lucy could see the little pouch that was forming in her midsection. "I'm pregnant."

At the same time that Lucy's mouth flew open, her arms circled Adel and they hugged tightly.

"A baby? Are you serious?" Lucy beamed.

Adel nodded. "Very serious."

"When is it due? Why didn't you call me?"

"In June, seven months from now. I've been sick as hell, so I haven't had a chance to tell hardly anybody."

Lucy sniffled, a signal that her eyes would soon tear up. "I'm so happy for you, Adel," she squeaked. "What's the proud papa doing? Probably strutting around like some vain peacock."

Adel waited a moment before she responded. "I haven't even told him yet."

Lucy's forehead creased. "What? Why not?" she asked.

"I guess it's because he won't commit to our life together and I'm not sure if we're going to make it, Lucy," Adel admitted.

Two older women in nearby chairs had stopped their own

conversation to listen, so Lucy got up and led Adel out on the deck for some privacy.

"Now what happened to 'I love the man and I'm going to stick by him'?" Lucy teased while they wiped off the seats of two patio chairs to sit down.

"He's a big old baby himself, Lucy, and I don't have the time or energy to take care of two of them."

"Well, maybe if you tell him you're pregnant and give him a chance he might step up to the plate and hit the ball."

Adel chuckled. "The question is, will he bunt it or knock it out of the park?"

"You won't know until you give him a chance."

"The subject came up not too long ago and he told me not to expect him to stay at home and take care of a baby. He said he needed his freedom."

Lucy reared her head back. "Damn, he said that?"

"Yeah, but it was before I actually knew I was pregnant. I keep hoping he didn't mean it."

Lucy's lips curved upward and she pulled Adel close again. "Well, no matter what Thad does, you know I'm here for you, right? I'll even babysit just as soon as the diapers and poop stage is over."

"Gee, thanks," Adel grunted.

"You know I'm kidding. I got your back and your front," Lucy added, patting Adel's stomach. "You're my girl."

When the patio door opened and Spencer came out onto the deck, he greeted Adel with one of their normal hugs.

"Hey, haven't seen you in a while," he said.

Adel nodded. "I'm really sorry about your mother, Spencer."

"Thanks. Did Lucy tell you the good news?" he asked, grabbing hold of Lucy's hand.

Adel looked at Lucy questioningly and Lucy looked clueless, so they both gazed up at Spencer.

"We're back together," Spencer said with a face so straight it could have been true. "I can't let this woman go. I love her," he continued, grabbing Lucy and kissing her passionately.

"Oh, that's great news!" Adel said excitedly. "You two need each other. Lucy, I'm so happy for you."

When Spencer finally let her go, Lucy fell back down on the chair like a wooden puppet, numb from the shock of his declaration. There was a tiny part of her that wished for it to be true. She could do a lot worse than spending the rest of her life with a gentle, caring man like Spencer Gray. But most of her knew that staying with Spencer was an impossibility, especially now that she knew Kuba could make her life complete.

31

✳

At eleven o'clock Sunday morning, Adel found herself sitting in the third pew at Spruce Street Baptist Church. It was the largest and oldest brick chapel in the fifth ward. Thad's father presided as pastor, relishing the many stories about how influential the church was in the early 1900s. When white radicals adopted violent lynching policies as a means to force blacks back into subservient positions, twenty churches in the area, led by Spruce Street Baptist, formed a resistant bond and successfully fought the hatred. Hundreds of husbands, brothers, uncles, fathers, and sons found shelter at the church and strength in Christian unity.

Adel wasn't sure why she was there, except that she had had an overwhelming urge to be in the house of the Lord that morning. She had only attended Reverend Kelly's church four or five times since her marriage to Thad.

Her wedding took place here. Adel summoned those memories. The sculpted wooden doors and pews were laced with yellow satin bows. Long streamers danced from the ceiling to just above the top of the average six-foot head. Her dress was white satin with a laced bodice, sleeves and train. She could still smell the bouquets made of golden roses and white buddleia, sprinkled with baby's breath, that were positioned along each window ledge throughout the room.

What she loved most about that day was how the light had reflected so beautifully through the colorful stained-glass windows. The large cavernous openings worked with the glossy wooden floors to capture the soul of the sun and hold it inside that room for her pleasure. She looked around now, noticing that the sanctuary did not seem as bright or as beautiful as it did on that day, her day.

When she and Thad stood in front of his father, Reverend Kelly, and vowed to love each other, it was a true cliché. Their talks about the importance of communication, compromise, and respect before they decided to take that final step seemed like drifting illusions now. They had come to this crossroad much too quickly. She hated it when her father used to tell her that "talk was cheap," but now she was starting to understand how cheap it really was.

Growing up, Thad couldn't see how the word of God helped him out on the streets, so he and his father had never gotten along very well. Most of the time Thad would refuse to even attend church, so when Adel came she usually came alone. Sometimes Thad's mother would invite them to a service or Adel might show up on special occasions like Easter or Christmas. But mainly she stayed away to avoid the drama.

As the choir stood vigorously singing "For God's Glory," it seemed like an invitation for Adel to tap her foot and hum along. She glanced around watching others in the sanctuary and wishing she could be like them. They seemed to be deep in the spirit, standing, swaying, shouting, and praying: "Praise God!" "Hallelujah!" "Amen!" She delighted in the music and relished God's word, but just couldn't let go completely, not like that.

Once the song was over and the choir had taken their seats, Reverend Kelly stood up to offer greetings and announcements.

"Good morning," Reverend Kelly roared in a prolific voice.

"Good morning," a few in the congregation offered back.

"I said good morning!" Reverend Kelly repeated even more forcefully.

"Good morning!" The congregation finally responded to his satisfaction.

The reverend spoke in a normal tone. "Today is a beautiful day, amen?"

"Amen!" The congregation echoed.

The reverend got a little louder. "Today is a blessed day, amen?"

"Amen!"

The reverend's voice boomed and his shoulders dipped with the rhythm. "Today is a hallelujah day, amen?"

"Amen!"

"We all woke up today, so it must be a beautiful, blessed, hallelujah day, praise God?"

"Praise God!"

"We have a few announcements to make and it is important that you pay attention because a church is only as strong as the work of its congregation. Let me say that again in case you didn't get it. A church is only as strong as the work of its congregation. Now, we need more volunteers to feed the needy this holiday season. Why? Because this season is not about taking, it's not about all the turkey and sweet potato pie you plan to eat; it's not about all the presents you hope to get or the New Year's Eve parties you want to attend. It's about giving to your fellow man. Jesus came to give. He didn't come to take. He gave us everlasting life and we all need to be more like Jesus. Amen?"

"Amen!"

"We need to walk like Jesus and talk like Jesus and think like Jesus and love like Jesus. Hallelujah!"

The congregation responded in abundance. "Amen!" "Praise God!" "Hallelujah!"

"Also, with your regular tithing there are baskets circulating today for a special offering. We're trying to build our scholarship fund for next year and we all know what that means. It means you need to dig deeper because the more you give the more you get back in return. It's a natural law of the universe. You may not get it back in the same way you gave it, but it always comes back. Why? Because you can't beat God's giving, no matter how hard you try. My God is a giving God! Say it with me."

The congregation joined in: "My God is a giving God!"

Once the baskets were collected, Reverend Kelly announced altar call and people gathered in the pulpit to kneel in individual prayer. While the pianist played quietly, Adel slipped out to go to the restroom. That was a major hazard of pregnancy, she'd quickly figured out. She was constantly on the toilet. She nodded as she passed Mrs. Kelly, who jumped up and followed her.

"Well, hello, daughter-in-law," Mrs. Kelly whispered, pulling her into a big bear hug.

"Hi," Adel replied briskly.

"You're not leaving, are you?" Mrs. Kelly asked with concern. "We have a visiting minister today and he's excellent."

Adel shook her head. "No, I just need to go tinkle. I'll be right back."

Mrs. Kelly looked at Adel curiously. Adel glanced down while she scrutinized her from head to toe. Feeling self-conscious, Adel tugged at the lavender jacket, which was pulling apart at her chest. Once she shifted the hem it sat awkwardly on top of her stomach.

The smile on Mrs. Kelly's face was followed by watery eyes. "I'm guessing I got a little grandchild growing in there," she said happily.

Adel panicked, but tried not to let it show. "Yes, you do," she said. "But, Mrs. Kelly, I need for you to keep it between us for a couple more days. I just found out for sure and I haven't told Thad yet."

Mrs. Kelly frowned. She linked Adel's arm in hers. "Well, sweetheart, you need to tell him. He'll be thrilled. Thad has always been great with kids."

Adel was bouncing in place by now as her bladder reminded her of the original purpose for their trek. "The anniversary of our first date is on Tuesday and I want to tell him then," she continued. Adel wanted to restate her plea, but didn't have time. "I really gotta go," she added, and rushed away.

The sermon had already begun when Adel returned to her seat. She was surprised that the preacher looked like a young kid. His hair was cut very close to his head with a trendy diagonal part in front. He wore wire-rimmed glasses that accented his compassionate eyes. Adel loved the dark lavender cassock he wore. The dark blue collar and matching navy shoes suggested impeccable taste. His voice surprised her too because it wasn't the voice she would expect to come out of that body. It was much more mature and robust than she would have guessed. His diction was distinct, with pulsating words that grabbed her and held her attention.

"I want to talk about God's call today because somebody out there may be missing it. What is God's call and where does it come from? How do you know He's sending you a message, inviting you to believe, expecting you to obey?"

As Adel opened her mind to the word of God, she suddenly felt lightheaded. At first she blamed it on the pregnancy, until an unshakable joy surged intensely through her body.

"God's call can come from the pulpit, but it can also come from the street. God's call can come from your family or it can come from a stranger. God's call can come from the Bible or it can come from a newspaper headline. This morning when you woke up and felt the sun shining brightly on your face, if you didn't take a moment to say, "I hear You, Lord," you probably missed God's call."

Adel trembled with an unfamiliar delight. It was as if God

knew who she was and he was right there, offering to take care of her every need, promising her true fulfillment.

"God's call is for everybody, sinners and saints. He called Moses to come to Horeb, the mountain of God, and lead his people out of bondage. He called David and changed him from a shepherd into a king. He called me from the hazardous, war-torn streets of the inner city to this mighty pulpit of peace. Is God calling you?"

There was an instant oneness, a unique sensation of yearning that Adel had never known before. She stood without thinking and lifted her hands high into the air, welcoming God's love into the core of her existence.

The memory of her tenth-grade geography teacher emerged unexpectedly. Mr. Roberts had been a former missionary in Africa who would probably be kicked out of the classroom today because so many of his lessons included explanations and stories from the Bible. He used to say all the time that ordinary people could do great things. He would tell the class that ordinary people in Christ often became extraordinary people in the world. He talked about Elijah's challenge to the prophets of Baal when he lead a lost people back to God, and told the story of Peter, an ordinary man that God used to heal a crippled beggar.

Adel didn't know what came over her minutes later when she walked toward the front of the church during the invitation of Christian Discipleship. She suddenly wanted to join Reverend Kelly's church. She needed to accept God's spirit within her. Reverend Kelly, along with the visiting pastor, rushed down to embrace her. Mrs. Kelly also hurried to her side, offering comfort and tissues. Adel surveyed the room and took in the uplifted souls surrounding her. She knew she had been blessed with this day and she thanked God for another miracle.

32

*

Adel thought Lucy had finally lost it when she first talked about scheduling a workshop at the fitness center on magnetic healing. But it was obvious from the very first session that the instructor, Nigel Quinlin, knew his stuff. He was a short, balding man in his late forties who moved more like a twenty-year-old. Adel was fascinated with the idea and especially found it interesting that Cleopatra had used magnetic lodestones to slow the aging process in her body.

Quinlin described two theories to the class of how magnets were supposed to work to improve health. First, they increased the circulation of the blood through the stimulation of the body's electrical system. Second, that stimulation released endorphins similar to the feeling one gets when acupuncture or massage is used at certain relief points.

This was Adel's first day trying out her new health improvement mentality. With the pregnancy, she had finally decided that health and wellness should become a primary part of her life. A moderate exercise routine had been drawn up by Lucy and they agreed to meet every Tuesday and Thursday. Adel sat in the magnetic healing class only because Lucy needed a few more bodies to fill the room. She wasn't allowed to wear any of the magnetic gear because there had not been enough research to determine how magnetic therapy might affect the baby.

After class Adel and Lucy went into the cardio room to begin their thirty minutes on the treadmills. Lucy wrapped thin strips of magnetic discs above each knee like an adhesive bandage before she started.

"So, does it work?" Adel asked as she straddled the treadmill next to Lucy.

Lucy adjusted the right magnetic strip, which threatened to slip down. "It's kind of awkward," she replied, "and takes some getting used to, but my knees are feeling better. It's like they're getting stronger somehow."

Adel nodded. "Nigel was pretty convincing," she concurred. "I never knew that magnets could be used to help heal broken bones or soothe muscle pain. I'm actually glad you talked me into listening."

Lucy stuck out her chest and walked faster. "I've ordered a pair of the magnetic shoe insoles and one of the studded facial masks."

"I'm not that convinced, Lucy," Adel continued. "You always take things to the extreme. You should wait to see a doctor and make sure this doesn't have some detrimental effect before you go all out."

Lucy winked. "When are you going to learn to trust me?" she teased, then turned her treadmill up higher and began a low-impact jog. Enjoying the lines of sweat that ran down the side of her face and disappeared into the collar of her T-shirt, Lucy concentrated on her breathing. She was lost inside a natural stride when she heard the three loud pops in the lobby behind her. It sounded like firecrackers being set off, nothing serious, but Lucy instinctively knew better. She turned off her machine and whirled around to head up front, and was frozen by his voice.

"Where are you, bitch?" Birch Tallan called as he stormed into the room. He searched the area until his eyes rested on Lucy. "Well, hello there," he called, walking fiendishly toward her. "You thought you had gotten rid of me, didn't you?" he smirked.

When Lucy's eyes moved over him and landed on the shiny, silver object in his hand, she panicked. She stepped back and tripped, falling off the treadmill and slamming her head into the foot pedal of a nearby StairMaster.

Birch lifted the gun into plain view, causing others in the room to drop to the floor or run. He sauntered across the floor until he stood over Lucy, holding the gun close to her temple. "I have been dreaming about death lately and I thought it might as well be yours," he spit out.

Lucy held on to her forehead, trying to ignore the lump that now caused shooting pulses of pain. She had read about disgruntled people coming back into the workplace and killing bosses and coworkers, but she had never imagined Birch might be capable of something like that. She should have given the situation more attention. Postal employees, day traders, accountants, even construction workers had all snapped, so why not Birch?

He ordered one chubby man slumped in the corner to shut the door, then he motioned for everyone else to move to the right side of the room.

"I want all of you to lie down in a line, right over there," he said, gesturing. "Lie on your stomachs and keep your eyes to the floor."

Adel had stopped her treadmill, but stood frozen in place. She couldn't leave Lucy with this madman and she was too afraid to try and help, so she just stood there, waiting for something to happen.

"Get going!" he shouted at Adel, who jumped, then glanced quickly over to Lucy.

"Go on over there like he says," Lucy told her in a voice that sounded calmer than she actually was.

Adel slowly stepped down and walked over to the other hostages. She wasn't sure how she would lie on her stomach, but she knew she had to try.

"What do you want, Birch?" Lucy asked, trying to summon her strength back.

"That's obvious, I want you dead," he replied coldly.

Lucy sat upright. "So, if this is about me, why don't you let everyone else go?" she asked in a slightly annoyed tone.

"I need them here to witness your death. I want to make sure people understand why I had to do this," he replied.

The sound of police sirens whirling in the distance was suddenly clear and getting closer.

"And why do you have to do this? Explain it to me," she requested while wiping at the trickle of blood that flowed from the throbbing lump on her head.

"This is a warning to all you niggers who think you can come in and take over. We are not going to sit back and just let it happen. This is about preservation. The fears of our fathers and grandfathers and great-grandfathers have all come to pass. This world is going to hell and your kind is taking us there. You try to look and act like you're the same, but you're not. You infiltrate our lives, spreading your filthy ideas about sex and violence to our young people."

Lucy shuddered. This was not only about her, it was about her culture, her race, and the need for some white people to demonize others to maintain their superiority. If she had been in that room by herself, she might have spit in his face and told him he was a racist asshole, but since there were other innocent people involved it was best to try reasoning with him.

"You're wrong, Birch, we're just trying to survive in this messed-up world the same as you."

Birch narrowed his eyes and kicked a pair of tennis shoes and a plastic bottle of water out of his way.

"You don't want to do this," Lucy continued softly. These are innocent people. Let them go."

"Shut up. You don't know me. You don't know what I want."

"You want me to die, that's what you said."

"I'll let all the white people go," he said with a sarcastic jeer. He spun around and waved the gun in the air. "Go on, get out of here, all the white people. You're free. Free at last, free at last!" He laughed a sick, pitiful laugh while half of the people in the room hopped up and hurried to the door. Lucy tried to count the bodies that were left without being obvious.

"Now I can get rid of some more niggers before I go," Birch informed her.

"What do you mean more?" Lucy stopped counting at eight to ask.

"I've already killed two of your kind out front and I plan to take care of a bunch more in here."

Lucy was instantly grief-stricken. That must have been the firecracker sounds she'd heard earlier. But who did he shoot? Maybe Mario at the snack bar or Elaine in the office. She wanted to cry, but refused to do it in front of him.

"Why would you kill other people, if this is about me?" she screamed. "What sense does that make?"

The police sirens stopped and Birch looked over at the front door. "It makes a lot of sense to me," he retorted while shifting behind a large mirrored platform. "Get over here closer to me!"

Lucy followed his directions. She watched Adel through the corner of her eye and saw the tears streaming down her face. Lucy suddenly worried about the danger not only to Adel and herself, but to Adel's unborn baby.

When Birch crouched down to get his body further out of the line of sight, his shirt sleeve rose upward and Lucy noticed a light scar on the inside of his left arm. It looked like a pentacle, not well defined, but she could make out the encircled star. She knew the symbol because she had seen the same thing on Kuba's altar a few days ago. He told her that it represented an end result or the manifestation of one's final efforts. Lucy reached out to touch the scar and Birch flinched.

"What are you doing?" he hissed, snatching his arm away.

"Where did you get that?" she asked, pointing to the mark.

Birch pulled his shirt sleeve down to cover it. "It's nothing," he bellowed.

Lucy recognized the fear that registered briefly across Birch's face when he knew that she'd seen the symbol. She interpreted the mark more through intuition than reality. It was a talisman, a protective charm, and somehow she sensed it was a message from Kuba. She stood abruptly, suddenly grasping the fact that Birch could not kill her even if he wanted to.

"Look," she warned. "Save the drama. If you want me dead go ahead and do it, but you're going to let these other people go!"

Birch was taken off guard by her unexpected aggression. He practically cowered on the floor, but kept the gun and his eyes glued toward her. "Keep it up and you will die sooner than you think," he threatened.

"This is the police," a male voice shouted through a bullhorn from the lobby. "Come out, now, with your hands in the air."

Birch glanced at the door, then back in Lucy's direction. "You think they're going to save your black ass, don't you," he asked, cocking the gun and holding it tighter. "Well, think again, bitch."

Lucy took a step toward him and spoke with a renewed determination. If he were going to kill her he would have done it already. "You're nothing but talk. You don't have the guts to kill me, Birch. And I'm not afraid of you!"

Birch turned and shot twice in the direction of the hostages. A curdled scream came from a man who was hit in the shoulder. "How about I kill some of them," he rebutted, aiming his gun in that direction again. "We'll see what it takes to make you afraid of me."

Lucy immediately lunged forward and grabbed at the gun in

his hand. Her small body fell on top of his and they both held on
to the pistol as they rolled and twisted about on the floor.

Several hostages saw the struggle as their chance to escape,
leaping forward and sprinting toward the door, while others in
the room joined in the tussle. The scene looked almost funny, like
a pile of football players after a major fumble, until a shot rang
out.

Adel had been carefully making her way to the front of the
room, but the shot stopped her. She wanted to leave for the safety
of her baby, but she had to know if Lucy was okay. She wheeled
around and watched as layers of people peeled off the pile. A
"thank you Lord" flew from her lips when she saw Lucy stand,
triumphantly, with the gun in her hand.

The police rushed in and handcuffed Birch, who was moaning
and holding his bloody neck. An emergency medical team looked
at the gunshot wound and wrapped it quickly before moving him
to a stretcher. Lucy handed the gun to the nearest officer and
Adel hustled over to her side.

"Oh my God, are you okay?" Adel asked, out of breath.

"Yeah, I think so," Lucy answered, suddenly remembering
that people had really been shot. She hurried over to the last guy
hit and waited for the medical team to lift his body to a gurney.
He was alive and the technician told her it was only a flesh
wound. She apologized to him before running out to see if Birch
had told the truth about the others.

The lobby was utter chaos as people were everywhere, crying
and hugging and rejoicing. She found Elaine sitting among the
police and embraced her.

"You okay?" Lucy asked.

"I'm fine, but he shot Mario in the chest. An ambulance took
him away about ten minutes ago."

"Is he going to be okay?"

"I don't know. It was pretty bad. Blood was everywhere."

"Was anybody else shot?"

"Marian, the lady that always buys papaya juice after her workout, was hit in the leg, but apparently it went right through, which the medical people said was a good thing."

Lucy's eyes locked on Kuba, who stood in the doorway with the sun framing his celestial body. She dashed into his arms.

"Somehow I knew you were here," she whispered.

"I will always be here for you," he pledged.

33

✳

It had been a week since Lucy had seen Kuba. The Birch incident really spooked her. It had proven that Kuba had powers she
couldn't even begin to understand. Despite the constant yearning
for him that wouldn't be ignored, she was also scared. An abnor-
mal hunger clung to her like a fire that Kuba needed to ignite on
a regular basis. She called his home a number of times that morning and left messages, with no response.

Later that evening under the guise of being worried she called
the psychic hotline and talked to several people before she
reached Kuba's friend Shaela. Shaela was obviously annoyed with
her call, but she eventually told Lucy that Kuba had gone to New
Orleans to become an *ounsi*. Lucy didn't grasp all of Shaela's explanation, but it had something to do with Kuba deepening his
connection to the spirits. Under the guidance of a sponsor he was
to be initiated as a true *ougno*, or African priest. The ceremony
would strengthen his rapport with his guardian, Lwa, and he
would learn the gestures and behaviors appropriate for communication with the other side.

In the middle of the night Lucy again woke from her dream of being chased. It was such an intense experience that the collar on her pajama top was sopping wet. In the dream she was running naked. Every time she found something to cover herself with it would dissolve or disappear. While running across a field she could feel the air rushing through her lungs and the sweat pouring from her body. At one point, her tormenter got so close that she could sense the heat from his heavy breath on the back of her neck. Lucy wanted to stop and face whatever it was. She even ordered her legs to be still, but they didn't listen. They lifted themselves up and down without acknowledging her demand. When she woke there was an intense anxiety that heightened her desire to make love, real, physical love, with Kuba.

She had seen him in her dream this time, but she couldn't reach him. He was always in front of her, far off in the distance. He stood under some kind of sheer material. It was draped over him like a protective shield while his body emitted a radiant light promising glorious blessings.

Lucy called information to get the number for the hotel where Shaela had told her Kuba was staying. When there was no answer in his room, she slammed the phone down. Her emotions shifted from sadness to worry to anger and finally delirium. Lucy was so out of control that she ultimately convinced herself in those early morning hours that going to New Orleans to find Kuba was a rational and essential act.

After throwing a few clothes and personal items in a suitcase, she tried his room once more and got only the voice mail system again. That was all the push she needed. She tossed her suitcase in the trunk of the car and steered toward Interstate Ten. As hours passed in the darkness, she pondered the warning signs. Shaela's willingness to be so helpful bothered her. And the fact that Shaela knew where Kuba was and what hotel he was staying in while Lucy didn't even know he was gone was also a problem.

Restaurants, motels, and houses blurred into each other as she zipped by. Lucy found herself fighting with her own sixth sense as it admonished this rash decision. She wasn't sure how Kuba would react to her showing up unannounced, but she was confident that it wouldn't matter in the long run. She wanted to be with him and because of their special link, she knew he would understand that implicitly.

Four hours down the road sleep crowded her thoughts. Lucy stopped at a well-lit truck stop to shake it off. She dragged herself inside, pulled a large plastic cup from the cup dispenser, and dumped ice into it. The cup was then filled with iced tea and several bags of pink and blue artificial sweetner. Lucy mixed it all together with a straw, then took long hard swallows until she was satisfied. The tea was thick and strong, nothing like the colored sugar water she usually drank, but she didn't care. In fact she preferred it that way lately.

Back on the highway her thoughts became more complicated. Her mind drifted back and forth between Spencer and Kuba; comparing, analyzing, and praying. How wonderful things would be if she could combine them both into one man, the perfect man.

No matter how hard she tried, Lucy couldn't let Spencer go, especially based on what happened the night of the funeral. She had helped his aunt Wanda clean up after the service, washing dishes and putting away food, then she went home, stopping only once at the gas station to fill up. At first, when she walked through her patio gate and saw Spencer waiting by the back door she thought something was wrong. She waited for him to explain.

"I wanted to see you," he said in a trembling voice.

"I just left you," Lucy reminded him.

She was actually pleased. She was glad to see him too, even though those feelings confused her more.

"Is something wrong?" she asked, slipping her keys out of her pocket.

"Yeah, us," Spencer responded gravely.

Lucy tried to step around him to open the door, but he didn't move. "Spencer, I'm not sure what you were talking about this afternoon with Adel, but we're not back together. There are a lot of issues to deal with before we could even have a small chance of reconciling."

It was a surprise when Spencer didn't respond to her words, but stepped up instead and grabbed her tightly around the waist. Lucy was tired and she said so, even though the feelings stirring in her body said something different. He pulled her to him, whispering over and over again between kisses. "I love you, Lucy, and I need to be with you."

It seemed natural for her to stroke the back of his head gently as their lips met. And when Spencer's breath turned hot and heavy, she found it hard to resist kissing him back with the same intensity.

"I can be the man you need, Lucy," Spencer told her as he pressed her body up against the door, rubbing himself up and down her thigh. He moved slowly at first, then stronger and faster.

"Is this the way you want it?" he asked as he pulled up her skirt and slid down her panties.

In the back of her mind Lucy was shouting: "Yes, yes, Spencer, baby, this is what I want! This is exactly what I want!"

She wasn't sure when he opened his zipper and freed himself, but suddenly their bodies were tangled together in frenzied delight, rocking back and forth until a series of muted screams came one after the other.

Afterward, she hated the fact that Spencer apologized, saying he was sorry to have done such a thing, and left abruptly. As his apology reverberated in her head, Lucy didn't want to feel sorry. She wanted to feel great. She wanted to feel happy. That was what she had needed from Spencer all along: an uncontrolled, passionate, amorous kind of love. She refused to accept the sadness that came when she finally admitted to herself that Spencer was only trying to please her.

Lucy flinched when it suddenly became clear that that was not the Spencer she loved. A stabbing pain moved through her chest and forced her to accept this conflicted reality. If she truly loved Spencer, why was she on the road to New Orleans to find Kuba?

At 11:30 that morning Lucy pulled up in front of the Bosen Plaza Hotel. She sat and watched the doorman open car doors, carry bags, and hail cabs until she finally built up enough courage to go inside. She had just reached for the door handle when Kuba strolled out onto the sidewalk. She scooted down in the seat, noticing that he wasn't alone. He was with a young girl, barely eighteen, and they were much too friendly as far as Lucy was concerned.

They hailed a cab and got inside. Lucy followed, trying to stay a car or two behind. The twenty-minute drive took them to a nicely kept, lower middle-class, residential neighborhood. Kuba and his friend got out of the cab in front of a vacant lot. They walked casually over a small hill. Lucy waited until they were out of sight, then she parked at the curb and trotted after them for a few minutes, until she spotted the two of them standing outside a large white church with a hundred or more other people.

The crowd was milling around in front of Good Hope Fellowship Church in the musty, humid breeze. A group of men carried base horns, snare drums, trumpets, trombones, and cymbals. They sported large, floppy, cool, Pappa straw hats and used pieces of towel to sop the heated sweat off their foreheads and noses. The ladies had their hair slicked down, pinned up, swirled around, and hanging loose. They held colorful umbrellas trimmed in gold with beaded lace. Lucy knew right away that it was a funeral party; a jazz funeral like Madea had talked about many times. People waited out in that hot sun for the large, oak-carved doors to open so they could begin the celebration of a life made new rather than mourning the death of a friend or family member.

As soon as the doors opened, the drum roll commenced. A slow dirge played while the family of the deceased emerged from inside the church with tears flowing. The casket was carried out behind them and lifted into the back of the long, black hearse. A heavyset woman in her mid-fifties, probably the deceased's wife, laid a bouquet of yellow and blue flowers across the top of the casket in a final tribute to the soulless body inside.

People had obviously come from all walks of life. Mixed generations and blended classes prepared to experience joy. Jazz funerals were so big in New Orleans that they were announced in the newspaper. Two police motorcycles led the way, followed by a young man on foot holding a large orange-and-white tattered flag. Walking behind the young man were family members and close friends. Next several kids carrying a banner that announced the Dumaine General Band in large black-and-white letters fell in line with the band playing loudly at the rear.

The music blended into a song that Lucy recognized, "Just a Closer Walk with Thee." But it was played so slowly that it sounded like a warped recording. The hearse inched forward, claiming its spot in the parade and signaling to everyone else that it was time to celebrate. Masses of people flooded the empty street behind the hearse with two additional motorcycle police closing off the procession.

Lucy kept herself hidden behind the crowd, maintaining a safe observational distance from Kuba and his woman friend. As the jazz funeral continued she couldn't help but get more into it. The music steadily built in tempo until the band was playing an upbeat tune, "Over in Gloryland." Lucy caught the melody swimming around in her head as she bopped along.

She watched mothers bouncing sleeping babies and elderly sisters dancing with pluma fans. Both sides of the street had sidewalks lined with people gyrating, singing, humming, twirling, and tumbling in the spirit. Old men waved their brightly colored handkerchiefs up over their heads and shuffled with the beat, while young men buck-jumped in line, throwing their hats high into the air and catching them right on time.

The spectacle passed beckoning to the swelling crowd through the tree-lined streets until the band took its cue to cut the body loose. The deceased had apparently been a musician and he or she probably even played with that specific band because on one corner, each band member stepped to the side and allowed the procession to continue without them. As the hearse passed, one by one they took a moment to lovingly touch the side of the vehicle. That touch was a special good-bye to a friend, encouraging his soul to rise up into heaven contentedly.

The hearse continued to the cemetery while the band turned around and played its way back to the church along with most of the audience. Lucy had somehow forgotten all about Kuba and when she searched the crowd she couldn't find him. She jogged back to her car, hoping he had returned to the hotel.

34

*

Lucy still couldn't get up the nerve to go into the hotel once she made it back. She wanted to burst into Kuba's room and snatch that woman bald-headed, but it was bad enough to imagine him in bed loving someone else; she didn't know what she would do if she actually saw it. She waited outside nodding off and on into a light sleep, until Kuba emerged again much later. Her hopes were lifted and then dashed as the same woman slipped out of the revolving doors behind him. Lucy kept her body hunched down behind the steering wheel until the valet pulled a dark blue sedan around.

The woman got into the driver's seat and they drove out into the street. Lucy checked the traffic, then pulled away from the curb. They made two stops before they got to the final destination. The first was at the International Shrine of St. Peter's Chapel, where Kuba emerged with a small plastic container that Lucy imagined held holy water.

The second was at a tiny house in Old Algiers across the Mississippi River. Lucy stopped a block away to watch Kuba go up to the door. An elderly woman materialized with a small gunnysack thrown over her shoulder. Kuba helped her into the car.

A strong aureole emanated from the old woman. She was obviously very powerful in her magic. Her celestial light was almost as brilliant as Kuba's. She wore dreadlocks, thick and mangled around her head. They were so long in back that they practically dragged the ground.

They drove for more than an hour, into a very secluded area. It was late by the time they arrived, almost midnight according to Lucy's watch. St. James Parish was the last highway sign Lucy remembered seeing and that was more than an hour before they stopped. She parked quite a distance away and watched the three bodies disappear into a large cane field. For a while she wasn't really sure that she wanted to go any further.

She sat in the car trying to decide what to do, weighing the potential consequences of her actions for the first time. It was a vibrant spark of light that caught her attention and moved her to continue. Lucy couldn't see anything from where she was parked, but that light up against the dark sky caused her curiosity to take over. She quietly got out of her car and snuck closer.

Making her way through the cane field, Lucy was surprised to find that it butted up against a tiny, unkempt graveyard. Lying down flat on the ground behind the stalks of cane, she scanned the area. She couldn't see Kuba, but the young woman he had spent the day with was preparing dishes of corn and rice, probably for the ceremony. The old woman opened her gunnysack, pulled out a chicken, and slit its throat with the ease of an expert. Then she stoked the fire and waited for the chicken to die.

Several voices called out in the darkness and two additional men, along with another young woman, appeared in the clearing. Both men carried drums that would be used to call Kuba's Lwa. Based on its shape the larger drum was an *asoto*, which would serve as an idol for the Lwa. The other smaller drum was a *bamboula*, like the one her cousin had played years ago. Its rhythm would bring the heartbeats of the faithful together in a spiritual dance.

When the new woman stepped further into the fire's light,

Lucy could see that she was holding a tiny *asson* rattle, probably made from a calabash shell. It would be stuffed with ritual objects like grain, stones, dried bones from frogs or chickens, and snake vertebrae to please the Lwa. The *asson* would then be used to maintain power over any unwanted spirits that appeared during the ceremony.

When the drummers beat their rhythm, the two younger women initiated the dance. They were both wrapped in a white flowing material that resembled large cotton sheets. The two drummers wore black pants and red shirts with red bandannas tied around their arms.

Kuba appeared out of nowhere. He stood out among the group in a loosely flowing black shirt and pants. A black bandanna was tied around his head, making his eyes seem larger and darker than usual. He sat down on a small, three-legged stool and motioned for the ceremony to begin. The two men lifted Kuba up in the stool three times to perform the priesthood rite called *haussement* as the rattle of the *asson* harmonized with the flames.

Suddenly the older woman began singing a litany of hymns and prayers, one right after another. Her words slurred together as she sprinkled holy water from the container on the heads of Kuba and each dancer and drummer. Kuba stood slowly and purposely walked to the center of the clearing. The two women danced closer, effortlessly propelling the warm air with their sexual innuendoes. The steady rhythm of the drums seemed to sink into Kuba's being and he was soon convulsing and jerking in what looked like a fit of possession.

The two dancers spun him around between them. They were humming as each used her body to express compulsive desires. They rubbed and massaged magical places that belonged to Lucy alone and the contact drove her wild. Their fingers pressed and slid across his body while he contorted and twisted to their will. When Kuba stripped off his shirt and submitted his flexing muscles as part of the arousal, Lucy fell into a jealous rage.

She was suddenly burning up inside. It was as if a fever dominated her brain. Lucy struggled to stop herself from watching the ritual, but couldn't pull away. With the women's dresses raised and straps lowered, the trio rocked together in a heightened, animated frenzy.

When Lucy could no longer be still, she stood up and approached the scene. She felt like she was in a hypnotic trance, no longer directing her own body movements. She glided toward that supreme light like a moth to a flame.

The two drummers saw Lucy first and their beat changed suddenly to thrusts that were slower, but more forceful. The older woman continued to chant, although her words no longer made sense. They now sounded like they were from a different language and time. Kuba opened his eyes and spotted Lucy. He motioned for her to come to him. With one look the other two women fell away and Lucy became his primary focus. She continued toward him, but it was not of her own free will. And when he held out his hand, her fingers reached for his automatically, claiming his powerful touch. Kuba pulled Lucy to his chest and whirled her around and around.

She wasn't sure how much time had passed as she and Kuba danced like possessed lovers. She hadn't even noticed when the drumbeats or the humming or the chanting stopped. All she knew was that suddenly she and Kuba were alone. Lucy looked into his eyes and saw for the first time a river of darkness rushing through them. He forcefully pushed her down in front of a large cement headstone and peeled off her clothes. As he sucked her breasts and stomach and thighs, Lucy closed her eyes, not knowing how to stop the vibrations that consumed her and not really wanting to anyway.

"This light of love is a burning fire, to spark our deepest soul's desire, each day our devoted fire burns true, and strengthens the love from me to you." Kuba's deep sexy voice brought their love chant to life.

Lucy swore she could once again hear the motion of the train from their first meeting. *Shoooo, shoooo, shoooo. Shooo, shooo, shooo. Shoo, shoo, shoo.* She repeated the chant along with him the second time. "This light of love is a burning fire, to spark our deepest soul's desire, each day our devoted fire burns true, and strengthens the love from me to you."

Without warning Kuba thrust himself inside her. It felt equal to the force of a lightning bolt, and she responded just like a torched tree. Her body wilted from the heat of his desire. Their moaning replaced the rhythm of the drums and their breathing brought back that exalted hum. She held on to him in a desperate effort not to pass out as his throbbing body strained harder and deeper, until there was an explosion of brilliant rainbow colors.

Moments later as Lucy pulled her pants on and buttoned her shirt, it was beginning to sink in. They had made love, the real, physical love that she wanted, and she still felt the smoldering embers of fire that Kuba left inside her. Searching his eyes, she looked for the man that she had conjured up in her heart, but he wasn't there. Instead she saw the dark river still running. She started to move closer to him, then stopped, noticing that his aura was not the same. It was dim and unstable. Kuba kicked dirt over the flickering warm light from the fire and it died, making the night so dark that Lucy had to struggle to see anything.

Kuba lowered his eyes. "You shouldn't have come, Lucinda," he said in a deeply disappointed tone.

Lucy tried to reach out and touch his arm, but he pulled back. "I love you, Kuba. I wanted to be with you," she explained.

"You should not have come, I said!"

"But I needed to feel your power."

Kuba shot a disgusted look in her direction. "You don't know anything!" he spit out. "The power is not in the sex, it is in the control! We have lost that now and we can never get it back!"

"But, it was wonderful, Kuba. It was what I wanted."

Kuba glared at her when he spoke. "This is not about what you want, Lucinda. It was never about you. Now go home, please, just go home!"

With that declaration Kuba turned and left Lucy standing next to that headstone where they had shared what she thought was a powerful beginning. She couldn't move at first. She called out to him, but he didn't respond.

Lucy stood sobbing in the darkness of that graveyard for a while as a sickness enveloped her. When she finally stumbled back to her car that sickness told her what his anger truly meant. What they had just experienced wasn't love at all. Spencer's words came back to haunt her. "What we do in bed is make love. Everything else is just fucking."

35

✳

Adel knew that Thad would probably not remember the anniversary of their first date, since he wasn't good with specific dates. So she wanted to surprise him by making the night special. She thought if she set the mood just right, their baby's impending arrival could be slipped into the discussion with ease.

Four boxes of Christmas paraphernalia had to be pulled out of the downstairs closet. Thad was two hours late for their first date, and by the time he arrived, Adel had put on her pajamas, poured herself a glass of wine, and was setting up her Christmas tree and lights.

The knock on the door startled her because she had given up on him. She was expecting a phone call with some kind of lame excuse. She looked out of the peephole and chuckled when she saw the warped face of a man who apparently didn't know how to tell time. She opened the door only because he wouldn't go away when she ignored him for the first five or six minutes. Plus, she had to admit he was cute. She twisted her smile into a smirk, so that he couldn't tell that she found him adorable.

"Please accept my sincere apology," Thad had begged, with a wilted yellow rose drooping sadly from his right hand.

Adel rolled her eyes. "I'm not going anywhere tonight. I'm going to finish my Christmas decorations and go to bed. Maybe we can try it some other time."

Thad flashed her an innocent cherubic smile. "I'm great with Christmas decorations," he said. "Can I help?"

Adel took another look at those bedroom eyes, that shapely charcoal gray Armani suit that framed his body nicely, and his big feet, then let him stay.

She laughed now, remembering how wonderful that night turned out to be, then slipped into the bathroom to shower before Thad got home.

When Thad entered their house, he recognized the Christmas boxes in the hall right away and went straight to work just like the first night they met. Christmas was his favorite holiday and he loved decorating almost as much as he loved his old 1967 Chevy Malibu.

Adel came out of the bathroom surprised to hear him singing "Jingle Bells."

"Hey, baby," Thad said from the top of the ladder where he was starting to loop the Christmas lights around the seven-foot Douglas fir. It was artificial because Adel's family had used fake trees to help save the environment for as long as she could remember.

"Hey, I didn't hear you come in."

"Tonight is a great night to start decorating," he continued.

Adel handed him another string of lights. "I think that's what made me fall in love with you."

"What?"

"Christmas."

Thad wrapped the lights as far around as he could go, then stepped off of the ladder and moved it to the other side. He continued the same way until he had circled the entire tree with blinking, multicolored sparkles.

Adel put on *The Christmas Soul* CD and they listened to "Silent Night" from the Temptations and "We Wish You a Merry Christmas" by the Whispers. Adel carefully unwrapped each ornament. She looped the hooks inside, then handed them to Thad to hang until they were all gone.

She held on to the two most important ornaments until last. They had been gifts to her from Thad for each Christmas anniversary. One was a chiseled gold-and-white ball that said "Merry Christmas, My Love," and the other had red and yellow flowers surrounding the words "You Are Loved."

When the tree was done, the two of them sang "Merry Christmas, Baby" along with Charles Brown and slow-danced blissfully around the center of the floor.

"I'm going to get some wine. You want some?" Thad asked when the song ended.

"No, I can't drink wine for a while," Adel replied, hoping he would catch the hint and get curious. He didn't.

While Thad was gone, Adel plugged in their culturally correct nativity scene in which everyone from baby Jesus to the three wise men had brown painted faces.

"I have some great news for you, Del," Thad declared as he headed back into the living room with the bottle of wine and two glasses in his hand.

"What kind of news?" she asked.

"Wait a minute. I want to make a toast," Thad continued.

He popped the cork on the wine and poured one glass, but before he could pour the second Adel spread her hand over the top.

"You don't want any?" he asked curiously, finally paying attention.

"Just a tiny bit for the toast," she instructed, then strolled over to light the three thick white candles on the fireplace mantel.

"So, what's your news?" she asked, joining him again on the couch.

Thad clicked his glass to hers and shouted, "The investors are in! We signed the contract today!"

Adel screamed and threw her arms around his shoulders. "Oh, that's fantastic, baby," she said. "Why didn't you tell me when you first got home?"

Thad took a big swig of his wine. "I wanted to wait for the right time."

Adel set her untouched glass on the coffee table. "I didn't even know you were supposed to sign the contracts today."

Thad lay back against the fluffy pillows. "I wasn't sure if they were going to come through, so I didn't want to get your hopes up. I'm tired of disappointing you, Del."

Adel moved over and sat down in his lap. They kissed with an unspoken promise that more would follow.

"I'm not disappointed, baby," Adel clarified. "Just a little frustrated sometimes. I'll always be by your side."

He ran his fingers over her hair and down the side of her full face. "I know you will and that's why I love you."

They shared another kiss and this time Thad's tongue explored the inside of her mouth. Adel enjoyed the teasing penetration.

When they came up for air, Thad shifted his leg to ease the pressure from the weight of her body. "You know I must be tired tonight because you feel heavier than usual."

"Are you trying to say I'm getting fat?" she teased, moving her hand to her hip.

"You know how crazy I am about that big behind of yours, girl. Don't even go there," he answered in an effort to clean it up.

"Well, I have to tell you that you're right. I am gaining weight," Adel said softly. She got up off his lap and stood facing him. "But there's a very important reason for it."

Thad looked at Adel inquisitively. He gently touched her slightly rounded belly.

Adel took a deep breath and nodded yes.

A tiny smile formed on Thad's expectant face. "Oh, shit!" he mumbled. "Are you . . . ?"

Adel giggled. "Yep, he's in there, or maybe she. I go for an ultrasound in three weeks and if we're lucky the doctor will be able to tell us if it's a boy or a girl."

A full grin spread across Thad's face, then it disappeared suddenly. "You sure this is what *you* want?" Thad asked with concern.

Adel hesitated. "Yes, but it also has to be what you want, Thad," she replied. "I can't do it alone. I don't want to do it alone." Adel held her breath, waiting for his response.

Thad stood up and walked across the room. "I have to be honest, Del, I still feel the same way. Of course I'll be here for you and the baby, but this can't be about forcing me to change."

Adel sighed. She didn't want to argue. She didn't want to fight. She wanted to enjoy this moment with the man she loved. So she motioned for him to come to her.

Thad strutted back over to the couch and sat down.

"Just tell me you love me, Thad." Adel said, brushing her lips across his eyes and nose and mouth. "And that you will love our baby."

"I do and I will," he answered. "I swear it to that God that my father seems to love so much."

The next kiss was deeply emotional with tongues intertwined. They exchanged breath and hope and affection and love.

36

✻

The conference was scheduled to last all day, but Adel had made up her mind that she was going to leave at lunchtime. A huge ethanol project was about to get under way in Iowa, but she couldn't imagine what they had to say that would take all day. Ethanol had been used effectively as an additive in gasoline for a number of years. It helped to lower the pollutants in gas and was great for farmers because they'd been able to double and triple their agricultural output.

She pulled into the parking lot of the hotel, where the event had already started. Rushing in the front doors, Adel found the ballroom and slipped into a seat in back. She listened to the presenter describe the fifty-six-million-dollar ethanol plant they were about to build. He said it would be the first of seven new plants in the Iowa/Illinois area. The four plants that were currently in existence produced about 425 million gallons of ethanol a year, and once the additional seven plants were operational a total of 170 billion gallons would be produced on an annual basis.

Adel squeezed her eyes shut. Even though the information was mildly interesting, she hated that the company hadn't bothered to find an exciting representative to present it. She had never understood how anyone could design multimillion-dollar projects, then allow somebody with the personality of a slug to try to sell it for them.

One of the first things she did as vice president of human resources at American Oil was to offer workshops on presentational style to the managers and other interested employees. She recognized the importance of having the right pitch person. Voice tone, inflection, projection, rhythm—they all played a crucial role in convincing people that you are someone who should be listened to.

Glaring up at the gray-haired, monotone-voiced man slumped down at the table in front of the room, Adel wanted to leave right then. One simple change could make a world of difference. All he had to do was stand up. She always stood when she presented to any group because it created a more vigorous image and suggested that the topic was a more exciting one. If the presenter doesn't act or sound excited about his own presentation, how in the world could he expect anyone else to feel that way?

She stopped her mental criticizing long enough to hear that California might be interested in the project because a different fuel additive that had been approved for use in that state was not effective. Apparently, MTBE, a petroleum-based product, had actually made things worse by polluting the water in the Golden State region. If that was the case, up to 3.2 billion gallons of ethanol-based gasoline would be needed to meet that demand alone.

The morning dragged by slowly as Adel took a few notes, filed her nails under the table, and skimmed the subpoena report she planned to turn in to Hunter that afternoon. Her mind drifted back to the fitness center. She had never been so afraid of anything in her life. But the fear was not for herself, it was for her baby. She had an obligation to protect, care for, and love the life inside her.

That mystical word interfered with her thoughts again. Faith. Why didn't she have the faith she needed? The faith that God would protect her. The faith that Thad loved her. The faith that her life had substance. Webster had once told her that faith was like an instrument. It only worked if it was played.

People received the answers they sought according to the strength of their faith. Lucy had faith. She didn't back down from Birch despite the gun that was held to her head. She questioned him, pushed him, and eventually overpowered him with her confidence.

Adel was trying to believe in the power of faith, but she didn't know how to find it within herself. God's miracles were all around her. She was pregnant, she had joined a church, she had not been killed by Birch, she and Thad were working things out, yet the substance of her faith was still not evident.

Once again she focused on her surroundings. According to the annoying voice in the front of the room, the feasibility study for the ethanol plants had already been completed. They were in the implementation phase, trying to secure the engineering design, construction, start-up, and operation components. Finally he got to the punch line. They needed investors, and who better than oil companies, especially since that is where most of the benefits would go. Adel liked the idea and thought she would make a positive proposal to Hunter about supporting it. The market was there, the technical production was in place, and it had already proven economically feasible.

When the group broke for lunch, Adel picked up the information packet and headed for the parking lot. She could not take another three or four hours of that man droning on and on. She'd read the rest of the proposal for herself later.

She reached into her jacket pocket for the keys to her car, but they weren't there. She checked her purse and they weren't inside the change pocket, either. Adel thought maybe she had left them on the table in the ballroom, so she ran back into the building. Her panic button lit up when she didn't see them anywhere. She dumped her purse out and sorted through the various items carefully: billfold, lipstick, mirror, address book, no keys. She turned her coat pockets inside out and tapped the sides of her pants, but didn't hear the rattle she hoped for.

Standing in line at the front desk, Adel wanted to cry. How could she have lost her keys? Things like this had been happening a lot lately: forgetting and losing stuff. When it was her turn she stepped up to the counter and asked the guy if they had a lost and found. He directed her to housekeeping.

She was frantic by the time she got to the basement, where the tall, thin woman in housekeeping tried to calm her down. Adel had worked herself up into a haze of negative thinking. Maybe something was wrong with her. Maybe she was sick or something. Her father called it CRS, "can't remember shit," but he didn't start losing and forgetting things until his late sixties. She was still young.

After hearing what the problem was, the woman told Adel that she had not received any keys that morning, but retrieved the lost and found box to look anyway. When Adel peered inside and saw they weren't in there, she cried. She hadn't planned it, but it couldn't be stopped. A thin comforting arm rested on her shoulder, led her to a chair in the back of the room, and thrust a handful of tissues at her. Then the woman left to give her some privacy.

A few minutes later, Adel tried to pull herself together. She took several deep breaths, but the sobbing persisted. She cried about her recent brush with death, she cried about the job she hated, and she cried about the loss of balance in her life. When she had run out of tears, Adel used the phone to call a locksmith, who agreed to meet her in twenty minutes in the hotel parking lot.

The clear blue sky and bright yellow sun were a stark contrast to Adel's increasing depression. As she trudged toward the car, she noticed faint puffs of smoke coming from the tailpipe. She moved closer and was startled when she realized the car was running. The door was unlocked, and the keys were still in the ignition. Adel opened the door and slipped inside. She sat astounded by her blunder. How could she have been in such a hurry this morning that she got out of the car and didn't turn it off? She didn't take the key out of the ignition or even bother to lock the door.

She lifted her right hand into the air and prayed. She prayed for spiritual healing and inspirational faith. She prayed for guidance and God's love. When she had finally gotten everything out, it was a verse from Matthew that told her what she had to do: "He that loseth his life for my sake shall find it."

Adel entered Hunter's office that afternoon with a purpose. The completed subpoena papers were in her hand and the four layoff files were under her arm. Hunter was finishing up with a telephone call, so he motioned for her to sit down.

"Sure, sure we'll finalize everything later. Okay, bye," he told the person at the other end.

"I have the subpoena responses for you," she said somberly.

"Great! How does it look?"

"It looks fine, I guess. Depends on what you want it to say."

"I was just wondering if you found anything in your research that didn't add up."

Adel took a deep breath. "I couldn't get all the details on why production over in Venezuela was stopped for almost a month, and that looks suspect in my opinion. Is there anything you need to tell me?"

Hunter cleared his throat and shifted in his seat. "No. No. There is nothing to tell," he replied.

"I'm sorry to hear that, because I had our detective friend do some snooping around and he found some things that don't fit quite right. It could be something or it could be nothing. Maybe we should let the Federal Trade Commission sort all that out."

"Are you blackmailing me?" Hunter asked tensely.

"Nope. I'm warning you that God don't like ugly and you have some important decisions to make."

"So, what did you put in the report?"

Adel smirked. "I actually wrote two reports. One that covers your behind, making the reformulated gas process the bad guy because it takes longer to manufacture, so the time is a catching-up period. And a second one that lets it all hang out. Including my detective's notes about strange meetings and employee pay-offs."

"Are you serious?"

Adel tossed the day care proposal and several files onto his desk. "This company needs to start a day care rather than firing people to maintain the vice presidents' bonuses," she replied. "I just want you to do the right thing."

Hunter spoke in an agitated voice. "It sounds like blackmail to me!"

"It's just a suggestion," she snapped.

Hunter frowned. "I never thought you'd turn on me like this, Adel. Not the way I've nurtured and supported you in this company."

Adel shook her head. "I appreciate the things you did for me, Hunter, but I don't want to play this game anymore. I've had enough. If you think that the working class is expendable and people's lives don't matter, then you've got a problem and I refuse to be a part of that problem any longer."

"What are you talking about?"

"My baby and I don't need this negativity in our lives."

"Your baby?" Hunter asked with raised eyebrows.

"Yes. It's the kind of revelation that makes you see the world very differently."

"But, Adel, your job is to hire and fire people. I'm not asking you to do anything out of the ordinary."

"And that's the point, Hunter. It's the ordinary people that matter; the people who have families and mortgages and decent lives. They've worked hard for this company and they don't deserve to be kicked in the behind."

"Maybe you should take the day off, Adel. Maybe your condition has your hormones out of whack," Hunter mumbled.

"I'm serious. This is not in God's plan for my life."

Hunter took a deep, exasperated breath. "Do you want the day off or not?"

Adel cocked her head to the side. "No! I want the year off. I want the rest of my life off!"

Hunter looked surprised. "You can't quit for no reason, Adel. Why don't you talk to a counselor or something?"

"I have a reason. I have a lot of reasons. How about the minority training program that you and the good old boys threw out a couple of years ago? How about this ritual of firing good people because of your insensitivity and greed? How about choosing an executive spa over a day care center?"

Adel handed Hunter a piece of paper with her signature and a two-line resignation on it. "I quit, Hunter," she told him. "I can't say it any clearer than that."

"You'll never find another position like this one," Hunter said in a condescending tone.

Adel walked over to his desk and stared into his flustered face. "To tell you the truth, I don't want another position like this one," she replied.

Adel had no idea what she would do next, but she felt great. It was that potent feeling of control that let her know she was finally on track. She thought about the resignation letter. It was probably one of the most unprofessional things she had ever written. It said simply: "I submit this as my official letter of resignation. 'Faith is the substance of things hoped for, the evidence of things not seen.' Hebrews 11:1." She laughed, knowing that Hunter would probably never understand what it meant.

Taking several empty boxes from the copy room, Adel sorted through her memories. She wrapped the crystal pendulum clock that she received on her five-year anniversary with the company in newspaper to protect it. The wicker-framed picture of Thad and her on their honeymoon in Egypt slid easily down the side. In the photo they were standing in front of the Giza pyramid, another miracle that Adel had failed to appreciate until that moment. They were standing in front of one of the original seven wonders of the world, built five hundred years ago as the tomb for Pharaoh Cheops, and at the time she didn't have a clue of how blessed she was to be there.

She unplugged, then emptied the water from the stone pond fountain that Thad bought for her birthday last year to calm her nerves. The file cabinets and desk drawers were harder to clean out. She settled on taking only those files that she thought she might need. When the phone rang, she knew who it was because she had informed her secretary that she didn't want to be disturbed unless it was Webster.

"Mrs. Kelly?" Jane questioned.

"Yes," Adel answered.

Jane spoke quickly. "Mr. Hudson is on his way to your office."

"Fine."

Webster burst through the door just as she hung up the phone.

"Yes, it's true," she said before he could open his mouth.

"Hunter called and asked me to come talk to you," he said with concern. "Why are you quitting?"

"Why not?" she replied flippantly.

Webster sat down on the couch. "Have you thought this through?" he continued.

"I'm not strong enough for this industry, Webster. We both know it. I feel like I'm dying inside."

He shook his head. "I just wished there was something I could do. I hate to lose you."

"You mean the company hates to lose me, don't you?"

Webster's face blushed red. "No, I said what I meant."

Adel stopped packing and went to the couch to sit next to him. "You'll never know how much your friendship has meant to me, Webster. But you can't change my mind. This is the right step for me and all you can do is wish me well."

Webster hesitated, then with a heavy sigh accepted her resolve. "So what are you going to do?"

Adel shrugged. "I don't know, but it will be something that makes me feel good. Something that brings me the peace and joy that I deserve."

"So things are better with Thad?"

Adel patted her stomach. "Yes, we're going to have a baby. That's why I've been so sick lately. There's a tiny little human being growing in here."

Webster hugged her. "Well, congratulations!"

"Thanks," she whispered.

Webster shook his head. "To be honest I've always wondered why you stayed around here. You've never really fit into this dog-eat-cat lifestyle."

"Isn't it dog-eat-dog?"

"Not around here."

They both chuckled.

"I've sometimes wondered the same about you," Adel said. "Why do you tolerate this place?"

"Somebody has to keep them on their toes," he replied with a wink. "And now that you're leaving that means I'm stuck."

Adel kissed him on the cheek. "And you are the best person I know for the job."

She finished packing about an hour later, slipped her office keys off the ring, and tossed them onto the top of her desk. Taking one more look around at the life she was giving up, Adel turned and walked out, ready to build something new with God's blessings.

37

✱

Lucy didn't drive back to Houston. Instead she went to the place where she knew she could sort things out. She went home to Madea. The front door flew open the minute she stepped in the yard. Lucy hurried up the stairs and into Madea's sympathetic arms, where she felt safe and secure.

Lying across the full-sized bed in her old room, Lucy stared at the scar on her inner thigh. It resembled an encircled star, the same symbol that she'd seen on Birch's arm and on Kuba's altar. What was going on in her life? Was she under some kind of spell? Since meeting Kuba her senses had not developed more keenly, but had dulled and sometimes disappeared completely. She was acting like a pawn, allowing Kuba to move her from one position to another at his leisure. Who the hell did he think he was to say something like that to her? Especially after she had given herself to him totally.

This is not about what you want, it was never about you. Lucy cursed Kuba, remembering how his voice shaped each word in a biting tone. Another thought instantly formed in her mind. She had heard similar words before. They came from her mouth and through her heart when she was talking to Adel about Spencer. She had dismissed his sacred love in the same despicable way.

Lucy's mind came back to reality when she heard Madea's soft voice on the other side of the door.

"Lucy, can I come in?" Madea asked.

"Sure, come on," she called, trying not to sound like she was upset.

Madea had already zeroed in on the source of her pain and spoke immediately, but cautiously. "He has you convinced that he's in control."

"Yes," Lucy agreed. "But I'm not sure how he did it."

Madea smiled because she knew. "He is powerful in his charm, and that's what you were looking for. That's what you've always wanted, Lucinda, to be charmed," she told her knowingly.

Lucy dropped her head. It was Kuba's charm, his magic, that had seduced her. But she couldn't put all of the blame on him. It was her willingness to be seduced that had ultimately led her down this path.

"So what do I do now?" Lucy asked.

Madea lifted her granddaughter's chin up slightly. "That depends on whether or not you still want to be charmed."

Lucy shook her head and forced the final remnants of sadness out. "Tell me, Madea, what can I do?"

"The first step is to remember that his power is only power if you believe in it. You must stop believing."

Lucy listened as Madea went on to explain the three ways that Kuba could potentially manifest his power over her. She talked first about how feelings and actions are recorded in the mind. Madea explained to Lucy that everything that happened between them has settled. Some memories might be out front and others might be buried under layers of related experiences. She warned Lucy that she had to identify those memories and strip them of their power.

His aura was his second vestige of power. Madea described how everyone has a certain vibration and people have a tendency to seek out those with like vibrations. They attract to themselves the forces that control their own thoughts and behaviors, pulling kindred spirits into their space. The second step for Lucy was to change her vibrations to eliminate Kuba's attraction to her.

Finally, Madea reminded her that what goes around will surely come back around. Even though the consequences of a certain action may not be felt right away, the impact is inevitable. Misfortune, she continued, could come from past faults whether in this life or a previous one. According to Madea, the only way to stop this revengeful force is to pray.

Lucy stayed with Madea for the rest of the weekend, strengthening her determination to be free of Kuba. They planned ritual cleansing ceremonies, protection spells, and prayers to God for spiritual strength. By Monday morning Lucy had a greater confidence for the battle that she had to fight.

Back at home, as carolers sang "Oh Holy Night" and "Deck the Halls" outside, Lucy did everything that Madea suggested inside. She sprinkled the protection oil that they had mixed all around her house, then scattered pinches of blessed salt in the doorways and windowsills. As she worked she repeated the prayer they chose: "Dear God, please give me the strength to win your victory over this enemy. In Jesus' name I pray. Amen."

The ritual cleansing ceremony was next, as she gathered everything Kuba had given her, placed them into a box, took it out to her backyard, and set it on fire. This was necessary, Madea had explained, to end his connection to her. Lucy stood and watched the fire burn. She felt stronger as it grew larger. When the glow reflected brightly in the silver ankh that still hung around her neck, Lucy took it off and tossed it in the fire as well.

The creation of a protection spell was more difficult. Madea had written down the instructions and sent everything she would need. There was a white candle for protective light, a blue candle to fight against the charm that she found so irresistible, and a pink candle to overcome the evil that Kuba's love represented. The candles were set in a semicircle around her gold cross, which lay on top of her childhood gris-gris bag. A bowl of earth that Lucy dug up from the backyard and a cup of holy water that she had gotten from St. Mary's sat side by side on the table.

Lucy was about to mix the dirt with the water and recite the prayer again when the phone rang. She tried to ignore it, taking a pinch of the dirt and dropping it into the water. "Dear God, please give me the strength to win your victory over this enemy. In Jesus' name I pray. Amen."

When the phone stopped ringing, she lit the white candle and stumbled through the prayer again until the shrill sound of the phone tugged at her soul once more. This time she reached for the receiver and held it up to her ear.

"I miss you," Kuba's voice purred on the other end of the line. "Will you come to me?" he asked.

"I-I can't," Lucy stammered.

Kuba's moan was low and seductive. "You can, Lucinda," he said. "We need each other."

"I can't talk to you, please don't call back," Lucy told him, and dropped the receiver into its cradle.

The phone was instantly ringing again. Lucy clasped her hands over her ears and rocked back and forth, willing his voice out of her head. She resisted, but not for long. She felt as if she were having an out-of-body experience, literally watching herself pick up the phone even though she didn't want to.

"Have you ever heard of a West African spirit called Kworrom?" Kuba asked.

"No," she whispered.

"It is an evil spirit that can confuse life's travels. According to the legend, you know that Kworrom is in your life because he lives in the ground among the roots of trees and he will constantly reach out and grab your feet as you walk, causing you to stumble."

"Maybe you're the Kworrom in my life," Lucy suggested.

"It is not me, Lucinda, but I warn you to pay attention to your steps because you are confused."

Lucy closed her eyes without responding.

"Come to me, Lucinda. I need you," Kuba continued. "I need you, now."

The words sounded like music to Lucy's heart, lighting a familiar fire inside her soul. In a matter of minutes she was in her car driving toward the place where she knew she could satisfy the intense craving that was building like a volcano ready to explode.

Lucy slowly walked up to the house with her head down. She counted each step carefully. She wanted to turn around and run but knew it was not a possibility. She had to go inside just like the rain had to fall, the sun had to shine, and the grass had to grow. Not looking forward, she bumped into Ashon on his way out the front door. She looked up nervously and was immediately thankful that the python was not in its usual place. For a moment their eyes locked. Neither said a word. Neither had to.

Inside Kuba was waiting. He had no clothes on, and as soon as she entered the house he ripped hers off savagely. Lucy found herself shifting between an awesome fear and sweet ecstasy as an enormous energy flow bounced between them. She finally let go, helplessly lost inside him.

Once Kuba had fallen asleep, Lucy slipped out of the bed and dressed quietly. She tiptoed down the hall toward the front door. As she creeped past the altar room, a sudden urge to go inside overtook her, so she checked the hallway, then quietly opened the door.

The minute she saw the heart she knew why she had not been able to sever their connection. Cautiously she moved toward the altar. She snatched at the heart, but only a portion tore off. Looking around the room, she spotted a letter opener and used it to scrape the rest of the heart off the table. She jammed the pieces into her jacket pocket, along with the excess wax.

Once the task was complete Lucy whirled toward the door and tripped over a bump in the oriental carpet. She lost her balance and fell directly on top of a large wicker basket, tipping it over. As she reached for the edge of the table to pull herself up, she was suddenly frozen, watching the huge albino python that poured out of the basket and curled itself into a ball directly beside her. Lucy was horrified. She opened her mouth to scream but nothing came out. The python lifted its head as if watching her carefully. He sat perfectly still, ready to strike at any moment.

Lucy sat stiffly. She waited to see what the snake might do. She repeated the prayer under her breath. "Dear God, please give me the strength to win Your victory over this enemy. In Jesus' name I pray. Amen."

Lucy gingerly inched her body away from the creature. Seconds became minutes as she struggled to put as much space as she could between them. When the snake lifted his head again and stared at her for a moment her heart stopped. The snake turned and slowly slithered closer to the door as if anticipating her efforts.

Never taking her eyes from his pale yellow hide, Lucy shoved her body backward and used a nearby chair to carefully pull herself up onto her feet. The next few moments felt more like an eternity. She thought about all of the mistakes she had made in the last few months and prayed that she could change her life.

When she heard a noise outside the door, without thinking Lucy bolted forward. It took every ounce of strength she had to leap over the snake and dash into the hallway. She was so afraid of running into Kuba that she didn't even turn around. She ran as fast as she could, just like in her dream. Her heart smashed against her chest hard and fast, her feet hit the cement pavement outside one after another with arduous thuds. It was not until she was in her car and blocks away that she remembered to breathe.

Safe inside her condo, Lucy grabbed a pot from the stove and snatched the pieces of heart from her pocket. She knelt down at the altar and lit all three candles again. After dropping the heart inside the pot, she tossed a little of mother earth on top and was about to sprinkle on the holy water when the phone rang. Lucy didn't answer. It took three tries, but she finally struck the match and set the heart on fire. She crouched down on the floor as it burned, repeating the prayer for victory over and over again.

38

*

Lucy never made it to Paris. The days and weeks passed. Christmas, New Year's, and Easter were all a blur. She received fewer calls from Kuba and found that somehow her spirit became stronger until she was able to refuse to see him at all. At first, he occupied her every thought. Numerous times she picked up the phone to call or got in her car to drive over to his place, but she fought the impulses and won. Eventually she stopped hearing his voice speaking to her in those powerful, sensual tones. And when he stood right outside her door, she summoned the courage not to let him in.

She had gone back to work and continued talking to Adel on a regular basis, yet nothing felt the same. As hard as she tried to put her life back in order, the special comfort that Spencer had brought into her life was gone, and it was only now that she could truly admit it. She still loved him. She would always love him. Lucy wanted to contact Spencer, but she couldn't bring herself to do it. He probably hated her after all she had put him through, and who could blame him?

After receiving good news from Dana about the Austin center's third month of significant profit, Lucy decided to celebrate. She met Adel at a nearby restaurant and bar for happy hour. Lucy was finishing her second Long Island Iced Tea while Adel toyed with a virgin daiquiri.

"Have you heard anything else about the trial?" Adel asked.

Lucy shrugged. "Just that it starts next month."

"You think Birch will get life?" Adel continued, chewing on the straw in her mouth.

Lucy rolled her eyes. "He killed Mario. I think he should get the electric chair."

Adel frowned. "I thought you didn't believe in the death penalty."

"I don't know what I believe anymore." Lucy scowled. "It was such a senseless death and I feel responsible."

Adel took her hand and squeezed it. "You can't blame yourself, Lucy. You didn't know the man was that far gone."

"I should have known. What good is this sixth sense mess if I can't stop something like that from happening?"

"Have you talked to Madea?"

Lucy shook her head. "Are you kidding? She would be so worried, she would probably put a spell on me to make me come back to New Roads."

Adel laughed, dropping her straw on the table. "It was all over the news. She didn't see it?"

"Madea doesn't watch the news. She only watches those corny Nick at Night shows with Andy Griffith and The Fonz."

Adel laughed even harder. "It must be an old-people thing. My parents watch that stuff too, especially *The Jeffersons*. They say the sex and violence in most shows today is disgusting."

"It's not about being old. I don't watch a lot of that mess myself," Lucy corrected. "They don't leave nothing for the imagination."

"Yeah, I guess you're right. I mainly watch those mindless comedies so I don't have to deal with reality."

Lucy motioned to the waitress for another drink, then changed the subject. "So, how is Thad handling your joblessness?"

"I'm dropping you off at home, right?" Adel asked, looking prudently at Lucy's second empty glass.

"Sure," Lucy nodded.

"Girl, you know Thad. He lets everything roll off his back. He was the only person who was surprised when I quit. He actually said, 'I didn't know you were that unhappy.' Duh!"

"Now he really does have to shit or get off the pot. A kid coming and no more six-figure salary."

"He's handling it. The mortgage and other bills are his for a while. I filled out my application to Houston Baptist College and I'm starting classes this summer."

"I still can't believe you're going to preach. Aren't you scared?"

"Sure I'm scared, but I'm happy, Lucy. I finally know what is important in my life and I understand what direction I need to move in to find joy."

"I wish I could say the same thing. My life is truly messed up right now."

"Have you prayed about it?"

"Every night, with no answers."

"The answers will come, but in the meantime, as Iyanla says, you should start cleaning out your closets."

"I don't know. There are some doors you just don't want to open."

Both women laughed. Adel checked her watch and told Lucy it was time for her to go. Lucy felt a pang of loneliness. She wasn't ready for the evening to end. When Adel started her car and they took off toward her empty condo, Lucy realized that she had been alone often in her life, but this was the first time she had ever been lonely.

They stopped at a twenty-four-hour supermarket and Adel

waited outside in the car while Lucy strolled through the flower section. A bouquet of blue irises called to her. The color blue attracted
her because it matched her melancholy mood, and she chose irises
because they were named after Iris, the goddess of the rainbow, who
could relay a message to earth from Zeus if she wanted to.

The house was too quiet when she entered, so she immediately
turned on the stereo to a popular jazz station and clicked the bedroom television on. She emptied the almost-dead tulips from the
vase in the hall and replaced them with the tranquil irises. After
slipping out of her clothes, Lucy crawled into bed and pulled the
covers up over her head. Hours later when she woke up still feeling an intense sense of loss, she sobbed.

It was the middle of the night so she didn't want to call Adel
or Madea, yet she craved a familiar loving voice to comfort her.
She lay still for a moment and listened to the love song that played
on BET. Softly caressing the tips of her nipples, she floated along
with the melody.

She summoned the stroke of Kuba's gentle fingers, the feel of
his soft lips, and the lingering of that initial spiritual bliss. Then
closed her eyes and conjured up the motion of the train. *Shoooo,
shoooo, shoooo, shoooo, shoooo, shooo, shooo, shooo, shooo, shoo,
shoo, shoo, shoo, shoo.* Until the Sexy Soul Psychic network commercial interrupted abruptly.

Lucy reached for the remote. When she couldn't find it fast
enough, she covered her ears and closed her eyes, trying not to
see or hear the omen in front of her. She hummed and screamed
and cried, but by the time the commercial ended, Lucy held the
phone in her lap.

She moved as if in slow motion, dialing the number she knew
by heart. When the man's raspy voice on the other end spoke,
Lucy took a deep breath and whispered: "Will you marry me?"

She waited for a response from the other end and thanked
God when she heard Spencer say: "Yes."

39

✳

Every year black Texans celebrated their freedom with a June-
teenth festival and every year, since college, Lucy and Adel had
been eager participants.

On January 1, 1863 President Abraham Lincoln signed the
Emancipation Proclamation freeing all persons held as slaves in
the United States, but somehow Texas slaves remained in
bondage until June 19, 1865. It was two years later when Union
military forces arrived in Galveston and finally set them free. Adel
didn't know anything about this historical faux pas until she
moved to Houston. They didn't teach such things in the Chillicothe educational system.

After listening to a local blues band croon along with melodi-
ous riffs on the west stage, Lucy walked and Adel waddled
toward the other end of the park to catch a gospel group they
wanted to hear. Adel had to stop and rest at an exhibit booth
along the way. She stood there too long and ended up buying an
African Kota mask from the Congo River.

"You feeling okay?" Lucy asked.

"Yeah. I just need to rest these weary bones a minute. Carrying this extra fifty pounds takes its toll after a while."

"You probably shouldn't be out in this hot sun, either."

When Adel bent over to stretch her aching back, the owner of the booth saw her dilemma and offered an empty chair.

Adel nodded her thanks and took it gratefully. Any day now, she kept telling herself. The baby was due any day.

Lucy purchased a Kente cloth tote bag and eyed several matching pieces of Ghanaian pottery just to let the booth's owner know how much she appreciated her kindness.

"So did I tell you we reserved Spruce Street Baptist for the wedding?" Lucy asked after she paid for her merchandise. "I wish you were already a reverend so you could perform the ceremony."

"Then who would be your maid of honor?" Adel asked.

Lucy laughed. "I hadn't thought of that."

"I'm really excited for you and Spencer. I told you a long time ago he was the right one."

Lucy shuffled in place nervously. "Yeah, well . . . I had to lose my mind before I could see it."

"Have you heard any . . . ?" Adel stopped.

Lucy raised her eyebrows in a joking manner. They had decided months ago that the Kuba fiasco would not be part of their future. Lucy was getting on with her life, so the topic was off limits.

Authentic Mexican fajitas from one of the restaurant booths was usually the next stop, but Lucy tried to bypass it for Adel's sake.

"Hey, wait! We need to try this one," Adel said, grabbing Lucy's arm.

"Don't you think that might be too much in your condition?"

"We said we are going to do everything the same, didn't we? So stop tripping," Adel complained.

After they bought the fajitas, the search for a little shade to eat them in was next. Lucy and Adel were pleasantly surprised when a couple of young black kids with baggy pants and baseball caps worn backward jumped up to offer their picnic bench.

"Thank you very much," Adel said, lowering her bottom onto the seat.

"No problem," they replied, heads down as if they were embarrassed, then rushed off to join some friends.

Lucy smiled. "I guess things aren't as bad as we sometimes think they are."

"Thank God," Adel said, propping her feet up on a wooden box nearby.

Lucy leaned against a tree that was working as hard as it could, but ultimately did very little to cool the area.

"So October ninth is the big day, right?" Adel asked.

"Yeah. It's my birthday present, so I'm not going to change the date again. Wait till you see the cake I'm ordering."

"Is it something traditional or way out?"

"It's pretty traditional. A white cake with three tiers. A bouquet of light blue sugar roses on top and butterflies fluttering around in the beveled layers."

"Butterflies? Why butterflies?" Adel asked.

Lucy shrugged. "I don't know. I like butterflies."

"You mean they don't have some special meaning or association with something in the spiritual realm?"

"I don't know. I didn't look," Lucy assured her. "I just like them. Is that okay with you?"

"I'm surprised, that's all."

Lucy playfully tapped Adel on the shoulder, then turned serious. "I have a question for you. Do you feel like you know who God is now?"

Adel looked up into the sky for a moment before she responded. "I know who He is for me," she replied, then smiled when she saw the confused look that spread across Lucy's unsatisfied face. "Maybe this will help," Adel continued. "I heard this story at school the other day about a little boy who told his teacher that he was drawing a picture of God. The teacher tried to explain to the little boy that his task was an impossible one because no one knew what God looked like. The little boy frowned at first, then he finally looked up at his teacher and said, "They will in a minute."

They both stopped grinning long enough to watch a young teenage girl, no more than fifteen years old, strut suggestively through the grass. She was wearing a tiny black leather tube top, half the size of a normal tube top, and "Daisy Duke"–style shorts, with flesh showing through criss-crossed ties down each side. A huge silver chain with a finely detailed silver cross thumped up against her bulging chest with each step she took.

"Ummm, ummm, ummm," Lucy moaned. "Now tell me what that's about. How can she put on a cross and wear an outfit like that?"

Adel stared at the young girl for a moment. "It shows how conflicted our children are today," she explained. "The sad part is that she probably believes in God, but doesn't really know what He's all about."

Lucy smirked. "I think she knows and doesn't care," she retorted.

"Maybe she knows, but can't figure out how to make it all work. This is a strange time we live in, Lucy. You of all people should recognize that."

"You're going to be a good preacher, Adel, because you are always trying to make things fit."

"I'm just saying that we all struggle in a society where secular images overwhelm us. Everybody does things that they know may not be part of God's plan and they find ways to justify it."

"Well, I don't see how anyone can justify dressing like that and slapping a cross on their chest." Lucy grumbled.

"The same way you justify sleeping with Spencer before the wedding and the same way I justify not going to church every Sunday. Even though I'm studying to be a preacher."

"So are you calling me a hypocrite?"

"Most of us are hypocrites, but it's up to the Lord above to judge, not me or you."

"I hope you don't become one of those Bible-toting, morals-pushing preachers."

"Why? You gonna stop loving me if I do?"

"No, but I might have to stop hanging out with you."

Adel sucked her teeth. "I don't have to worry about that," she countered. "Who else is going to put up with you?"

Lucy leaned forward and got serious again. "Tell me the truth, aren't you scared?" she asked.

"Terrified," Adel answered. "There are so many contradictions I have to work through. How religious do I have to be? I know I can't curse anymore, but what about drinking a glass of wine or a frozen daiquiri every now and then? And what about playing Bid Whist?"

Lucy patted Adel's hand. "You'll figure it out because it's want you want to do," she assured her.

"It's what God is calling me to do, Lucy," Adel corrected. "And that's a very different situation."

Lucy fanned her face with a folded yellow flyer announcing the appearance of a popular gospel group, Donald Conner and Imani, from Memphis, on the east stage. It was almost time, so they started over toward the stage to make sure they could get good seats. After going only a few feet, Adel stopped to rub the side of her stomach where the baby was kicking viciously.

"She's ready to get out of there, huh?" Lucy joked, touching Adel's stomach to feel the kicking for herself.

"I'm ready for her to come out, too."

"What about a day care? Are you going with Happy Hearts?"

Adel took several deep breaths and waved Lucy forward. "Oh, I didn't tell you, did I? I talked it over with Thad and we're going to use half of our savings, then take out a joint loan with Liz to start a second facility not far from the house."

"It must be nice. We all ain't able to buy our own day care centers," Lucy clowned.

"Well, even though Thad's computer business is taking off, I still feel like I need something of my own. Let's face it, the ministry is wonderful, but it doesn't bring in a lot of money."

"That depends. There are lots of multimillion-dollar fellowships all over the country—Bishop Victor Curry in Miami and Bishop T. D. Jakes in Dallas. You can create video tapes, write books, sell T-shirts, get a recording contract for your choir, the sky's the limit nowadays."

"Lucy, you need to stop mocking the Lord's work," Adel warned.

"I wasn't mocking anything. I was simply stating facts."

They made it to the stage and grabbed two seats in the fourth row to wait for the show to start. The festival was obviously in full swing. An old-fashioned boom box played behind them with several kids dancing in the street. Booths were filled with customers, a merry-go-round's tune played sweetly in the breeze, and the grass was littered with trash.

"It's not really about money, anyway," Adel continued. "I wanted to help Liz get this new day care going because it can impact working women. Plus, I needed somewhere for my little one to go, so it just made sense."

"Ummm, hum," Lucy teased.

A black Harley Davidson motorcycle with silver trim and a long red stripe suddenly darted past. The rider wore dreadlocks and his dark jacket and jeans covered a familiar body that leaned forward against the wind. Lucy didn't get a good look, so she stood up and stretched, shading her eyes with her hands for a better view. When he turned the corner, she flopped back down and took a deep labored breath.

Adel raised her eyebrows, but didn't say a word.

40

*

The third Sunday in September was missionary Sunday, and since Adel was now heading up Spruce Street Baptist's Missionary Society, she was allowed to sit up front in the pulpit. Lucy and Spencer hurried into the sanctuary and found a couple of seats near the front. Adel sat ridgidly in one of the large, majestic-looking, red velvet chairs next to Reverend Kelly. Lucy glanced up at the pulpit and beamed at Adel. She winked back.

Thad nodded confidently at his wife from the front row. He was sitting next to his mother, who held their ten-week-old daughter, Faith, in her lap.

Adel looked across the many faces of the congregation. She didn't want to sit up front, but her father-in-law had insisted. Despite the fact that she was enjoying theology school, she was still concerned that her calling was not clearer. The guy who sat next to her in the philosophy of religion course talked like he knew exactly where he was headed: a Pentecostal ministry in Macon, Georgia. He seemed so much more organized and it worried her because doubt and conflict were still a part of her daily routine.

The only saving grace was that now she could better recognize the signs and determine which path was God's guidance and which was her own choosing. God's work was all around her, but she still wasn't sure what part she was expected to play. The conversation on the plane with the nun, her discussions about faith with Webster, and even that day when she joined Reverend Kelly's church were all part of the big picture. The Spirit of God not only told Ezekiel that he would be a prophet, but He gave Ezekiel the ability to spread his word.

Adel's eyes rested on her husband in the second row. It was an unbelievable sight to watch him now rocking their daughter in his arms. She had worried unnecessarily about so many things, only to have it all work out. Since Thad didn't marry a preacher and had such a poor relationship with his father, Adel was sure that her announcement to go to theology school would be the final wedge to drive them apart. Miraculously, it had the opposite impact. They had become much closer and Thad was even trying to find some common ground with his father.

Adel's faith seemed to get stronger as she realized that there was no other explanation but the power of God. Despite all of his macho posturing, Thad took one look at that tiny little baby girl and grew up. In the mornings she would drop Faith off at the day care center and Thad picked her up at night. Her husband and daughter were at home by the time she returned from class. She looked over at the old rugged cross hanging on the wall and thanked God for her ordinary life.

Reverend Kelly stood up and cleared his throat. "I know I'm supposed to preach the sermon right now, but the Lord has put something on my heart. Most of you know my daughter-in-law, Adel Kelly, was called by God a few months ago. Nobody could be more proud than I am right now, except maybe my wife and my son and my granddaughter. I know I'm putting her on the spot, but I'd like for her to come up here and say a few words to you."

Adel's eyes widened and the sweat on her neck grew thick. Even though Reverend Kelly had warned her that he might do something like this when he overheard her practicing a sermon she had written for class, she didn't think it would be today. Rising slowly, she walked up to the podium, barely hearing the members of the congregation shout their support.

"Take your time child . . ." "It's all right baby . . ." "Just let the Lord move you!"

As she stood next to Reverend Kelly in a daze, he started to talk again. "I want you to remember that this is a woman who gave up her corporate luxuries to serve the Lord. A woman who has learned firsthand what Roman's first chapter, seventeenth verse tells us, that 'the just shall live by faith.' "

Once Reverend Kelly had sat down, Adel shifted her body behind the podium. She adjusted the microphone closer to her mouth and coughed tensely. "Good morning," she finally said, just barely getting it out.

"Good morning," the congregation offered back loudly.

"Let the words of my mouth and the meditation of my heart be acceptable in thy sight, Oh Lord, my strength and my redeemer. Amen."

"Amen."

"I come to you this morning as a reborn child of God with a renewed faith. Since I wasn't actually prepared for this, I'll talk to you about something that is heavy on my mind. I was up late watching the Animal Channel last night. It was a show about the predatory nature of animals. I sat and watched in horror as a herd of antelope wanted to cross a river that was infested with crocodiles. The leader of the herd, along with several others flanking behind him, stepped cautiously but swiftly into the water. And moments later hidden crocodiles grabbed at their legs, pulling them under. Instead of turning and running in the opposite direction, the entire herd abruptly lunged forward into that death-filled river in a desperate attempt to cross. Only about half of them made it safely to the other side."

"That scene brings forth these words today," Adel continued. "We need to choose the miracle of life over the spectacle of death. I was stunned by the tragedy of it all, but I was even more disgusted when I thought about the difference that could have been made if that camera person would have scared the antelope away from the water rather than simply watching and taping such a gruesome event."

"Lord have mercy," an elderly lady in the third row shouted, waving her hands up in the air.

"We need to realize that as human beings we make choices everyday, just like those antelope. Even though we know that something is not good for us, we bolt forward and buy it or participate in it anyway: cigarettes, alcohol, drugs, violence, sex, and so much more. We're all guilty on some level, and just like those antelope, only half of us will make it through this river called life."

Lucy sat proudly listening to her best friend preach as if she had been doing it all her life. She held on to Spencer's arm tightly, glad that he was a man with a forgiving heart. She knew how blessed she was to have him back in her life.

Lucy envied the courage that Adel had to have to choose God, unconditionally. She planned to move closer to God's positive spirit herself but there were so many different ideas that had to be sorted through first. She would have to analyze each belief, custom, and folktale that she had learned from Madea.

Adel's voice softened a bit. "As Reverend Kelly said, I left a job in the corporate world with a six-figure salary and twenty-thousand-dollar holiday bonuses. I don't tell you that to brag. I tell you that to let you know the depth of my sincerity and commitment in helping people better understand what life should be about, what happiness must include and what love has to mean. When I was vice president of human resources for American Oil, I felt like I was one of those crocodiles waiting for someone, anyone, to step into the water so I could feed."

As her voice dipped and crooned, hitting the right syllables with proper inflection and spin, Adel eased through the words with a natural grace.

"The faithlessness, self-centeredness, and greed of our society today is overwhelming. We've forgotten important scriptures like 'Do unto others as you would have others do unto you' and 'Do not be conformed to this world, but be transformed by the renewing of your mind' and 'Behold, I send you forth as sheep in the midst of wolves.'"

Adel stood mesmerized by the crowd, thinking about the power of God's love. It didn't matter if people were worshipping across town at a Quaker meeting or in a West African village in the Catholic church, they were all seeking the same thing—God's love.

"I understand the miracle of life because my standing here in front of you today behind this pulpit is a miracle of life. I know the spectacle of death because I was dying, spiritually dying every time I stepped into that company. We can't explain the miracles that occur in our lives, just like we can't explain God, but through faith we can believe. And it is ultimately through belief that we will receive his blessings. Amen."

Adel lifted her right hand into the air, then sat down. She smiled at Lucy and silently thanked God for taking much of the conflict out of their friendship. Adel had agonized for weeks about how Lucy's extreme leaps into the supernatural and bizarre would fit with the new life she planned to lead. Finally, she turned it over to God and he fixed it. Late one night as Adel meditated on that very dilemma, Lucy called and left a message on the answering machine. When Adel listened to the message the next morning she was amazed by God's glory, because Lucy wanted to be baptized again.

Lucy stood up first and clapped enthusiastically. Spencer stood next, draping his arm around Lucy's shoulders. Adel watched that loving act and testified: "He may not come when you want Him, but He's always right on time."

41

Lucy primped in her bedroom, trying on her wedding gown. The silk dress with a cowl back and a crystal beaded yoke had been her second choice until the day she pulled out her credit card. She wanted to simplify her life, but not that much.

There were only three days left before the blessed event when she would become Mrs. Lucinda Marie Gray. Madea would arrive tomorrow and Spencer's aunt Wanda was already in town helping with the various details. Lucy reached into her closet for the matching beige silk pumps and brushed against her navy blue jacket. It wobbled for a moment, then fell off the hanger and onto the floor. She bent down to pick it up and noticed a small piece of red paper sticking out of the pocket. She pulled out the paper and stared. It was the tip of the red heart.

Lucy gazed at the smooth round edge that ended too abruptly. She rubbed her finger lightly across the soft lump of wax stuck on top. Sometimes it seemed like it was all a dream. Sometimes late at night when everything was quiet, including her thoughts, Lucy's soul could still sense his energy surrounding her. Madea's only warning about sex was how the power of such a spiritual connection lasted long after the physical was gone. She had never really understood Madea's meaning until now. Lucy crumbled up the scrap of paper and tossed it into the trash can.

Adjusting the waistline of her wedding dress, she had to grin because her image in the full-length mirror said, "Lucinda Marie Merriweather is all that." She ambled out of the bedroom and twirled around several times to get Spencer's attention.

"Girl, what's wrong with you?" he asked after he glanced up. "Don't you know it's bad luck for me to see you in your wedding dress before the ceremony?"

Lucy leaned over and kissed his lips several times in a quick, exaggerated manner. "I don't believe in all of that superstitious mumbo jumbo anymore," she said, then strutted back to the bedroom with a renewed air of confidence.

She had driven her wedding planner crazy when she decided to eliminate the superstition and ritual. She would be preceded down the aisle only by Adel, her maid of honor, and Spencer's best man because bridesmaids and ushers were out when she discovered an old Roman law that said their purpose was to confuse the Devil so he wouldn't know who was getting hitched.

Matching wedding bands would be exchanged only because they were a symbol of the love and commitment she and Spencer would share, plus Lucy had already found a set that she really wanted.

Lucy chose to walk down the aisle alone, at least physically alone, since her father would be by her side in spirit. She didn't plan to wear a veil because the veil was historically used by the Greeks to keep the evil eye away from such festivities.

She would carry a bridal bouquet made with lilies of the valley, lady's slippers, and white sweet pea to represent her and Spencer's growth together. However, rather than throwing the bouquet to all of the single ladies to see who might catch it and marry next, she planned to simply hand it to her best friend and maid of honor, then wish Adel and Thad many more years of love and happiness.

When Madea told her that the phrase "something old, something new, something borrowed, and something blue" was rooted in magic and superstition, Lucy started to write her own phrase. "Something sacred, something sweet, something blessed, and something . . ." She hadn't quite finished it yet.

Finally, all rice throwing was eliminated because in some Oriental cultures it was meant to chase evil spirits away from the couple. Instead the well-wishers would cheer the couple off to their honeymoon. Of course the honeymoon stayed the same, except it was extended from one week to three at a beautiful Grand Bahama Islands resort.

Lucy slipped out of the dress and hung it carefully in the closet to avoid wrinkles. She had planned to join Spencer on the couch, but he was watching golf and she could only watch as long as Tiger Woods was on the screen. Everyone else was boring. She sat down on her bed and flipped through a *Today's Black Woman* magazine, stopping when a sex quiz caught her attention.

The first question asked, "Does your partner treat your body as: a) a toy; b) a new piece of jewelry; or c) a household appliance?"

She quickly answered "b."

"When you fantasize sexually is it with someone from your: a) past; b) present; or c) future?"

Lucy thought for a moment, wanting to be honest. She marked the "a" at first, but scratched it out and circled "b."

"Would your partner compare your sexual encounters to: a) a sizzling steak; b) a warm cup of soup; or c) cold mashed potatoes?" Lucy laughed out loud and added a third "b" to the page. Then she shook her head and tossed the book on her nightstand. She went into the living room and kissed Spencer passionately.

"What was that for?" he asked, turning away from the television for just a moment.

"For ever," she replied, snuggling up under him, thankful for the steady, comfortable love he offered.

Later, when Lucy found herself in the kitchen making iced tea, she had to chuckle. The glass was half full of tea when she tore open one pink and one blue package of sweetner and dumped them both into the liquid. Next she added a handful of ice cubes and filled the rest of the glass with mountain spring water. She stirred the bland concoction and watched it twirl, then enjoyed a sweet sip.

42

✻

"**S**even no trump," Lucy bid and looked around at her opponents to judge their reaction.

"Girl, you're lying," Susan snapped before Lucy could get it out of her mouth good.

Lucy snorted. "Ain't nothing you can do about it so just give up my kitty."

Susan rolled her eyes. "You really gonna bid that mess?" she asked Lucy.

"That's the name of the game, Bid Whist, right?"

Susan leveled her eyes with Lucy's. "Well I'm gonna set you," she promised.

"You gonna try!" Lucy snapped.

Adel took another look at her hand and frowned briefly. There was absolutely nothing she could do to help her partner make such a ridiculous bid, but she put on her best face. "You should know better than to call my partner a liar. She's been baptized and has God on her side," she added with a cocky air.

"God don't have nothing to do with this whoopin' I'm about to put on them," Lucy teased.

"Which way are you coming?" Elaine asked with a scowl.

"Downtown," Lucy sang from the popular song and swiveled her head.

Elaine tossed the six-card kitty over to Lucy. "I hope you can stop this Boston, partner," she mumbled to Susan.

"Ain't no hill for no stepper," Susan bragged.

Lucy organized her hand, keeping three cards from the kitty that could help and throwing away the other three along with three losers from her hand. She started with a run of spades, playing the ace, two, three, four, and so on until everybody ran out of that suit and had to throw off. Next she played her hearts and again the cards fell perfectly and everyone around the table ran out. The ace and deuce of clubs were the last of her roll and the game came down to the very last card.

"Okay, Adel, this is the only book you need to get," Lucy pleaded across the table.

Adel grimaced. "I don't think I can help you, partner."

"Why don't we just stop the game so you two can take all the time you need to discuss your problems," Susan taunted.

Lucy hesitated, then tossed out the two of diamonds. Susan didn't even wait for her turn to slam the ace of diamonds on top of it and yell, "Stopped that Boston!"

Lucy grunted. "I don't care, it was a pretty hand and I had to bid it."

Susan continued her tirade. "Yeah, well, pretty is as pretty does and my ace of diamonds is gorgeous!"

"Amen," Elaine responded, and they gave each other a high five.

"For somebody who needs a ride home you sure are talking a lot of mess," Lucy teased Susan.

"Sorry, I forgot when folks get their behinds beat they don't care to hear about it. Too bad!"

"You'd be standing there crying if my partner had had that ace," Lucy joked.

"That's your dream world you're talking about. In the real world I had the ace, remember?" Susan shot back with a chuckle.

"Okay, okay you two, we've got to get out of here anyway, so I can meet the children's choir over at the church," Adel cut in.

"Sore losers first," Susan said, holding the front door open for Lucy and grinning.

"Next month I'm gonna turn that grin upside down," Lucy teased and walked past her with her head up in the air.

"How's Webster doing?" Adel asked out of curiosity, as they all got in the car.

"He's well," Susan answered. "You know, he's engaged to that woman in accounting, Lenore Bagby."

"I'd heard that." Adel nodded and took the car out of park. "I hope she makes him happy."

Susan giggled. "He walks through the hall with a perpetual grin on his face all the time, if that's any indication."

Adel turned onto the 610 freeway, then continued the conversation. "Are you guys coming to church this Sunday? We have a visiting gospel choir from Dallas that is supposed to be excellent."

"I'll be there," Susan said excitedly. "There's a single father in the congregation that I have my eye on."

"Girl, how are you going to church looking for a man!" Lucy chastised.

Adel laughed. "There are some good men in church, so why not? As long as that's not the only reason you're coming."

"Of course not. God's word is why I come and this cutie-pie just makes the experience that much more heavenly."

"All right, now," Elaine teased.

"Is it that guy you were grinning at last Sunday? He usually sits in the third row to the left with his daughter," Lucy said.

"That's the one."

Adel shook her head. "That's John Washington, and his daughter is Tamara. He is a real nice guy. He joined the single parents' ministry last week, so maybe you need to get involved too, Susan."

Susan nodded. "I sure will. Good looking out!"

Neither Lucy nor Adel had ever been to Susan's house before, but they immediately recognized the Missouri City area. As soon as they turned down the familiar block both heads looked in that direction. They rounded the corner and the house appeared. Lucy and Adel glanced at each other with surprise because it was in such bad shape. The grass must have been three feet high, the roof on the porch had caved in on the left side, much of the siding was chipped off, and the beautiful ivy-covered gazebo leaned sideways, covered now by dried-up vines.

They dropped Susan off farther down the street, then with just a glance at Lucy, Adel turned the car around. When they got back to the house, Adel slowed down and pulled over to the curb so they could get a closer look. Lucy hopped out of the car first and Adel followed, trudging across the grass where a sidewalk had once been.

The long wooden swing no longer hung from the ceiling and the shiny brass chains were hopelessly rusted. Stepping around a pile of debris on the porch, they finally reached the front door. It was locked, so each moved to a window, amazed to see that the inside looked worse than the outside. There were huge holes in the floor, flowered wallpaper was peeling, lights were dangling from sockets, and trash was everywhere.

"What do you think happened?" Adel asked, walking up behind Lucy.

Lucy jumped from the sound of her voice. "I don't know," she answered softly.

"Excuse me, can I help you?" a man with a gruff voice asked from the driveway next door. Lucy craned her neck, but all she could see was brown skin and a head full of white hair.

Both girls walked cautiously back down the steps, out to the front sidewalk, then over toward the man.

"Hi," Lucy said lightly. "Do you by chance know what happened to the man who lived here last year?"

The old man scratched his head and leaned against his lawn mower. "Nobody lived in that house last year. I live right next door, so I ought to know."

Lucy frowned. "But there was a man living here late last year. He had chocolate skin, wore long dreadlocks. He had a motorcycle."

The old man shook his head. "I'm sorry, miss. The family who lived in this house has been gone a long time, probably five years or more."

"Are you sure?" Lucy had to ask again.

He eyed both of them carefully before tilting his head upward to think. "They did have a son who looked something like that and he rode a motorcycle too, now that I think about it. The damn thing woke me up many a night."

"Do you know what happened to him?" Adel asked.

The man sighed. "He died in a really bad accident. He was on that motorcycle. I think he was around thirty years old when it happened. The family moved up north not long after that. They had his funeral here in Houston, but shipped the body to be buried up there."

Lucy and Adel thanked the old man and moved slowly back to the car. They took one last questioning look, then drove away.

As the sun was fading and the moon claimed its place in the sky above them, they reached the freeway in silence. Both sets of eyes were simultaneously drawn to a huge purple billboard up ahead on which stark gold letters boldly asked the question that weighed heavily in their hearts: "What do you believe?"

About the Author

Venise Berry is an associate professor of journalism and mass communication at the University of Iowa in Iowa City. She is the author of two *Essence* magazine Blackboard bestselling novels, *So Good: An African American Love Story* (Dutton, 1996) and *All of Me: A Voluptuous Tale* (Dutton, 2000). *All of Me* received a 2001 Honor Book Award for the Black Caucus of the American Library Association.

Berry is also published widely in academic circles in the area of African-American Cultural Criticism. Her most recent co-authored project is *The 50 Most Influential Black Films* (Citadel, 2001), and her coedited book, *Mediated Messages and African-American Culture: Contemporary Issues* (Sage, 1996), won the Meyers Center Award for the Study of Human Rights in North America in 1997.

She teaches a one-week workshop called Writing the Popular Novel at the University of Iowa Summer Writers Workshop each year and conducts a number of seminars: Weight and Wellness: Challenging Myths; Racialism and the Media; and Success in the Twenty-first Century.

For more information visit Venise Berry's Web site at: www.veniseberry.com